Praise for *Lesson Plans*

Editor's Pick, *Library Journal*

"Homeschooling will never be the same after Suzanne Greenberg's hilarious, poignant, and cinematic debut novel about three families whose lives change profoundly through the wild, exhausting and redemptive journey that home-schooling actually requires. This bittersweet novel is a survival manual for intelligent parents willing to take a hard road, and for any reader, a sheer delight."

— Howard Norman, two-time National Book Award finalist for
The Northern Lights and *The Bird Artist*

"A wonderful book about the world of parenting, told with grace, humor, insight, and empathy. Suzanne Greenberg gets it, and she makes her readers get what's at stake for parents and children alike. A good read that makes you think, smile, and turn the page quickly right to the end."

— Mimi Schwartz, author of *Good Neighbors, Bad Times* and
Thoughts From a Queen-Sized Bed

"In her new novel *Lesson Plans*, Suzanne Greenberg brings her slyly humor-ous eye to a group of homeschoolers in Southern California. Following three families whose lives are unraveling, Greenberg lays bare the illusions and despair of these characters, their loneliness and longing for love. But she also shows us hope springing to life as reliably as vacant-lot weeds. Greenberg is an unapologetically honest writer, with a sharp eye for how easily any life can veer off course."

— Cai Emmons, author of *His Mother's Son* and *The Stylist*

"*Lesson Plans* is a complex, character-driven story written with clarity about the intersecting lives of ordinary parents, the choices they make, and the long-term effects of these choices on their children. Author Suzanne Greenberg mines the territory of Tom Perrotta with a fresh take on today's suburban subcultures and entwined family relationships. Crafted with skill and depth, the characters stay with you long after the book ends."

— Lian Dolan, author of *Elizabeth the First Wife* and
Helen of Pasadena

"All good parents want to protect their children from the perils of the world around them. Not all parents put their children's needs before their own. Or find the balance between the two. A story set within the arcane world of homeschooling, *Lesson Plans* is rooted in place and time and misplaced love. There are no heroes or villains in this heartbreaking tale of families torn asunder by the conflict of good intentions and desire."

— Peggy Hesketh, author of *Telling the Bees*

"Reading *Lesson Plans*, I was schooled in the nuances of the human heart and privy to the most illuminating of chalkboards. Suzanne Greenberg possesses a satirist's wit and a realist's sharp eye for details. *Lesson Plans* has everything: depth, humor, insight, a compelling, page-turning story, and deftly crafted, unforgettable characters. This is a brilliant debut novel, a completely engrossing look at contemporary suburban America."

— Lisa Glatt, author of *A Girl Becomes a Comma Like That* and *The Apple's Bruise*

Praise for *Speed-Walk and Other Stories*

"Greenberg's characters and the crises they go through are enigmatic and unique."

— *Booklist*

"If you enjoy reading quiet, contemplative pieces that take an intimate look at another person's everyday life, you're in for a treat."

— *Pitt News*

"[Greenberg] might be best described as a visual eavesdropper who uses her imagination to describe and inhabit her characters' lives.... Her attention to detail is mirrored by her ability to find stories in ordinary situations."

— *Pittsburgh Tribune Review*

"The remarkable and heartening debut of a major new voice."

— *Orange County Weekly*

"Poignant and yet occasionally comical...her stories are a juxtaposition of the melancholy and the mundane, with a little of the absurd thrown in."

— *ForeWord Reviews*

LESSON PLANS

a novel

SUZANNE GREENBERG

PROSPECT
·PARK·
BOOKS

Published by Prospect Park Books
969 S. Raymond Avenue
Pasadena, California 91105
PROSPECT
·PARK·
BOOKS   www.prospectparkbooks.com

Distributed by Consortium Book Sales & Distribution
www.cbsd.com

Library of Congress Cataloging in Publication Data
Greenberg, Suzanne.
    Lesson plans / Suzanne Greenberg.
        pages cm

    ISBN 978-1-938849-24-4 (pbk.)
    1. Families--Fiction. 2. Domestic fiction. I. Title.
    PS3607.R4525L47 2014
    813'.6--dc23
                                            2013039281

Cover design by Howard Grossman. Book layout and design by Renee Nakagawa.
Printed in the United States of America.

For Michael

UNSCHOOL

When his four-year-old, Katie, rammed a piece of chicken wire into her finger one hot October afternoon as they finished their snail fences, David called Madeline and Emily over and let them take turns wrapping the wound.

"See how much pressure it takes to stop the bleeding," he told his girls. "Try different amounts."

Maybe the girls would grow up to be doctors, David thought as he watched the care they took wrapping the kitchen towel around their sister's finger. Maybe they'd be Peace Corps volunteers or veterinarians or candy stripers. Did hospitals use candy stripers anymore, he wondered? How old did hospital volunteers have to be anyway? When he got online later, he'd have to look this up. Each day David was filled with a deep sense of possibility for his girls.

"I think the holes are too big," Emily said. She stared critically at the circular enclosures the four of them had worked on all afternoon. "I bet the snails will climb right through and eat all the fall tomatoes."

David began to suspect as much himself about ten minutes into the project, but he figured it would be a learning experience for his girls, and they could always reuse the chicken wire later for something else. Hadn't he just read something somewhere about making lampshades out of recycled stuff?

"And what would we learn from that?" David asked. "If the snails did get through?"

"We could try cheesecloth next time," Madeline said, twisting the kitchen towel tight around Katie's punctured finger.

"Good thinking. We could experiment to see if enough light gets in for photosynthesis," David said.

"It's my turn to stop Katie's blood," Emily said, elbowing Madeline out of the way.

"I want a band-aid now," Katie said, pushing both her sisters and the kitchen towel away. "I want a real band-aid, a Star Wars one, and I want Daddy to put it on. Not either one of you."

"Daddy to the rescue," David said, picking up his youngest duckling, his baby, and carrying her inside to the bathroom, where Katie climbed up on the toilet seat and pulled a box of band-aids out of the medicine cabinet. David centered the padded section over the small dried-up puncture on his daughter's fingertip.

He heard the television set blare on in the living room. They had decided to hold onto cable for the first year of homeschooling and had never really revisited the issue. David thought he and the girls might watch selected documentaries on the History Channel and have interesting discussions afterward, that they could all study Spanish together on the public station and maybe even have some fun with their new skills by following a telenovela. And what harm could there be if the four of them spent a half hour a day watching *Sesame Street* or some other educational programming?

But instead of doing any of those things, the girls ripped open bags of organic trail mix and sat down to watch the cartoon channel every time he left them to their own devices. And the truth was, David was relieved to have the down time. Sometimes he watched cartoons, too, the four of them sprawled across the couch in the middle of the afternoon, his index finger poised above the "off" button of the remote in case he heard his wife's car pulling up in the driveway.

He wasn't sure when Deborah had become the authority figure in their household, but no matter how much he tried, he couldn't seem to help thinking of his wife as *the man*. Once in a while he even slipped and called her that to the kids. "The man is home," he'd hear himself say as the front doorknob turned.

David had always assumed he'd end up in Oregon or perhaps in a foggy coastal area north of San Francisco, somewhere like Mendocino, where rocky cliffs jutted out over the ocean. His future children would grow up collecting rocks and building forts in the woods. He'd made it as far north as Santa Cruz for graduate school, where the coastal fog-loving banana slug was the university's official logo.

And he planned on heading farther north still as soon as he completed his master's. He imagined a life with rain and redwoods and plenty of community activism and liberal free-thinking neighbors and a surprising abundance of small companies eager to hire people with MAs in comparative literature. But, instead, after graduate school, he'd somehow wound up right back in Long Beach, living in a crappy tract home ten minutes from where he'd grown up.

The somehow part was not a complete mystery, of course. Deborah, the law student he'd begun dating while in graduate school, had passed the bar and, after sending out two rounds of resumes, had landed a job working at a law firm in nearby Cerritos. Although the job was corporate and dull and had nothing to do with the legal work she planned to pursue—environmental law—with their first baby already on the way, they'd snapped up the offer. They reasoned that it was a first job. It didn't have to be a dream job. And they reasoned that with Deborah's parents retired in Florida, having at least one set of grandparents nearby had to be a good thing for children. Then they sealed the whole suburban deal by getting married at the Lakewood Country Club, a glowing Deborah then eight months pregnant.

Their three daughters had been born two years apart nearly to the day. Deborah called them their lucky ducklings, using the phrase for the first time when she surprised them all by getting off work early one Friday afternoon to find the girls trailing after David on their way home from the corner playground.

He was the stay-at-home dad, and Deborah went to work and made enough money to pay for bicycles and vacations to San Diego and rectangles of sod to cover the dry dirt David unearthed by drilling through the concrete of the backyard. He planned the playdates, made the doctors' appointments, and found the waxed paper cups stowed away in the garage for the lemonade stands. In this way, at least, they weren't their neighbors. But in every other way, he had relented. The tract house, the kind of vacations where the only surprise was how long the lines would be at SeaWorld, the cable television, none of it was anything he had ever imagined.

A year before it was time to enroll their oldest daughter, Madeline, in school, David decided he would finally take a stand. Even if his children had been born and raised in dry, paved-over Southern California the way he had been, he still imagined his idealized elementary school in the redwoods. The principal would have a Question Authority bumper sticker peeling off his back windshield, and the teachers would be young and enthusiastic and attractive, although, of course, he knew he couldn't quite justify this last wish.

And because their city offered school choice, he began searching for just this school. He visited a French immersion charter school, a K–8 arts magnet, and their own neighborhood elementary school, where the moms with whom he organized playdates planned to send their children. Some already had older children there, and they gossiped freely and, it seemed to him, a bit too happily about the tyrannical nature of the PTA board.

None of the schools David visited seemed right to him. Instead of meeting actual teachers, he was forced to interview assistant principals and other beleaguered administrators, city employees who sucked breath mints and had bad haircuts, and who glanced too often at their watches. When examined closely, the "magnets" themselves, he decided, were little more than sales ploys to attract parents from middle-class neighborhoods like his own to the grim neighborhoods they could otherwise safely avoid. No matter what they claimed to be, every school he visited had standardized testing, and virtually the same grading system, the same hoops at the end of the day that each kid had to jump through.

Having jumped diligently and unhappily through plenty of those hoops himself as a child, David decided to say no to all of it and homeschool his girls instead of sending them anywhere. They may not be able to roam freely in nature the way he'd hoped, but he could make sure that their imaginations weren't killed the way his own had nearly been with rote memorization. They wouldn't sit for hours while he flipped flash cards in front of their faces so they could learn their times tables. In third grade he'd used his own subtraction flash cards to build an entire city across the floor of his classroom during after-school "math club," and, instead of being praised for his creativity, he was sent the next day to practice math facts with the second graders.

Who cared what the names of the fifty state capitals were if you never got to leave your own confining desk? His girls would be able to get up and sharpen pencils without raising their hands. They could walk down the hall and go to the bathroom without enduring the humiliating choice of requesting a bright yellow hall pass or risking an accident. They could pursue what they loved at their own pace. Everything they did would be about learning.

"We'll get rid of cable, of the television set entirely," he had told Deborah, formalizing his plan even as he talked to her.

"One year," she told him. "Try it with Madeline for one year and then get back to me with the full report, and we'll see."

Screw you, he thought. Deborah had never talked this way before they were married. They'd met during a beach clean-up and shared equal parts raw idealism and lust. Back then, he thought it was sexy, in a feminist sort of way, how she told people to pronounce her name, Deb-OR-ah, with the accent on the middle syllable. Now, it just seemed affected. Back then, they used to stay up all night having sex and plotting how to change the world. They didn't *try* anything.

"Okay, *Deb-OR-ah,*" David said. "We'll try it for a year."

Three years later, David couldn't believe he had ever considered sending his daughters into classrooms. He shuddered when he imagined them forced to sit on hard wooden chairs for six hours a day. He was certain that one day humans would look back at schools the way society now looked at foot binding or public stoning. Human beings were the only animals who treated their own in such cruel ways.

Now four, six, and eight, his daughters spent their days any way the four of them saw fit. They took field trips to the nature center to look for garter snakes and egrets. They studied planets by driving up the mountains of the San Bernardino National Forest with their sleeping bags and a telescope, noting the changes in vegetation as their car climbed. They studied earth science by pulling out carefully laid sod and planting an organic vegetable garden. They found geometric shapes in the patterns of spider webs. They soaked old newspaper in warm water and broke the blender trying to make their own recycled paper.

They spent an hour each week eating free samples and tracking the life span of the humble doughnut in their local Krispy Kreme, following the same doughnut from its flat beginning to its full glazed glory. When they became bored with their own company, they participated in the occasional half-price homeschool restaurant dinner or a midweek homeschool day at the Lakewood Ice Palace skating rink.

And sometimes they stayed home and did very little.

"Why don't you and your boo-boo watch TV with your sisters for a while," David said, giving Katie's band-aid one last kiss, "while Daddy does his computer work."

Katie nodded and said, "That's a good idea. I need to take it easy for a while."

He watched his youngest daughter wander into the living room, feeling dizzy with love for her and the stoic temperament with which she was clearly born. While they physically resembled one other and their mother, with their sandy blond hair, small waists, and larger bottoms, it seemed to him that each of his daughters had a strikingly different personality. Madeline, easily overstimulated by the outside world, was the first one to pop on the television set. Alert Emily always counted the most pelicans at the bay. And Katie was the rule-follower, the one who probably would have done the best in an actual classroom.

David went into the bedroom and logged onto his computer. He thought having children would make him more of an activist. Didn't people want their families to inherit a better Earth, with healthy air, good daycare for single mothers, and political leaders whose names they wouldn't be embarrassed to utter?

But he found that becoming a father had actually made his world smaller. He cared so intensely about his own children that he had to remind himself to consider anyone else's. And even then, after the birth of his first daughter, his concerns felt abstract—the world's poor, the homeless, the disabled—and were usually in the context of teaching his girls something.

He knew he should care, so when his youngest daughter, Katie, was three and David deemed her old enough to participate, he made it a project to get the girls involved in a more direct way. When it turned out that they were too young to volunteer in person anywhere meaningful (the local homeless shelter insisted that children be fifteen), David decided to let his daughters pick charities online.

They made one of their first donations to teenage girls in foster care who wanted new prom dresses. "I like the one whose mother is a drug addict," Madeline said, pointing to a moon-faced girl on the computer screen.

"I want the one who got straight As," Emily said, touching the screen where a girl's hopeful smile revealed a need for braces more urgent than her desire for a prom dress.

He felt overwhelmed with the luck of his children's lives.

"Who do you want?" he'd asked Katie.

"I want them all," she said.

The girls counted up the coins they had amassed between sofa cushions and under the seats in the family minivan. They paid for prom dresses.

Then they found more causes.

They manned lemonade stands each Saturday until they could afford to buy a bicycle for a man in Ethiopia who had started a small business delivering coffee beans to a bed-and-breakfast that catered to a surprisingly regular tourism industry in Addis Ababa. They bought prescription glasses for women who sewed clothes in sweatshops in India. They bought winter coats for a family of eight in Appalachia.

David praised his daughters for their efforts, but he knew the truth:

He had become one of those *distant givers* he and Deborah used to deride
as they speared plastic bags and the occasional used condom around the
fire pits of Seacliff Beach with other environmentally conscious UCSC
students. His point had been to get his children directly involved. He
finally found a homeless shelter in Inglewood that didn't care how old
the volunteers were as long as a parent supervised them. But after just
one afternoon spent attempting to organize clothing donations—this
had devolved quickly into a spontaneous and disorganized game of
dress-up—he realized the truth: They really were too young to do
much good in person.

They went back to their online charities. David vowed to teach
his girls how to make a difference in the larger world without leaving
their own small one. And in the process, he had become the kind of
person he used to criticize. Home with daughters, he rarely left his
own comfort zone to pull on rubber gloves and pick up syringes in a
city park or mop a sticky, peeling linoleum floor at the kind of shelter
that smelled like barley soup no matter what was on the menu.

He gave money instead of time. Of course, everyone's contribution
was *needed*. And it could be argued that money was way more valuable
than time. It could be argued particularly now that he was the one
giving it.

While the girls were nearly as instantly thrilled and subsequently
bored with their small donations as if they'd purchased something
for themselves, none of it felt like quite enough to him. They were
all out there pleading with him to give them more, to make a real
difference in their lives, the children with cleft palates and big empty
bellies, the Latin American men with their modest needs for an ox or
a wheelbarrow.

Late at night, while Deborah and the girls slept on their thick
mattresses in their suburban neighborhood, David logged onto glossy
nonprofit websites the way some men logged onto porn. And he said
yes. Like Katie, he wanted them all, too.

He'd held onto several of his own credit cards when he and
Deborah married. Feeling righteous and sneaky in a way he knew was
more adolescent than adult, he maxed out those cards one by one on
his causes. Now he was chiseling away at the small retirement fund

he doubted Deborah even remembered he had, one he'd accrued at meaningless jobs before he quit pursuing outside work to become a full-time father.

But no matter how many goats he secretly bought for struggling villagers in central Mali, no matter how many bath towels and teddy bears he bought for a women's shelter in Oakland, he felt that his one real connection to his old activist self, the person who used to man the suicide hotline on New Year's Eve and dish out mounds of wet stuffing on Thanksgiving at shelters, his one real, nonmonetary contribution to the larger world that existed outside of his daughters, was to homeschoolers.

He posted his email address on every legitimate website and chat group he knew of, and every day he made himself available to answer questions. So he didn't feel overwhelmed, he made a schedule, checking for questions in the afternoon and once again later at night when the girls were asleep.

Each day he had at least several messages. There were leisurely comments about curriculum—along with occasional book recommendations—from a group he thought of as hobbyists or would-be homeschooling experts themselves. Then there was an entirely different set of messages from the desperate people whose emails felt nearly as urgent to him as the suicide-threateners had seemed. *Help me!* they wrote. *No one understands why I want to do this. I'm all alone.*

He answered the desperate ones first, of course, today's leading contender a triple threat of a woman named Beth who had a daughter with nearly constant asthma and potentially life-threatening allergies, a husband in the process of leaving her, and no connection at all with other homeschoolers.

I don't know where to start, she wrote. *Can you help me?*

Of course, David typed back, the screeches of revved-up cartoon voices in the background and images from his most recent charity, famine victims trekking across a desert in northern Kenya, calling out to him from a window on his computer that he would reopen as soon as he finished this email. *No matter how you feel now, you are not alone!*

METEOROLOGY

Jennifer Wheeler had not had asthma for three days and missed the rattling company of it. Her mother, Beth, lay next to her in bed, flipping through stations on the television. They had all the basic cable channels plus the movie package, but the sound had gone out a week ago, and now they had to watch the whole thing on mute.

Some of the channels showed words at the bottom of the screen if her mother pushed a certain button on the remote. But for Jennifer, trying to piece together those words was like trying to hear the other side of the conversation when her mother talked on the phone. Once in a while, she could make out a word, but she couldn't read well enough yet to follow all of it.

Her mother finally settled on the Weather Channel, putting the remote down between them on the bed. Jennifer tried unsuccessfully to find their exact place on the map, but geography was her worst subject in first grade. Jennifer found California, but where was Long Beach, above or below Los Angeles? She forced a deep exhale, but nothing caught in her throat. Without her asthma to listen to, Jennifer focused hard on the muted television, trying to block the other noises.

Outside their windows the wind was still howling, but on their soundless television, everything seemed under control. Jennifer watched the weather pulsing through the country while the forecaster motioned with her arm as if she was causing the clouds to move all by herself, and making the sun beat down on entire outlined states.

"Would you look at that," her mother said. "Winds this loud and they don't even make the radar."

The winds were worse at night, but it was the mornings Jennifer dreaded. Yesterday morning she looked out the window and found the pansies she and her father had planted under the lemon tree uprooted, the flowers glued with their own pollen and nectar against the white stucco wall of the patio, the stems scattered like knotted witch's hair across the brick walkway.

Tonight, in bed with her mother watching the Weather Channel, Jennifer remembered leaving her doll stroller in the backyard. She listened for it between the sounds of branches snapping off of trees. She thought, *Please*, just this one word alone in its own sentence. If the doll stroller broke, she was too old to ask for a new one. As it was, she hid it under her skirts and dresses in her closet when certain friends from first grade came over, the kind who had moved on to Monopoly Junior, video games, and handball.

"How are you feeling, baby?" her mother asked, her eyes still on the television weather.

"A little better, I guess." Jennifer chose her words carefully. Her mother might look like she wasn't really listening, but she couldn't tell anymore. Before her mother decided to homeschool her, she never knew if her words had any effect on her mother at all. She could plead for chicken nuggets and be served soy spaghetti, ask for a Siamese cat and be given a goldfish, beg to stay up until ten and be tucked in at eight. All she had said this time was that school was boring. Everyone said that. All her friends.

Her mother's bedroom was hot, but they couldn't open the window because these kinds of winds blew in filthy air. The Santa Anas were desert, as opposed to ocean, winds, her mother explained to her in that new tone of voice she'd begun using now that Jennifer was being homeschooled. The winds were full of negative ions, which caused static electricity and erratic moods. Jennifer nodded as her mother had explained, even though she didn't understand most of what she was talking about.

All Jennifer knew was that their yard smelled smoky for days after the winds stopped, and at this very moment the thin metal legs of her baby stroller were probably being ripped off at their hinges.

"Shh," her mother said, although Jennifer hadn't said anything. "Time to sleep, baby." Her mother turned off the television and the room went dark. Since her father had left them, her mother had kept her close by. Jennifer didn't bother to get up and walk down the hall to her own bedroom, although, in truth, she missed her Pocahontas pillowcase and the way she could adjust her curtains to make a shadow on the wall by her bed that looked like an elbow. And she missed taking out her emergency flashlight in the middle of the night and sliding under her bed to look at the souvenirs she stored in a shoebox.

Jennifer collected slick packs of gum from pharmacies when she and her mother waited to pick up prescriptions. She collected a collapsible magic wand a rented clown forgot at her sixth birthday party. She collected sealed packets of hot pepper and dried parmesan cheese from pizza restaurants, ticket stubs from movies, and key cards from hotel rooms. It all was equally important, and it all was there, in her own room, under her own bed. But her mother wanted her with her. She never told her she had to stay, but her mother never walked her down the hall and tucked her into her own bed either.

Her mother slept with her back to her on her separate half of the mattress, but Jennifer still couldn't forget she was there, that she might turn in her sleep and bump into her. Since her father had left, this is where she'd been sleeping and where they'd been eating most of their meals on TV trays. Her mother's room felt like a hotel room, but a maid never came to clean up after them. Instead, once a day, after the soundless soap opera ended at 3 p.m., her mother took their dishes down to the kitchen sink and fluffed up the pillows behind their heads.

When Jennifer woke up in the morning, for the first time in over a week, her mother was already out of bed. She felt strange in the room without her mother in it, as if she were trespassing and would soon be discovered the way Goldilocks had been by the bears. This was a kindergarten story she knew she was supposed to have outgrown, but before he left, she still asked her father to read it to her at bedtime because of the special way he had of making each bear's voice sound different.

The night he moved out, Jennifer was asleep in her own bed, but she had felt him kiss her forehead and whisper that he'd be back. She was too tired to open her eyes and ask him where he was going, what he meant. She was in the middle of a dream she couldn't remember anymore, but she hadn't wanted to leave it. She hadn't worried. She'd used the last of the soy milk to dip her cookies in before bed. Probably he was just going out for more so she could have cereal in the morning.

Now, two weeks had passed since she'd seen him. Unlike some of her friends' fathers who disappeared regularly on business trips, her father had never been gone before. At the end of each day, she waited for the sound of his car door shutting and the snap of the deadbolt unlatching. Instead, much later at night, close to the time he should be reading her a story, the phone would ring and her mother would whisper angry-sounding words into it before using her fake-happy voice to call out to Jennifer to come talk to her father.

I'm okay, she told him each night on the phone, skipping the part about the asthma attack that had sent her to the nurse's office the day after he left. Careful not to seem like the trouble she was.

When are you coming back? she asked.

I miss you. Be good, he said, which wasn't an answer.

Where are you? she thought but didn't say. She liked to imagine him on an airplane, high above their house, circling, even though she'd been on an airplane before and knew you couldn't make phone calls from them.

Jennifer heard the vacuum cleaner running downstairs, and even though the winds were still blowing, she thought maybe this was a good sign, her mother cleaning the house. Maybe if it was cleaned up enough, they could leave and come back home the way they used to.

Maybe she could even go back to real school.

She missed lunch and recess and music. But mostly what she missed was the coming and going, the sound of the front door opening and the surprise of her own living room. The magazines stacked on a chair no one ever sat in, the mail scattered on the coffee table, the photograph of Jennifer in a fat diaper sitting on the edge of her father's old kayak in front of the bay. They'd been inside for four days in a row now, and the house had begun to feel like clothes that need washing.

All she wanted was corn flakes with a tiny bit of soy milk on them, but when Jennifer came downstairs, she saw her mother had made one of her breakfasts that looked like it was for company: toast on the edge of her plate, scrambled Egg Beaters heaped in the center, orange juice in one of the goblet glasses they usually only took out of the china cabinet when they were making ice cream sundaes.

"Eat up, sleepy-puss," her mother said as she rinsed the plates they'd accumulated over the past several days and stacked them in the dishwasher. "Eggs are brain food."

Jennifer thought about brain food, how the food could get up there, how stupid she was, how much she didn't know. She hadn't eaten out of bed for nearly a week now, and sitting up at the kitchen table under the bright hanging light, she felt confused and disoriented.

"Okay, I'm thinking categories," her mother said, shutting off the water and rubbing her hands down the sides of her jeans. "Here's what I've got so far." Several index cards were spread out on the counter by the toaster oven. Her mother leaned over and read them, still wiping dry her hands.

Her mother's belly was soft and large, pushing against the kitchen counter. Early in the school year, Jennifer's teacher asked her if her mother was having another baby, and she'd felt embarrassed for her mother. "I don't know," she told her teacher, even though she did know. *I already have my perfect child,* her mother said whenever Jennifer used to ask her for a little brother. *Why would I want another?*

"Geography, Math, English, Spanish, Social Studies, Science. Okay, that's as far as I've got. What am I missing, honey? Can you help me out here?"

The eggs tasted sour, and Jennifer wondered if Egg Beaters could go bad the way real eggs could. Once, at her neighbor Lauren's house, Lauren's mother, Darla, had found an old Easter egg in the back of the refrigerator. The egg had been dyed purple and was still pretty, but when Darla pulled it out, saying *Here's the culprit*, the smell was so thick and rotten that Jennifer had touched her throat, thinking she might have an asthma attack.

"Food," she said to her mother. "I think that's a category."

"Hmm," her mother said. "Why not? Who says we can't have a little fun while we're learning? After all, isn't that the whole point? Let's come up with some more. How about foreign movies? How about anatomy, animals. What about dachshunds? I've always thought they were so cute, haven't you, sweetie?"

"Dachshunds?" she said, having no idea what her mother was talking about. Was this something else she was supposed to know?

"Why the heck *not* dachshunds?" her mother said, as if she were arguing with someone. "We could research how they're bred, how much they eat. You name it. That's the whole idea, isn't it? Making this fun. Going with the tangents? And P.E. for Pete's sake. How did I forget P.E.?"

"And dance," Jennifer said, remembering all at once something else she loved about school: her dance teacher, who wore the special soft black shoes that made her sound smaller than she was when she walked down the hallway. In dance class you were allowed to be little the way Jennifer was little. Petite, it was called. All the words in dance were velvety and foreign. The first grade class learned a dance that came from Morocco, another from Portugal. The boys pushed each other around and laughed when the teacher demonstrated the steps, but they did the dances, too. Everyone did. This was the way things were at school. "We have dance every Thursday," she told her mother.

"Well, let's tackle that one pronto," her mother said. And she watched her mother switch on the radio by the sink and skate around the channels until she found something she liked. Soon, she knew, the Santa Ana winds could make her mother's mood shift and they could go back to bed and forget about dancing and probably about P.E., too. But for now her mother, who was not petite and who wore thick white sneakers, not small black slippers, was shuffling around the kitchen, her arms holding the air out in front of her.

Jennifer did not want to dance with her mother in the morning on a school day in their kitchen. She touched her throat, found the soft, round place at the base of it, pushed into the curved bone beneath, and breathed out until she found a familiar hiss.

"I think it's back a little. I'll just watch," she said. The toast tasted like vitamins or some kind of herbs. She thought about the school lunches she was allowed to eat and the ones she took her chances on and bought anyway sometimes, emptying her lunchbox into the first grade girl's bathroom garbage can. There was so much she missed: the seedless hamburger buns, the shiny packets of ketchup, the Styrofoam cups full of syrupy fruit salad.

She wished she had taken a ketchup packet to keep in her souvenir box. She hadn't realized that school was a place she was only visiting.

Holding her arms out as if they were around someone, her mother was showing her something called the box step.

"The whole thing is in the timing," her mother said, and Jennifer nodded, although, once again, she wasn't sure what her mother was talking about.

They didn't go back to bed. Instead her mother made more lists, and they went to the grocery store after the winds finally calmed down. Her mother made Jennifer weigh out a pound and a half of oranges. Then she told her to read the signs until she found the plum tomatoes and to count out a dozen of them for gazpacho while she priced detergent on another aisle. Her mother never used to price anything. She just bought the brand they always got. But on the one other grocery-store trip they'd taken since her father left, she had compared the prices of blocks of goat cheese, corn flakes, baked beans, ketchup.

The pricing was supposed to be educational, but Jennifer knew the truth. Since her father left they weren't sure where they were getting their money. This is what her mother told their neighbor Darla one night when they were all outside on the sidewalk, eating the bitter-tasting orange-juice popsicles her mother had made. Lauren made a face because her popsicle tasted sour, which was rude because she was in kindergarten and old enough to know better. Little Jeremy stuck out his tongue to see if it had turned orange, which was different. Her mother said, *We don't know when the next check is coming.* This was right before the winds started up.

Whenever Jennifer knocked on Lauren's front door to see if she could play, she hoped Lauren wouldn't be home so she could play with Jeremy instead, pushing him on his little swing out back or helping him build a fort with pillows in the living room. Lauren hated Jeremy because he was younger and everyone said how cute he was, even though he still wet his pants after he was supposed to be potty trained. How could Lauren like playing babies so much with dolls and not like playing with her real live little brother?

Jennifer could feel the produce man watching her as he unloaded his trays of lettuce. She whispered the tomato names—hothouse, vine-ripened, cherry—until she finally found plum and silently placed each tomato in a bag, keeping track in her head. Probably he had a daughter her age in school and wondered why she wasn't sitting at her very own desk right now, copying an addition problem from the overhead. Maybe, because she was petite, he thought she was just five and only in kindergarten or still in preschool. Or maybe he thought she was held back and kept in morning kindergarten because she couldn't even write her name yet, because she couldn't tell a circle from a triangle.

She stopped picking tomatoes from the big pile and put her hand in the pocket of her shorts and felt the yellow whistle she'd taken from the little hanging display near the grapes. This was something she liked about grocery stores, the way they had toy surprises scattered everywhere, hanging down on hooks by the rice or soda or paper towels. Souvenirs. Each time she went somewhere she might not go back to for a while, she tried to find one. This seemed to her different from stealing, which was obviously wrong and bad. Each time she took only one small thing. Today the plastic whistle was it.

"Didn't they teach you what a dozen was yet?" her mother asked, back from another aisle with a brand of dishwasher detergent Jennifer had never seen before in her arms, the word *DETERGENT* written out in big capital letters large enough for her to read quickly. "We definitely have some catching up to do," her mother said. "One dozen is the same thing as twelve."

Jennifer looked down at her bag and realized that at some point she'd stopped counting, even though she knew since kindergarten that a dozen was the same thing as twelve. The thin plastic bag she was holding was way too full of tomatoes, but she couldn't figure out how to subtract the correct number to make twelve without emptying out the entire bag and starting over. She already hated everything about gazpacho soup, its mealy texture, the way you could taste it in your throat for hours after you ate it, how the leftovers looked like blood in the plastic container in the refrigerator, and now they would have even more of it. Last summer her mother had made too much and froze the extra into rancid-tasting popsicles that Jennifer now worried she had pretended too hard to like.

She handed the bag to her mother and said, "I need to go to the bathroom."

"Of course," her mother said, and they left the cart and were off together into her favorite part of the grocery store, the not-quite-public area behind dairy. It was like a secret passage they walked through behind the moveable shelves of shiny, day-old cupcakes and pies.

Her mother pushed through rubber doors that smelled like gummy bears and rain boots, and Jennifer was face to face with the Employee's Tracking Log, which she scanned to see who had tardies. Jennifer loved the word *tardy*. She loved the way it sounded, mean and final.

"It's just impossible to get away from, isn't it?" her mother said. "That punishing school-based attitude is everywhere."

You do not know what I'm thinking, Jennifer thought, turning away from the Tracking Log. Her father never acted like he knew what she was thinking the way her mother did. She shut the bathroom door behind her and leaned against it in case her mother had ideas about following her in there, which was something else her father would never do.

The bathroom was large and messy in the same way it always

was, with paper towels balled up on the floor in one corner and none in the paper towel holder. She read the sign on the wall that told customers that the store took pride in its bathroom being clean and to let the management know if it wasn't. Because she could take her time, she could read most of the words on the sign, unlike the words that scrambled on their television when it was stuck on mute. But she never told anyone that the bathroom wasn't clean. She liked the word *tardy* but didn't want to get anyone in trouble.

Outside the door, her mother was humming something Jennifer almost recognized, a theme song to one of the television shows they'd been watching on mute. Her father was the one who did things like make the television work and fix the vacuum cleaner and put air in the car's tires, and Jennifer wondered what else might go wrong now that he was gone.

Jennifer flushed the toilet and washed her hands. Then she stood on her tiptoes and practiced making faces in the blurry mirror above the sink.

"I thought I lost you in there," her mother said in her almost-kidding voice when Jennifer finally came out. But she could tell by the way her mother wrapped her arm around her back that she was worried, even though there was nowhere to hide in a bathroom.

When she was younger, Jennifer hid in racks of sweaters at department stores and in tunnels at indoor playgrounds at fast-food restaurants. Sometimes she hid so long in her own house that her mother called Jennifer's father at work crying, and then she would come out from a kitchen cabinet or under the couch. She was petite and could make herself smaller by listening to her own breathing. Once she hid so long in the back of the coat closet under piles of her father's old ski clothes that her mother had already hung up on her father and was on the phone with the police.

Even though she was old enough to know better and tried not to hide anymore, her mother was always breathless when Jennifer didn't answer right away, as if maybe she had asthma herself. And now, in the grocery store, this made Jennifer inexplicably happy, the happiest she'd been all day. She grabbed her mother's hand and made her skip with her through the cereal aisle back to their cart. And for just a minute, instead of a punishment, homeschool felt like a surprise recess right in the middle of a math facts review.

The parking lot was full of shopping carts scattered by the Santa Anas. Even though the winds had died down hours ago, no one had bothered to put all the carts back in their proper places yet. The carts reminded Jennifer of the woolly mammoth skeletons she'd seen on a class field trip to the tar pits, and she kicked one just a little to prove to herself that it was a cart. A minivan careened around near them, and her mother told her to stay close while they loaded the groceries into the trunk of their car.

Her father left them with the Camry, the good car, the one Jennifer and he cleaned together every Saturday, but it had already begun to look run-down during the two weeks he'd been gone. The trunk was full of half-empty water bottles and old newspapers that her mother planned to drop off at recycling, and she had to push it all out of the way to make room for their bags. Jennifer missed her father all at once, the way it sometimes happened since he'd left. She cleared her throat, checking for a rattle, but she didn't find one.

Because the wind had finally stopped blowing in bad air, they rode home with the windows open. Her mother counted the downed tree limbs they passed, and Jennifer was supposed to count the garbage cans left turned on their sides by the curbs. Her mother was talking about graphs, how they could compare the number of downed limbs to downed garbage cans on a graph using colored pencils. "I think I have some graph paper at home, don't I?" she asked. "I need to get organized, figure out what we already have, what supplies we need." Her mother tapped her finger on the steering wheel while she was talking. Jennifer lost track of her counting. She decided she would make up a number that sounded believable. Not one hundred or one thousand or one million, but something like thirty-eight or twelve. A dozen.

"Or, I know, maybe instead of using colored pencils, we can glue on actual bark," her mother said.

Jennifer sat in the back seat and thought about her purple glue stick that smelled like grape jelly in the art drawer at home, about whether she'd remembered to put the top back on it, about how the bark would stick all over it and mess it up forever. When they turned the corner that took them to their own house, she shut her eyes for a minute, opening them only after making a wish that she was amazed to see come true: her father's car parked in his regular space out front.

"Daddy's back!" she shouted.

"Will you look at that," her mother said. "Parked right out front. Just like he never left."

Jennifer had her hand on the door handle, ready to jump out and find him. She wondered if he had shaved yet today. Would his face feel scratchy when she rubbed his cheek? She wondered if he'd have a present for her the way her friends' fathers sometimes did when they came back from business trips. A souvenir.

Once, Lauren's father had brought her a heavy, clear bubble paperweight with a tiny Statue of Liberty inside of it. Lauren carried it in her jacket pocket for one whole Saturday. She held onto it when she skipped rope and played hopscotch.

Jennifer felt the outline of her souvenir from the grocery store, her plastic whistle, in the pocket of her shorts. She tried to see her mother's face in the rearview mirror, but she could only see her eyes and part of her nose. But even without seeing her mouth, she knew her mother wasn't smiling, and she tried not to smile either.

"My dad's back," she said, quieter this time, holding her excitement in now. "Dad's home."

FOREIGN LANGUAGE

Surfing was not supposed to become religious. Even Winter seemed to appreciate that Patterson hadn't set out to change the language of their marriage. They had shared the same mutual hands-off approach to religion when they met, a vaguely confused guilt about *not* being guilty about any of it. They agreed they would always avoid the stale air inside churches, and they talked about raising whatever future children either of them might have—they still were too new as a couple to be discussing shared children—with good manners and a respect for all religions.

Religion had come upon Patterson in a way neither of them quite understood, although late at night when he lay next to his gently snoring wife, their twin sons, Aiden and Nolan, asleep in bunk beds down the hall, he knew he should try to explain it to her. He owed Winter that much, and he worked on a way to translate into a shared language the first time he felt God's determined grip.

His twins had been born through an emergency caesarean six weeks early, after Winter's blood pressure had suddenly dropped, and Patterson had felt so relieved to see them yanked out shimmering and whole that when they cried, he wept, too. But instead of thanking God, he felt grateful to the doctors, and later to his insurance company when huge zeroed-out balances showed up in the mail. Religion came upon Patterson years later, when his twins were five and he'd begun routinely leaving for work two hours early so he could surf before sitting in an office all day calculating insurance risks.

Winter had laughed when he showed her the ad for a surfing class in their local newspaper. But when she saw he wasn't kidding, her laugh turned into a baffled smile. Then any discussion they might have had was quickly aborted, the way most of their discussions were when their sons interrupted them with one of their endless needs.

Patterson had needs himself, not that anyone had noticed in the past five years. One of those needs was to get off his increasingly big ass and do something. So he took Winter's smile for a nod of acquiescence and signed up for surfing lessons.

He had grown up in Riverside, where he spent his childhood summers skimming brush lizards off the surface of his family's backyard pool so many miles from the ocean that he may as well have lived in Missouri. After his one introductory class, he'd opted for an extended series of Saturday group lessons, enduring the embarrassment of paddling out with a group of twelve-year-old boys and an instructor who didn't look much older.

And he had finally begun to get the hang of the thing, standing up a few times long enough for the instructor to high-five him on shore when the classes had ended. To keep up his progress, each weekday morning he zipped himself into his wetsuit, hung his work clothes on the hook in the back of his car, and continued to practice alone.

The twins were easier in the morning now without diapers and bottles to deal with, and no matter what she really thought about Patterson surfing, Winter didn't complain about his new schedule. And he reasoned that by surfing close to work, by going south on the 405 early before pulling off near San Clemente, he could count missing the bulk of rush-hour traffic as an added bonus.

Still, for weeks he felt thwarted and middle-aged out there, a kind of parody of himself, a balding insurance underwriter among the sinewy teenagers.

It happened only after he'd become so accustomed to defeat that he could barely imagine anything else. When his whole life looked like a series of poor decisions as he failed to catch wave after wave, as he fell again and again, his dull, repetitive work, the needy family he thought he had wanted. All wrong, each wave, all of it. But when he finally stood up on his board and took his first wave to shore without an instructor paddling next to him and cheering him on, he felt a fierce tug tight on his shoulder, as if he were being pulled up to the sky by an invisible hand. *This is it*, someone whispered. *Take it.*

He knew then that he wasn't alone out there, even when he was. He knew this as he paddled back out, as his board slipped through and over a wave. Even as he fell and tumbled the next time, his mouth filling with seaweed and salt, he knew. Patterson knew how it felt to walk on water with that grip on his shoulder, with that voice in his ear. *God*, he thought. *You* are *there. Fuck.*

At first he'd been happy to find a group, Christian Surfers of Southern California, and leave his family out of it. "Join us," they said as he lingered near their morning circle, feigning interest in a small tear on the sleeve of his wetsuit. And he tried. Despite feeling alienated and a bit embarrassed, for four Sunday mornings in a row, he held hands and prayed with this group before heading out into the waves with them.

But the group had taken him only so far. The members pestered him to join them in church after surfing on Sunday mornings and seemed more interested in praying in general than in experiencing the transformative power of each wave in particular, whether it was faultless or only half formed.

They were Christians before they became surfers, and they seemed to him like a fraternity to which he would never quite belong, even after he had paid his dues and pledged.

He only really understood the true extent of his conversion when he finally began to tell Winter about it. He felt himself beam as he described the surprising, sure grip of God's hand on his shoulder, guiding him to shore, and, increasingly, guiding him on land through the morning and into the lunch hour. Routine job tasks like running actuarial tables on clients felt more meaningful now that he was partnering with God in calculating mortality, he explained. His own family waiting for him to arrive safely home from work seemed a daily miracle instead of three people ready to pounce on him and fight for his attention.

"You're fucking with me, right?" Winter said. They were lingering at the breakfast table one hot late-October morning. Kindergarten had been canceled for the day district-wide, some kind of teacher training, and Patterson had decided, at the last minute, to take the day off, to spend it with his sons, who were now plugged in, playing video games in the attached family room.

"I wish I were," he said.

His wife stared at him hard for a minute, the way she stared at the boys when they'd done something she wasn't sure they should be praised or punished for, like writing their names in perfect print with oil paint on the driveway. Then she said, "Well at least you're not having an affair. I was beginning to get worried."

"Let's go," he said. "I'll show you what I mean."

"But we don't go to church," she said, gripping the side of her chair. "We're not church people."

"No," Patterson said. His wife was right. They weren't church people. What he needed to show her wasn't anything that could be found in a building. "We're going to the beach."

While Winter dug out the boys' swimsuits and greased their bodies with sunscreen, Patterson loaded up the car with beach supplies. He strapped his board to the roof and his boys into the booster seats they were clearly outgrowing.

As they neared the beach parking lot, he slowed down, wondering exactly what he could show his wife. He parked the car, and the boys took off toward the ocean, running and stumbling through the sand. He looked out beyond them to the unreliable chop of the afternoon waves and realized how ludicrous and incomplete any explanation would sound.

He turned to Winter. "Let's all just have some fun together."

Patterson set up the umbrella and chairs, then watched his wife pull off her shirt and rub on sunscreen. She'd done something new to her fingernails. They were long but flat instead of curved at their white tips. Fake, he assumed, like the long ponytail she sometimes attached over her own shorter one.

He looked at his wife again, forcing a smile. Winter had quickly lost her baby weight after the boys were born, but something unpleasant had happened to her body. Or maybe her body had always been that way and he had only begun to notice after they had children. It seemed to him that her posture had shifted, that her pelvis had thrust forward somehow. Could carrying twins have done this? The C-section itself?

"Want me to do your back?" she asked.

"Sure." Patterson felt his wife's hands on his back and tried to shake off his judgments of her. He ran his tongue over the bridge that connected four fake teeth to two worn-down real ones on the lower left side of his mouth. He was imperfect, too. He knew he shouldn't be so critical. He thought about what one of the young Christian Surfers had said. Patterson had asked him if it was hard to surf with eyesight so bad that he had to wear his glasses in the water, goggles stretched over them. *God doesn't make mistakes.*

He was lucky with his decent eyesight and two healthy boys. And Winter, he reminded himself, who was so good to him. She never called him at work to berate him about something he forgot to do at home the way some of the wives of the men he worked with did. He was lucky she was still thin, pretty. He willed the feeling of God's hand onto his shoulder.

"This was a good idea," Winter said, rubbing her palms down her thighs to get rid of excess sunscreen. "Just look at them. This is so much better than cranking up the AC and letting them play video games all morning."

Patterson watched the boys running back and forth in front of them as waves broke at their feet. "Let's keep them home," he said, surprising himself. Among the Christian Surfers he had met during his weeks of trying to belong, there were homeschoolers, of course. He remembered one family with five homeschooled children, the youngest surfer just six, but until just now he'd never actively considered the idea of homeschooling the twins.

In fact, for as long as he could remember, Winter and he had talked about how much easier life would get when the boys started kindergarten. Preschool had been tough, with the boys often in trouble for doing what Patterson considered mostly normal boylike things:

refusing to sit still at story time, using finger paints to stripe their faces with war paint and crouch in wait for victims. Sometimes Winter kept them home to punish them, and sometimes she kept them home, he suspected, just to avoid the looks the preschool teachers and sometimes other parents gave her at pickup time.

But so far kindergarten had been a smoother ride. They'd been called in for a few extra parent-teacher conferences to discuss "aggressive playground behavior," which, as far as he could tell, amounted to hogging a handball. And the teacher sent occasional terse notes home about the boys making "inappropriate bathroom sounds" during afternoon quiet time, but it seemed, with regular discipline at home, like things had started to ease up over the past few weeks. Winter seemed more relaxed when he came home at night, having spent only part of the day picking up after the boys. She had even started highlighting her hair again and making his favorite meals. Hadn't the neighborhood's excellent, full-day kindergarten program been a large part of the reason they'd chosen their house?

Still, he found himself feeling more confident the second time he said it. "Let's keep the boys home."

"What are you talking about? It was your idea to go to the beach. We just got here."

"I mean from school. Let's pull them out."

"For a trip? Because they frown upon that, you know. Remember what their teacher said at Back-to-School Night. No ditch days. We have to schedule our trips to Disneyland and vacations when everyone else does now."

"No, I mean let's pull them out forever, or try it at least. Home-school them."

"Are you shitting me?" she said, turning away from watching the boys to stare at him and sounding much more alarmed than she had when he'd told her about his religious awakening.

"What the heck are they learning in that place anyway?"

"What do you mean, what are they learning?" she said. "It's kindergarten. They just started two months ago. They're learning to cut in a straight line. They're learning how to wipe their noses."

"I just mean, what are they learning that we couldn't teach? You could do better with them. I think God would want it that way, that's all. They're such a gift, our boys," Patterson said. "They're our gift, aren't they? Who could teach them better than us?"

"What about our plan? I thought I was supposed to start looking for a job."

"We can work it out. I'm making enough now to support us all."

"I have to think about this one," she said, but he could tell the thinking would wait, that Winter was done with him for now. Two revelations in one day had pushed her to her limit. She pulled a *Glamour* magazine out of their bag and flipped through the pages until she lit upon an article that could hold her attention longer than he could right now.

Later he would talk to her. His wife was easy to convince, really. Hadn't he talked her into getting engaged years ago when she was still intent on dating other people? Hadn't he convinced her to go with the store-brand appliances when they remodeled their kitchen? She'd just need to hear it all again, give it time to sink in.

Patterson picked up his board. He imagined his wife staring hungrily at his body, toned by so many weeks of surfing. He walked past his sons, who had dug an enormous hole and were now trying to fill it with buckets of water, half of which was quickly absorbed back into the sand.

"We're making a Jacuzzi," Aiden said.

"For Mom," Nolan said. "So she can relax more."

"That's very sweet of you boys," he said. Floating in the water were several small dead crabs, their limbs detached. "What happened here?"

"They're dead," Aiden said.

"They drowned," Nolan added, pouring another bucket of ocean water into the hole.

"Okay. Be good boys," Patterson said, watching the detached limbs bounce in the new wave Nolan had created. Then he walked into the ocean, slid onto his board, and paddled out past the breakers. Patterson half nodded to the other surfers who waited out there, the official noncommittal greeting he'd studied surfers using. And then he waited for his first wave to come, and for the singular, divine joy of riding it to shore.

MATH

The daytime world exhausted Beth with its groaning needs. Potted flowers shriveled up in only a matter of days if left unwatered. Laundry molded overnight in the washing machine if she forgot to transfer it to the dryer. A neighbor's cat brought over the remains of a mouse wedged tight in its clenched teeth. A toaster oven spewed out dark smoke and shut off forever. A dishwasher filled up with water and overflowed onto a mopped kitchen floor. Beth ate boxes of Girl Scout cookies and fat handfuls of goldfish crackers while waiting for repairmen who showed up hours late or not at all.

Still, there were the odd moments each day when she felt she was exactly where she was supposed to be, a necessary witness to the domestic world all around her. Beth never knew when one of these moments might occur. Once, she felt a sudden ocean breeze blow through her kitchen window as she was finishing her last sip of coffee at the exact moment the coffee maker's automatic timer switched off. Another time, she turned off the vacuum just in time to hear the 2 p.m. thud of mail through the front door slot.

Several times over the past year she found herself paying bills in the small office upstairs while Jennifer and her neighbor Darla's children, Lauren and Jeremy, played hopscotch in the street outside her window, and she knew at least a section of this background music wouldn't be possible without her. It all needed tending to, though, and that was the problem. The coffee grounds needed to be dumped, the pot rinsed out, the mail sorted through, her own daughter called inside to use her inhaler and start her homework.

Beth hadn't decided to quit her job after her daughter was born. She just couldn't quite figure out how to go back, how women actually did it. Not the emotional part. She hadn't gotten nearly that far. It was the basic moves she couldn't see getting through by nine o'clock or, in fact, reliably at all on any given day. Where did people put a squealing baby when they showered, shaved their underarms, searched for pantyhose without runs in them?

Her six weeks of paid maternity leave had turned into an unpaid leave of three months, then six months, and then a year. And finally she just stopped calling in to ask for extensions. In truth, it didn't matter. When she called back after six months to ask for the rest of the year, she knew by how quickly her boss agreed that she had already been replaced.

Still, she figured she might go back part-time one day, as soon as she could remember exactly how she used to function out in the world and how anyone had taken her, with her fat gut and meaty thighs, seriously. But back then, they weren't quite so meaty. After Jennifer was born, her previously dependable body had betrayed her. Not only did she keep the extra thirty pounds her obstetrician had assured her would slowly "melt away," for nearly a year her pores teemed, and she broke out like a teenager. When she tried to blow-dry her hair, strands loosened from her scalp and wrapped themselves in clumps around her curved wooden brush.

Much to her disgust, she had become one of those women who never quite recovers from giving birth, who becomes thick and matronly and weepy, and all this shocked her almost as much as Jennifer's enormous and unrelenting needs.

It wasn't just that Jennifer cried a lot. And she cried constantly, unless Beth held her with her arms out in front of her at an angle that felt stiff and awkward—as if her baby were something vaguely distasteful, like a stuffed animal bought at a yard sale that continued to smell soiled even after it had been washed.

Jennifer napped only when perched upright and continuously moving. This meant pushing the stroller for hours through their neighborhood, walking past the houses in which Beth imagined other mothers were home soaking in tubs and reading important novels or doing rewarding freelance work or at least getting the dishes done while their children slept soundly in their cribs. But the hardest part of being a mother was listening to Jennifer's labored breathing.

The first time Jennifer had a full-scale asthma attack, the pediatrician misdiagnosed it as normal baby's rattle and sent Beth home with one of his patronizing booklets, this one entitled "Your Developing Baby, Ages Six Through Twelve Months." The book told her nothing at all about baby's rattle and was clearly published by a formula company that was attempting to hide its obvious agenda, complete with coupons, behind disingenuous advice about the importance of giving your baby breast milk, "the perfect formula," whenever possible.

When Jennifer's asthma became so bad that she started choking one afternoon while nursing and then turned rigid and silent in Beth's arms, she skipped the pediatrician and rushed her daughter straight to the emergency room. Waiting for Keith to arrive, she watched a group of doctors and nurses take the baby, already on her way to becoming a ghost, from her arms. They stuck tubes down her throat and adrenaline into a tiny vein they finally were able to poke through on the damp underside of her forearm. Beth thought her secret was certainly out now, that everyone knew what a lousy failure of a mother she was.

Three weeks later, an allergy specialist handed her an indecipherable report, Jennifer's small back still pocked and speckled from tests. Her asthma triggers were numerous. Her future was unlikely ever to include peanut butter and jelly sandwiches or ice cream sundaes or chocolate-covered strawberries. And her present should probably—to be safe—include no more breast milk. It was, for Beth, confirmed. For nine months she had infected Jennifer with her obsessions over whether or not her baby would be normal or was missing something

the ultrasound had failed to catch, like a knee or a liver or the left
quadrant of her brain. And now she was poisoning her own child with
her preposterous body.

The new formula cost $340 a month, close to the amount she
figured they'd have to pay for childcare if she did go back to work part-
time. Relieved, she let the childcare math decide.

Before Jennifer, Beth worked in promotions for a department store
in Costa Mesa, a job that, with her BA in marketing, she felt both
overqualified for and terrified of losing. She roughed out pages for the
Orange County Register that advertised cooking demonstrations in their
Housewares Department and special appearances by Madeline and
Bob the Builder in Children's Accessories.

Once she listed the time for an appearance of a children's dog
puppet she had never heard of as an 11 a.m. when in fact he was
scheduled to arrive at 10. After this, she learned to double- and triple-
check dates and times. The puppet ended up leaving at 10:30 after
signing autographs with his mouth for the few Cosmetic Counter
employees who had children. A half an hour later, she tried to fend off
irate parents and their whining children with ten-dollar gift certificates
when they hunted her down personally through the vast office maze
behind Today's Hair to meet the apparently popular dog. "It's one
thing to inconvenience adults, but do you really think you can buy off
our children?" one mother said as she grabbed her gift certificate with
one hand and held tightly to her toddler's hand with the other.

Now Beth had only her daughter's schedule to keep track of, and
she still couldn't get it straight. She found tiny doctors' reminder cards
washed clean of dates and times in the pockets of her jeans when she
pulled them out of the dryer. She missed appointments for allergy
shots, playdates, haircuts, Tiny Tumblers gymnastic classes. She drove
to Los Angeles at 11 a.m. on a Wednesday for a Tuesday appointment
with an allergy specialist who was so in demand that his receptionist
not only billed her but refused to reschedule her.

She knew that part of her problem was sleep deprivation, brought
on by listening for any irregularities in her daughter's breathing. Each
night she stood by Jennifer's open bedroom door until she was certain
her breath wasn't raspy. The beginnings of asthma could be brought on

by any number of triggers Beth had failed to shield her from that day. When she was certain her daughter was breathing normally, she walked down the hallway and crawled into bed beside her husband. She lay there trying to sleep, but instead, she listened to the earth tremble.

Ten years before, in the spirit of newly married adventure, she had moved with Keith from the East Coast, back to Southern California, where they'd met in college. She knew earthquake faults veined the ground; she'd been woken in her college dorm room by the sound of a stack of textbooks tumbling off her desk. But it was only after she had Jennifer that she became aware of the faults' routine presence. While her daughter and husband slept, Beth swore she felt dozens of tiny shifts, all too minute to make the news.

To take her mind off the rumblings apparently only she could feel, she tried to focus on whether or not she was prepared to help her daughter in a medical emergency. A runny nose or a case of hives was easily calmed with an over-the-counter antihistamine kept in the medicine cabinet. Even asthma, Jennifer's most persistent and frightening allergic reaction so far, could be treated, if caught in time, with her prescription inhaler.

Anaphylaxis was what kept Beth wide awake at night. The possibility of her daughter's throat swelling up and strangling her. Beth slept with an EpiPen under her pillow. Its genteel name—EpiPen— sounded to her like something you might give a girl for a high school graduation gift. The name disguised what it really was: a loaded shot of epinephrine. She hoped, if she ever needed to, she wouldn't be afraid to stab it deep into her daughter's thigh.

She had watched the DVD that came with the drug, had practiced stabbing the empty sample into a stuffed bear the way the preternaturally calm voiceover actor had suggested. But still, she wasn't sure if the time came, that she could do what the woman on the DVD did: jab the needle deep into her daughter's flesh, straight through her clothes. Sometimes late at night, while Keith slept soundly next to her, Beth imagined practicing by stabbing the empty sample shot into her husband's shoulder. Once she tapped it against his flesh so hard he turned in his sleep and batted her hand away as if it were a mosquito. But he didn't wake up, and in the morning, the red mark that the point of the EpiPen had made on his shoulder had disappeared.

To compensate for her persistent lack of sleep, she made lists to keep track of Jennifer's appointments. She bought long, thin pads of lined paper and each day transferred information from her appointment book to a crisp new sheet that she hung on the refrigerator with a hot pink "To Do!" magnet. She set her cell phone's alarm, and several times a day when it went off she scrambled to find the matching task on the phone's calendar feature.

But nothing had prepared her for the complexity of keeping up with Jennifer's schedule once she started school. Beth missed spring kindergarten registration by a day, early summer registration by three hours, and finally had to wait in line with the anxious, fidgety parents who had just moved into town in late August. She showed up ten minutes late for parent-teacher conferences that were scheduled to last fifteen minutes, a half an hour late for back-to-school night, and the wrong day entirely for the Mother's Day brunch.

With homeschool, Beth reasoned, there would be far fewer of these humiliations for both of them to endure. If she forgot to pack lunch for a field trip just the two of them were taking, Jennifer's first grade teacher, Mrs. Miramir, would not have to check the ingredients before offering to share her own sandwich. They could just buy Italian ice at the snack bar. Who besides the two of them would even know if they slept past the seven o'clock alarm, or if they ate a real breakfast at 11 a.m. when they were finally hungry instead of cramming down wood-flavored, nut-and-dairy-free protein bars on the way out the door?

Homeschool meant there would be no more Hawaiian Shirt Days to remember, no more Bring a Flower for Your Teacher Days, Wear a Hat Days, Mom's Muffin Days, Geography Shirt Days, Pet Days, Career Days, Sport Shirt Days, Inside-Out Days, Sleeping Bag Read-a-thon Days, Late Start Days, and Early Out Days. There would be no more home-reading sheets to lose, volunteer hours to fill out, vaccine records to supply.

There would be no more sitting alone on the benches that bordered the blacktop of the playground in the punishing afternoon sun while mothers all around her were busy with their gossipy conversations and fundraising packets. There would be no more waiting for her daughter to wander out of her classroom, always last, her sweater left behind, some important notice stuffed into the depths of her backpack, where Beth would find it only when whatever crucial date had already passed.

There would be no need to explain to Mrs. Miramir that her husband had left them both two weeks ago, so please be patient if Jennifer seemed not quite herself.

But of course she knew that these were more fringe benefits than actual reasons to homeschool. She'd made her decision so recently that she was still sorting out those actual reasons. She imagined defending her decision to her good-naturedly overwhelmed neighbor, Darla, or to that mean-spirited woman judge on television. Or to her husband. She would talk about the need for creativity and flexibility, not to mention that Jennifer had already missed so many days with her asthma and was bound to miss even more.

In California, it turned out there were four legal ways to homeschool your child. While Beth was still calling the school each morning, telling the secretary Jennifer was sick, she was leaning toward what seemed to her the simplest solution, establishing what amounted to a virtual private school for one in her home. As far as she could tell, this school would never be visited by anyone like a principal or truant officer as long as she sent in the right paperwork, taught certain required subjects, and generally laid fairly low.

So far she'd been able to track down the information she needed online, which seemed a far better way to begin than talking to actual people and getting drawn into their messy agendas. She'd assumed other homeschoolers would be shy or at least private and defensive, but the homeschoolers she'd come across online had home pages so upbeat and group-oriented that she wondered why they didn't just stick with the public school system and run for PTA president. Just thinking about actually trying to meet them in person, or even over the phone, made her want to take a long midday nap on the couch.

The chirpiness of their websites did offer Beth a few solid phrases she had latched onto and found herself silently repeating whenever she felt dizzied by the double jolt of abandonment and doubt: "Relax! Who could know more about your child's personal learning style than you?"

"Every child deserves to feel like she's special."

And, perhaps her favorite: "You were your child's first teacher—why shouldn't you be her last?"

Beth decided that before she told the school, or Keith, about the decision to homeschool Jennifer, she would have to make sure she had all of her facts straight. She had emailed a man named David who made his contact information available on several different chat rooms and websites. David encouraged new homeschoolers not to be intimidated by the paperwork or the school systems. He said that, as parents, they were the ones who knew what was best for their children, no one else.

Beth liked the idea of contacting a man, someone who might be able to get right down to business and not get too chatty and personal the way a woman might. She knew this was a terrible thing to admit, her suspicion of women. Knew that she was supposed to have a close group of female friends to support her through difficult times. But the truth was, the only woman she talked to regularly was her neighbor Darla, and she confided in her mainly out of convenience, not any real sense of trust.

Earlier that day, before making Jennifer's breakfast, she'd read David's response to the email she'd sent him the night before, assuring her she was not alone and inviting her to stop by with Jennifer and meet his children. When she typed his address into her phone, she felt what she knew was a false sense of accomplishment, but she had let the feeling propel her through her day nonetheless.

Now, seeing her husband's car parked in front of her house, she felt the heavy weight of her own inefficiency. She had accomplished nothing today but grocery shopping, and she had been keeping her daughter home from school even though she hadn't been sick in days.

She spotted Keith's car at the same moment Jennifer did. It was a bright red Mercury Tracer station wagon, a model not even made anymore. She pointed this out in one of her arguments to upgrade to an SUV or at least a minivan before she gave up and allowed the car its natural de-evolution to becoming Keith's car. The wagon's rear door was closed, but she could see through the glass clothes from their closet still on their hangers, strewn across the back.

When he walked out two weeks ago, she'd said, *Go on ahead. It's not like you're really here anyway. What difference will it make?* But in truth, she never believed he would follow through. For the past two weeks, she had alternated between pretending he was away on an extended business trip and not thinking about him directly at all. Now here he was, back again, apparently only to show her he wasn't through leaving yet.

"Daddy! Daddy's home!" Jennifer screamed out her window, although Keith was nowhere in sight. Beth looked back at her daughter and watched her face slowly adjust to its more familiar blank stare. She suspected Jennifer had been practicing how she would greet her father since he'd left two weeks earlier the same way she practiced her smile, her look of astonishment, even her gum-chewing technique, in the upstairs hall mirror. This outburst was probably not what she planned.

She watched her daughter cross their front yard, first walking and then running until she disappeared into the house. Instead of getting out and unloading the groceries, Beth sat tight, kept her hands on the steering wheel as if she might just drive off. She imagined her daughter to be someone else's breathless, running-home child spotted in her peripheral vision. She tried to watch her in the same way she'd watch a pelican diving over the bridge into the cold water of Alamitos Bay or, back in Pennsylvania, a single deer bounding through a field.

She wondered how long it would take Keith and Jennifer to realize she was even gone if she did drive off. She knew how her personal math equation played out in public: The more weight she'd gained, the less visible she'd become. But now she considered what her private equation might be: The more she focused her life around Jennifer, the more Jennifer wanted her father. While she knew she should be grateful that Jennifer loved both her parents, she was jealous. No matter how hard she worked at making herself indispensable, Keith always won. What could be more proof than this moment? Even after he'd abandoned them both for two weeks, Jennifer still chose him.

Before Beth had time to pull herself together and get out of the car, Jennifer and Keith were walking back across the lawn toward her. Jennifer held her father's hand and skipped at every fourth step. Beth popped the trunk and slowly got out. She felt grubby and wished she had bothered to wash her hair that morning or at least put on makeup.

"Here, let me help you," Keith said, reaching in the trunk for grocery bags.

Like her, Keith wore jeans and a T-shirt and looked like he hadn't bothered to shower that morning either. He might have been a graduate student who'd just gotten out of bed after studying all night, while she was simply a middle-age woman, her body doughy with inattention.

"So, what's Jenny doing home so early? Teacher conference day?" Keith asked as they walked into the kitchen. Jennifer had run up the stairs to bring down a picture she drew for her father.

"Teacher conference? Oh, right." She suddenly felt crowded in the galley kitchen, wondered how the two of them had ever fit in there together.

"You should have called me," Keith said. "You know, I'm still her father."

Beth shook her head. "Not a conference-conference. They went to some conference," she said, surprised at how quickly she'd lied. "All the first grade teachers. Do you want to sit out back for a minute?"

The patio was still strewn with debris from the Santa Anas. She righted a plastic chair and pulled it up to the glass patio table, brushing leaves and twigs off the table with the side of her hand. Her birds of paradise and lemon tree looked scorched after the windstorms. She could almost taste their thirst. The recycling bin was tipped sideways, and she could see that empty plastic milk and juice bottles were wedged into the juniper bushes. Always, there was so much that needed tending to, so much to do. And, as always, he seemed not to notice any of it.

He pulled up a chair, sat down across from her at the table, and stretched his legs out on one of the chairs that were still tipped sideways. "It's amazing to see Jenny again," he said. "You can't believe how much I've missed her. We need to work out a schedule now that this is real, now that this is really happening."

"She's been wondering when she'd see you. It's not our schedule that's a problem."

"Okay, I get it," Keith said.

"You *get* it? What do you *get*?"

"I'm bad, you're good. I'm wrong, you're right. Why don't we get all that out of the way first, just put it all out on the table."

Before she could answer, Jennifer was out on the patio handing her father a stack of drawings and explaining each one. "Hang them up in your office, okay?"

"Gotcha," Keith said.

"Now watch me jump," Jennifer said, looking around the yard and finally locating her jump rope coiled in the dirt by the garbage can. "I can make it to one hundred now."

"Cool," Keith said.

Be careful about your asthma, Beth thought. Even if they'd been careful, and Jennifer hadn't eaten anything she wasn't supposed to, the thin, hot air could kick it up. Beth bit down on the inside of her cheeks instead of talking, a trick she'd taught herself to keep quiet and only silently predict the worst. She felt her belly pushing against the waist of her jeans and pulled her T-shirt down lower.

Upstairs in her bedroom was a drawer full of clothes she longed to climb into, stretchy pants and men's gym shorts and huge yard-sale sweaters. These were her post-maternity clothes, the ones she'd planned to wear for just a few months after Jennifer had been born. To get out of these clothes, she had purchased a three-year family gym membership. She had bought into one of those promotions she knew from her own marketing experience were designed to lure impulsive customers. They counted on her not to take up valuable floor space in an already crowded Pilates class or wear down the cardio machines by using them regularly. And instead of going to the gym, Beth remained scattered and busy. She dropped off and picked up Jennifer, refilled prescriptions, and spent hours on the phone with insurance companies. She became just the kind of no-show customer the gym had counted on her being.

Together she and Keith watched their daughter jump. "You're not coming back, are you?" Beth asked.

He didn't answer, but she could feel him shake his head even as she looked straight ahead at her daughter. The air was still charged with enough negative ions and static electricity for Jennifer's hair to shoot out like a sprinkler in separate, thin strands around her head. Under the lemon tree was Jennifer's doll stroller, its thin metal legs stretched too far on either side of it, split by the wind.

"You have to fix the TV before you go," Beth said. "We don't have any sound again."

"Can do."

And then Jennifer was on his lap, her arms wrapped around Keith's neck. "Did you see me do it, Daddy?" she asked. "Did you watch every second?"

"Absolutely," he said. "Every single second."

Beth tried to imagine being somewhere else, anywhere else, rather than sitting two feet away from her husband, who was really never coming back home. She had taken a meditation class in college. She'd had a mantra then. A word that sounded like a hum. But the word was gone. She tried to focus on a quiet place where she had felt tranquil, serene. She thought about the beach in Corona del Mar where she'd once made out with a boyfriend in college by a rocky cove, but she could only get so far as imagining herself stuck in a traffic jam on Pacific Coast Highway on the way there.

"I hear there's a television set that needs me," Keith said, standing up and putting Jennifer down. "You lead the way."

"I'll just wait down here," Beth said, or maybe she only imagined saying this. There was always so much she thought about saying. Her own voice sometimes surprised her when she actually spoke. *That's how I sound*, she thought. *Here I am.* It occurred to her for the first time that maybe she should have argued with Keith more, not less, that he wouldn't be able to walk out so easily if she had been louder, more insistent.

She walked around the yard, picking up the larger branches and breaking them in two so they fit in the garbage can. She stuffed the baby stroller in first, hoping Jennifer hadn't seen it snapped. She reasoned that at seven, her daughter was getting too old to play with it for much longer anyway, that maybe she wouldn't even notice it was missing.

Although the winds had ended, the air was still thin and hot, as if they were living in the middle of the desert, not just a few miles from the ocean. Beth heard her daughter giggling upstairs in the bedroom and then the sudden loud pop of sound as their television set finally started working.

PHYSICAL EDUCATION

The health club was such a different place in the late afternoon that Keith wondered if he'd accidentally stumbled into the wrong club or had come in a different entrance. Except for the desk clerk, he seemed to be the only man there. Women wearing tiny shorts and tops and large, complicated sneakers stood around the entranceway chatting, and he could have sworn that several looked him over when he handed the desk clerk his membership card.

Keith had been living in his office for the past two weeks. He'd been showering here. Irritated that Beth had signed up for a three-year family membership without consulting him, he rarely used the gym before this. He figured now that at least one of them was taking advantage of the place.

Since he'd left Beth, most mornings before officially opening up his office, he drove the several blocks to the traffic circle and headed straight for the locker rooms. Surrounded by other men finishing early morning workouts, he figured he didn't look so out of place in his sweatpants and T-shirt. Only someone following his moves a bit too closely would guess that he hadn't worked out before showering.

While he couldn't imagine investing the time it would take to learn how to use the exercise equipment, he'd discovered a small indoor lap pool, and a few mornings he actually swam two or three laps before showering. His slow crawl back and forth was hardly enough to constitute a workout, but he reasoned that it was a start, or at least an effective way to shake off the ache that came from sleeping on a cheap sofa.

Keith had skipped his morning shower the day he finally went home to pick up more clothes; he planned to take an afternoon one instead before he met with clients. He had left his family late at night with just an overnight bag and, despite the effort it took not to see Jennifer, until now he had avoided going back.

But he had meetings coming up and events for which he needed to appear in something other than sweatpants or jeans. When he found the house empty, he'd considered taking his things and leaving before Beth came home, but thinking about getting to see his daughter again helped him to stay put, act less like the coward he knew he was, and make things official, work out a schedule.

Their last fight hadn't really been a fight at all. *Why don't you just leave*, Beth had said, interrupting herself in the middle of telling him about some study she was thinking about signing Jennifer up for about tree nut allergies. *It's not like you're really here anyway.* At that moment he knew she was right. It had been years since he'd really listened to her. Leaving made such complete sense to Keith that, after he finally decided to do it, the only thing he second-guessed was how he had managed to stay so long.

He smiled at the group of women in the entranceway of the gym now and thought he heard a muffled giggle as he walked toward the men's locker room. He felt almost buoyed enough to try to figure out the weight equipment and work out before showering, but then he remembered the photographs he needed to sort through and opted for a few quick laps in the indoor pool instead.

When he walked into the pool area, a young woman in a red tank suit thrust a bright pink children's pool noodle at him. "A latecomer," she said. "No matter. We're glad you're here. Name?" she said to him.

"Keith?"

"Okay, Keith, jump right in," she said while he stared at her. "That's the best way to do it. Here, let me show you." The woman lifted his arms up and wrapped the noodle around his chest. "Now put your arms down. See, it's just like a life preserver. Don't you feel safe?"

What he felt was far from safe. The noodle felt like his daughter's legs wrapped around him, but instead of peeling the noodle off, he gripped tighter. Bobbing in the water were three women and two men, adults looking up at him, their noodles keeping them afloat. Here's where the gym men were in the afternoon, he thought, learning to swim with the women.

"Jump!" one of the men shouted. "Just do it, Keith, buddy."

Keith imagined this same man yelling at a suicide jumper. He angled his leap so he came down close enough to splash him in the face.

"Excellent," the instructor said. "Didn't that feel good?"

The man who had been shouting at him was wiping the water out of his eyes with one hand while gripping tightly to his noodle with the other.

"It did," Keith said. "It really did."

"Okay, here's our key word for the day. *Kick*. It's the only thing you have to remember. We're going to line up next to each other and kick our way to the end of the pool."

As he kicked to the end, he found himself bumping noodles with a woman wearing a flowered bathing cap and bright blue goggles that somehow lit up on the sides whenever she moved her head.

"I'm sorry," he said. "I'm not very good at this."

"Please don't talk to me while I'm kicking," she said.

"All right! You did it." The instructor applauded for each of them as they reached the edge of the pool. "Now go wash that chlorine off. I'll see everyone tomorrow for lesson numero three."

In the lobby as the girl at the counter handed him back his card, Keith felt someone tap his shoulder.

"I didn't mean to be rude," the woman said. "I just can't talk at all out there. I really can't."

"Oh, you're the lady with the goggles," Keith said.

"I thought they might be lucky," she said.

She still smelled faintly of chlorine, but he wouldn't have recognized her outside of the pool otherwise. He had imagined long hair under her swim cap. He assumed the goggles had sharpened her features. But the woman next to him now had short, spiky black hair and a face that was more angular than pretty.

He slid his membership card quickly into his wallet before she had a chance to see his scowling picture, taken in annoyance shortly after Beth had signed them up.

"So see you tomorrow, huh?" the goggle lady said.

"Right, tomorrow," Keith said. "I can't wait to find out our new key word."

"You missed *breathe*," she said. "That was our first class."

"No wonder I had so much trouble today. That was a bad one to miss."

They were the only ones in the lobby now, and Keith held the door open and watched the woman walk out in front of him. She carried a huge, zipped shoulder bag that looked like it weighed nearly as much as she did. Why was he flirting? She wasn't even his type. He waved goodbye as she got in her tiny, toylike car and drove away.

Keith was a wedding photographer, but he shot only in black and white and had refused to go digital. Not only could he develop the photographs himself without a lot of expense, but black and white was more flattering. And no matter what clients said about wanting to tell a story or capture the spirit of an event, the bottom line was that people wanted to look good at their own weddings.

At first he'd simply been too cheap to invest in the new equipment he needed to make the switch from film. But after an elaborate Palos Verdes wedding, word had quickly spread among people with unlimited budgets, the way things did in Los Angeles, that he was the real thing, an old-fashioned black-and-white film guy, a true wedding artist. One of his clients made a phone call, and he was interviewed for a piece in *Bride* magazine. When asked why he shot only in black and white, he talked about shadows. When asked why he hadn't made the switch to digital, he found himself rambling on about the texture of film, pretending to have based his decision solely on principle, even if the truth had more to do with money.

After the magazine article appeared, he joined the ranks of the lucky few, doubling his prices and choosing his weddings. Still, he was forced to turn down destination weddings in Italy and Costa Rica because Beth worried Jennifer would have an asthma attack and he couldn't get back in time. Instead, he photographed a model marrying a stunt man on a cliff in Malibu and a distant cousin of the Kennedy family getting married at the Ritz-Carlton in Laguna Niguel. And he shot several weddings at a hotel on a Coronado Island beach where Marilyn Monroe made *Some Like It Hot.*

His clients all thought they were being original, one of a kind. But the men all drank too much and waited until they were sure to have an audience to tip him. And the women blurred together, too. Most were pretty in the same way, thin, with highlighted hair, smoothed skin, plumped lips. If it weren't for the different bridesmaids' dresses, he might have returned the negatives from the wrong wedding when a client paid the extra fee to buy them.

He may be demanding more money than he had in the past, but in the end, it all came down to the same thing, work. He'd begun early that morning, developing film from a wedding that must have cost more than most people's houses. The party had taken place on the *Queen Mary*, a dusty retired cruise ship harbored in Long Beach. Brides loved the ship for weddings and booked it so far in advance that he wondered if some of them actually booked before they even found husbands. But he hated shooting on the *Queen Mary*. For daytime weddings, he tried to work with natural light, but the ship's rooms were dark, and he had no choice but to use artificial lighting.

He wouldn't receive the final third of his payment until the bride and groom approved the proofs, hundreds of 3 ½-x-5-inch photos. They had rented the ship's most ornate ballroom, and Keith had struggled to keep the chandeliers and heavy drapes well in the background, not to let the setting overwhelm his subjects.

It had been several years since the *Bride* article had appeared, and Keith could feel its effects waning. He hadn't had to lower his prices yet, but he rarely was double-booked on a Saturday anymore.

And he had committed what he knew was the freelancer's number-
one mistake: not squirreling away enough money. They hadn't done
anything extravagant—no big trips or new cars or remodeled kitchen.
They had gone through it by paying insurance premiums, buying
food for Jennifer at expensive health-food stores, and writing checks
for PTA memberships and wrapping paper drives and cable bills and
parking tickets, and doing all of it without paying attention. Still, until
recently, there always seemed to be more.

Now, for the first time in several years, Keith had reason to worry
about money. Even though all assets were split down the middle in a
California divorce, Keith knew that with child support and the likely
possibility of alimony, none of it would be cheap or easy. He had no
idea what divorcing his wife might eventually cost him. What was clear
to him was that their marriage had ended years before, and, no matter
what it cost, he wasn't doing much more now than formalizing the
situation.

Along with his daughter's drawings, he took all the bills that had
come in during the two weeks since he left. Before driving to the gym
to shower, the bed of his station wagon full of clothes, he'd handed Beth
a check for $500. He'd always filled her checking account whenever he
was paid, but now he felt he should do something more official.

She had looked at the check and then him and walked up the
stairs. Keith waited at the bottom for several minutes, thinking maybe
she was writing him a receipt. But she didn't come back down. He
wasn't sure if she'd been insulted by the amount or was just through
making small talk with him. Since Jenny had been born, he hadn't
been able to read his wife, and it seemed unlikely he was going to start
figuring her out now.

Sometimes he wished he had more of a problem reading his
daughter. When Jennifer wrapped her arms around his neck and her
legs around his waist, he couldn't pretend his leaving had no effect
on her. "I'll see you sooner next time, I promise," he said, giving her
one last kiss before peeling her off. "Your mother and I will make up
a schedule," he told her, although the truth was, they had gotten only
as far with that discussion as talking about having it. His visit had

accomplished nothing. He left feeling like even more of a shit, and his wife seemed angrier than ever at him.

Back at his office, Keith wrote numbers on the back of each print and arranged the best photos in an album, filling small, heavy black boxes with the remaining ones. Although this would complicate his search for negatives later, he placed the photos on the first pages that he hoped the couple might be compelled to order more of, the reprints for aunts and grandmothers and the 5 x 7s and 8 x 10s for framing. These were where he made his real money.

He had trained himself not to be disappointed. People rarely chose his best photos. Still, he took private satisfaction in them—the way the light fell across a bride's turned cheek, or a white chair with a piece of cake left on it, one bite missing. When they were first married, he would show Beth his work as they sat together on the couch at night, and she admired the best ones along with him. They had been a different couple then. He remembered her heels kicked off onto the coffee table, laughing about a best man's pot belly.

His clients wanted him to blow up the more predictable, sentimental photographs: the groom feeding the bride the first bite of cake, the requisite photo of the flower girl standing on tiptoe to kiss the bride's cheek when she bent down.

He had worried that arranging these wedding photos would make him finally sink into some dark abyss over the demise of his own marriage, but, as always, it felt like pure business. Keith had spread the photos out on two long card tables that morning, and he quickly got back to work.

There was nothing upscale about his office, just this room and the attached bathroom he had turned into a darkroom by stapling a dark blue towel over the small window. He rarely met with clients here, preferring instead to bring his portfolio and set up meetings in coffeehouses, where he could let his work, not his office, make the first impression.

Three weeks had passed since the wedding, and it was now more obvious that the bride was pregnant. No one he worked with seemed to care much about these things anymore, but in case prewedding pregnancy ever went out of vogue, Keith tried, whenever possible, not to highlight it, shooting the brides from the front, where their pregnancies were less obvious.

At six p.m. the coffeehouse wasn't crowded, just a few college students cramming for midterms and several stragglers hunched over books. He saw one customer count out his change for a coffee and wondered for the first time if the haphazardly dressed people Keith had always assumed were artists or students were actually homeless. Maybe he'd have to find another coffeehouse.

"Oh, look at that one," the bride said now, sipping her decaf latte. "We look so happy. We need an 8 x 10 of that, don't you think?"

Keith didn't bother looking at the husband before writing *large cake face* in his notebook. No matter what kind of plans the couple had for an egalitarian marriage, the woman always chose the wedding pictures.

An hour later, Keith left the coffeehouse with his final check and an order large enough to keep him holed up in his darkroom for the next several days. He was about to turn onto his street when he remembered that he didn't live there anymore. He made a sudden U-turn and heard a car honk at him.

He drove slowly to his office, knowing he should be relieved to have a place to go besides the coffeehouse but still not eager to spend another night on the couch he'd inherited from the previous tenant.

Soon, Beth and he would have to sort things out. He'd find an actual apartment somewhere and make a schedule to see his daughter. He'd never been away from her before this, and he couldn't quite imagine seeing Jennifer without Beth standing somewhere nearby, hovering, making sure he didn't get her too excited and start her asthma up, give her the wrong food, strap her in the wrong seat of the car.

He drove past Jennifer's school, something he'd done almost daily for the past two weeks while he'd stayed away. A big, crisp blue award-winning ribbon was painted on the wall by the entrance. Although the school day had ended hours ago, he pictured Jennifer in the classroom he'd visited on back-to-school night with the American flag hanging in the corner, the kids' crayon drawings of their families taped to the walls. He imagined her hunched over her little desk working while her teacher with the wide hips and long, blond hair walked through the aisles with her sheets of gold and blue star stickers.

He missed his daughter, but he worried that he didn't miss her as much as he should. With her tense, beleaguered face as she explained the latest Jennifer crisis, Beth had always made him feel like he didn't care about their daughter as much as she did. And he saw now that maybe she was right. Although Jennifer often seemed to choose him over Beth, she still belonged in some inextricable way to Beth, not him. And the house clearly belonged to the two of them. He already felt like a visitor in it.

The truth was that since the adult swim lesson it was the goggle lady he couldn't stop thinking about. He imagined he could lift her up easily, not just in the water, but right out of it. He could almost feel her thin legs gripped tightly around his waist.

And now he wasn't concentrating again, and he had to or he'd never finish when he got back to the office. For years, while Beth fussed with medicines and special foods and second opinions, he had made himself focus on work. And he'd do it again now, so Jennifer could keep her house and her school with the blue ribbon painted on it and her gold and blue star stickers, everything exactly the same, despite the fact he had left.

The next afternoon at swim class, the word was *float*. Keith had worked most of the night, slept late, and intended to come in to the health club only to shower, but he'd somehow arrived at the same time as the swim instructor. She winked at him and said, "See you soon, Keith Wheeler," in front of what seemed to be the same group of women as the day before loitering in the lobby.

"That's very brave of you," he heard one of the women say as he dug his membership card out of his wallet. "Most people never confront their fears."

Not knowing which woman had talked to him, he shrugged in the group's general direction. He heard someone whisper, "How cute is he?" as he walked into the locker room. The back of his neck ached from sleeping on the office couch, and all he wanted to do was pound hot water from the shower onto it. But instead, here he was, standing in the shallow end of a lukewarm pool, getting ready to float.

"We'll start with the back float today, so no one has to worry yet about putting his or her face in the water," the instructor said. She wore the same regulation-looking swimsuit, but like yesterday, she was on dry land, standing by the pool talking down at them. "What we're all going to do is just relax and lie down on top of the water like we're about to take a nice nap on the couch."

Having just gotten up from the couch in his office, Keith was uninspired by the analogy. He looked at the goggle lady, who seemed to be staring at a fixed point on the instructor's shoulder. He thought about whispering something clever to her about all of the instructor's "we" talk when only some of them were getting wet, but maybe the goggle lady didn't want to talk in the water even if she was standing up. While Mr. *Jump* looked like a napper, she definitely didn't. Keith thought the instructor might have tried to come up with something more universal.

"And, *float!*" she shouted. All around him, he felt the water move as if several small speedboats were racing through the pool in different directions. He was being splashed in the face so vigorously that for a moment he panicked and forgot that he already knew how to swim. "It's okay to take a minute," the instructor said. He looked around and saw everyone still splashing frantically about. He was the only one standing. She was talking to him. "Pace yourself. Visualize yourself floating in air if that helps. And remember to *breathe*."

"Right," he said. "I missed that lesson."

Keith found a less frenetic patch of shallow end and stretched out. He couldn't remember the last time he had actually floated, and now that he'd managed to edge away from the group, he saw its lazy appeal.

"Okay, that's it for today. Much better, Keith. I think someone remembered to breathe."

He found himself taking his time in the now-empty lobby. He scanned the ingredients on the protein bars that were for sale and carefully read each flyer promoting Zumba and yoga classes before he finally had to come to terms with two things: He had been waiting for someone, and he had missed her. She had hurried out of the pool, avoiding the crowded steps and instead hoisting herself up off the side before he had a chance to talk to her. And now, he realized, she must have skipped her shower completely.

Keith turned on his cell phone when he got in the car and found that he had three new messages, all from his daughter: a report of an injured knee from hopscotch, a lost baby stroller, and a huge crisis: Beth planned to get rid of the television he had just reset for them. "Call me earlier tonight, Daddy," she said in the last one. "I really need to talk to you."

ROCKET SCIENCE

"None of it is rocket science," David said to Beth as they sat at a splintery picnic table in his backyard and watched their daughters jump through a sprinkler. David's barefoot girls looked androgynous to Beth, with their long, stringy hair, boy's swim trunks, and flat, bare chests. If David hadn't told her on the phone the day before that he had three daughters, she might have wondered if they were actually boys.

In her skirted yellow one-piece, thick yellow hair band, and pink water shoes, Jennifer suddenly looked prissy to Beth. Maybe it was a good thing that they were rushing out the door and hadn't been able to find the matching flowered flip-flops. Beth had dressed up a bit for the occasion herself, squeezing into a pair of white jeans and ironing a blue sleeveless blouse that now felt too tight across her chest.

"We're trying to raise them to be liberated in a sexist world," David said, turning from the girls to Beth.

"I think that's terrific," she said. "Good for you." She hadn't thought about women's liberation herself in years, not since she'd been in college and, due to a late registration date, had found herself enrolled in the only history class that fit into her schedule, Reproductive History of the U.S., which had a decidedly feminist bent.

Over the past few weeks it had become clear to Beth that she'd been so caught up in trying to keep track of things that she'd barely been thinking about anything else at all for years. Now, here she was discussing feminism in the backyard of the house of a strange, bearded man who wore a T-shirt that read THROW OUT YOUR TELEVISION! Beth imagined saying something witty about birth control pills actually giving birth to the second wave of feminism the way her history professor had, but she couldn't figure out how to fit it in.

"All of this is particularly tough in So Cal, of course," David said, scratching at his beard.

"Really?" Beth said, feeling her initial enthusiasm for getting started on the homeschooling thing already beginning to slip.

"Oh, not the homeschooling part," he said, once again demonstrating his disturbing ability to read her thoughts. "That's just a matter of paperwork, like we discussed. It's the feminist part that's tough around here. I mean, it's not like the majority of our neighbors subscribe to the same idea. Or even the other homers."

"Homos?" Beth said, wondering if this man who called himself a feminist somehow managed to hate gay people.

"Homers. That's what the girls and I call them. The other homeschoolers. It's one of our little private language jokes. We have a load of them."

Beth smiled and sipped her tea, trying not to make a face that David might quickly read. It was some kind of herbal blend made in the sun by the girls, and it tasted leafy and vaguely medicinal. Still, although the winds had stopped, it was desert-hot outside, even in the shade, and she was thirsty. She didn't want to insult her host by asking for a glass of water instead.

David lived several more miles from the ocean than Beth did, and each mile in Southern California meant several more degrees of heat. Ten years ago, she and Keith had looked at houses in this same neighborhood, vowing only to buy one if it came with air conditioning or a backyard pool.

Long Beach had already been a compromise, a location they'd picked for completely practical reasons. They'd miss their old apartment in Santa Monica, but they'd reasoned that the trade-off was worth it: owning a house close to freeway access and with proximity to both

Orange County, where Beth had worked, and the South Bay, where Keith was developing a reputation. They'd had two incomes then, no child, and, in retrospect, they'd seemed to her to be another couple entirely, the kind of couple she now would be intimidated to talk to if she'd met them at a party.

"This table, for example," David said. "The girls made it. It was our math lesson one week. They measured everything, and they sawed and hammered the thing together themselves. I don't want them thinking that just because they're girls they can't build things."

"That's wonderful," Beth said. "So creative."

"That's the difference between the other homers and the un-schoolers. Creativity. We're not trying to *instill* anything. We let each day teach us, set its own curriculum. We needed a table. They made a table."

Beth felt suddenly dizzy and wondered if she was reacting to whatever herbs were in her iced tea or to so many new ideas coming at her at once. "Excuse me," she said. "I need to find the little girls' room."

Little girls' room. What had come over her? She felt like a foreigner of some kind, an exchange student from a ridiculously formal country or perhaps shot forward in time from the 1950s. *Bathroom*, Beth thought. *It's called a fucking bathroom.*

The inside of the house was hot and dark and cluttered with the extraordinary detritus of these three children. Brushes and paper plates filled with paint, open granola bars and wedges of brown apples, some of them with bites taken out of them, others dipped in paint, covered the dining room table. Beth tripped over a bucket and an open can of tennis balls on her way to the bathroom, and then she opened a door to a closet so full that two bath towels fell and covered her head. After pushing the towels back in, and securing the door against them, she tried another door and was relieved to see a toilet. She walked in and screamed when a huge turtle stared up at her from the bathtub.

"It looks like you met Iggy Stardust," David said, appearing suddenly at her side. "I should have warned you. We were playing car wash with him earlier."

"Car wash?" she said, leaning back against the sink and knocking a tube of organic toothpaste onto the floor.

"With toothbrushes, not the spigot, of course," he said, as if that explained everything. "He's a tortoise, not a turtle, and can only tolerate so much water play. Don't mind him. He can't get out of there himself. Right, big guy?"

David walked out, and Beth shut the door against him. She peed while staring at the tortoise and tried for several minutes to figure out how she might be able to wash her hands and splash water on her face without turning her back on him, and finally gave up.

"I think we'd better get going," she said when she came back outside. She picked up the small stapled stack of papers David had given her. "You gave me a lot to think about."

"Any time," he said. "I mean it. That's what I'm here for. See you later tonight?"

Beth felt a moment of panic. Had she already forgotten an appointment of some kind?

"Homers' night out? Half-price homeschool night at Hometown Buffet."

"Right. We'll see. We're on a bit of a budget right now."

"I hear you," David said.

Beth wondered if he really did hear her, or if he was just spouting a sympathetic-sounding line. He certainly didn't seem to be worried about the water bill. The sprinkler had been on so long that the yard was flooded in spots. The oldest girl had found a sunny dry spot on the patio and had stretched out on her stomach and appeared to have gone to sleep. The youngest girl sat in one of the largest puddles and splashed. The middle girl had taken Jennifer off to the garden in the corner of the yard and was pointing out something when Beth went over to tell her that it was time to go home.

"They eat the aphids and mealy bugs," the girl said, catching a ladybug on her index finger and trying to hand it to Jennifer, who took a step backward. "Don't you want to hold one?"

"No, thank you," Jennifer said.

"What, are you afraid of bugs or something?" the girl asked.

"Of course she's not," Beth said, taking Jennifer's hand. Although Jennifer had never had a reaction to any kind of animal, Beth felt a sudden flush of panic, as if these girls and their bugs might cause her daughter to break out in a strange rash. "We just have to go home now."

David walked Beth and Jennifer through the house to the front door, the littlest girl skipping alongside him. They passed a television set in the living room that Beth decided must have been disconnected or used just to show educational videos.

"Remember, any time," David said as Beth shook his hand goodbye. "You know where to find me."

"Was that a girl or a boy?" Jennifer asked as they drove away.

"That was a dad, honey," she said. "David's right. It's still a sexist world. You're not used to seeing fathers who stay home with their children, are you?"

"I mean the one that came to the door with him."

"Oh," Beth said, laughing. "That was a girl. They were all girls. Every single one of them."

As soon as they got home, Beth changed into her sweatpants and an oversized T-shirt and Jennifer stayed upstairs to watch TV. After reading an article about its negative effects on early childhood development, she'd gotten rid of the living room TV when she was still pregnant with Jennifer. And after her initial phone conversation the day before with David about homeschooling, she had decided to get rid of the set in her bedroom as well. Beth had told Jennifer about the pickup she'd already scheduled with Goodwill, hoping she would feel in on the decision instead of betrayed by it. But now all Jennifer wanted to do was watch the TV until it disappeared.

The truth was, Beth would probably miss the TV more than her daughter would. She was the one who relied on it for company. The afternoons felt shorter with voices chatting in the background. But with homeschooling, she and Jennifer would be having their own conversations. Although she wasn't exactly sure what they'd discuss, she imagined her daughter asking intelligent, startling questions about the universe that she would never have even contemplated as she plowed through the rote work required to get a stick-on star in her first grade classroom.

When Lauren came to the door, Beth was upstairs in her tiny office, trying to read the homeschool information David had given her. The brochures had a familiar patronizing tone, the same tone, she realized, as the brochures her pediatrician's office had sent her home with before Jennifer had been diagnosed with life-threatening allergies. Beth reached for the phone when she heard the doorbell. This was the problem with finally trying to concentrate on something other than her daughter. It threw off her sense of balance entirely.

"Mom, Lauren's here. Can I go over to her house and play?" Jennifer shouted up the stairs.

Beth walked down and saw Lauren standing in the entranceway, home from kindergarten, a look-alike doll stuffed in a stroller that was thrust out in front of her. Lauren was a year younger than Jennifer but already a head taller. Although her father was probably only five-eight, her mother, Darla, a varsity volleyball player in high school, was six feet tall. While Lauren's little brother, Jeremy, seemed average in height, small even, clearly Lauren was taking after her mother.

"We want to play dolls at my house," Lauren said. "I've got a new crib."

"Come get me when I have to go home, okay?" Jennifer said.

Beth gave her the thumbs-up sign. Then she went to answer the phone, which had actually started to ring. "You're calling early, aren't you?" she said to Keith.

"What's going on over there? Jenny left me three messages."

When had she done this? When she was supposedly watching television? "Everything's fine. She's playing at Lauren's. What did she say?"

"That you're getting rid of the television for one thing. Is the sound out again? Do you want me to explain how to fix it? It's just a matter of turning off the mute on the right remote. It's not that complicated."

"No," she said. "It's working fine. I'm just getting rid of it. I thought it might be better for Jennifer's development."

"Her development?"

"Her creativity."

"Her creativity?"

"Yes, her creativity. Why are you repeating everything I say? It's hardly rocket science, Keith."

"Isn't she going through enough right now," he said, "without having to be creative, too?"

"And whose fault is that?"

"Okay, once again," Keith said, "you win."

"I'll tell Jennifer to call you when she gets back." She hung up the phone. Even without living here, Keith was able to make her feel like she was the odd one out, the one who didn't have a clue.

Although she hadn't begun to make dinner yet, she cleaned up her office and walked across the street to pick up Jennifer. If she didn't get her on time, she knew from experience that her daughter would have already eaten at Lauren's house and, chances were, would be up itching and, worse, possibly wheezing later. Beth had gone so far as to make an extra copy of the list of off-limit foods she'd given Jennifer's teachers, but she couldn't bring herself to give it to Darla and risk alienating one of the few people she spoke to regularly.

Besides, she imagined the list would just migrate to the back of the same kitchen drawer where the class rosters and lunch menus were stuffed. Darla was even less organized than she was but, unlike Beth, managed to show up where she was supposed to when it mattered. Instead of giving the list to Darla, Beth regularly went over the off-limit foods with Jennifer, hoping she would eventually learn to monitor her allergies herself.

"Excuse the hideous mess," Darla said, letting Beth in. "I don't know why I'm still paying Becky to clean. It's not like I can exactly afford to pay her *not to clean* and hire someone else *to clean* at the same time."

With Darla it was always *I* and *My*. *I can't afford. My kids. My house.* As if she was a single mom, instead of one with a husband who traveled for work. It was the Darla show, and it was on twenty-four hours a day. The phone rang constantly. Disney songs blared out of living room speakers. Food burned on the stove. Friends and relatives constantly came by to drop off and pick up kids. Her husband, Trent, went away on long business trips, and when he came back, they had such loud sex that Beth could hear them from her bedroom window across the street. Things were loud and messy and chaotic, and her daughter never wanted to leave their house.

Darla cleared a living room chair for Beth by knocking a tennis ball to the carpet and picking up a tiny pair of shin guards. Becky, an ancient cousin of some kind who cleaned for them, had had back surgery a month ago, and until she came back to clean, nothing would be done.

"Aren't they adorable?" Darla said. "Trent thought we should start Jeremy with soccer earlier than Lauren. That maybe it would stick better."

Beth remembered Darla telling her that Lauren had refused to go back to soccer after the first week, claiming the coach was mean and she didn't want to play anyway. "Do they even have soccer for toddlers?" Beth asked.

"They have everything for toddlers somewhere if you look hard enough. Which I'm certainly not planning to do. Maybe they'd fit Jenny?" she said, holding up the shin guards and squinting at them.

"Too much running," Beth said, shaking her head. "It'll just kick her asthma up."

They both heard the screams from the side yard at the same time, but Beth got there first. Lauren was sitting on the plastic sandbox cover while Jeremy pounded up against it. "Get off of that thing this minute," Darla said. "He can't breathe under there."

Lauren stood up slowly, looking hurt. "He ruins everything. He wouldn't even let us play."

Instead of running to his mother, Jeremy brushed off the sand and ran to Jennifer, who bent down and picked him up. "I have to go home now for dinner," Jennifer said, giving him a hug.

She thought about saying *no, not yet*. They'd make them all promise to play nicely and leave the kids out back. Then she and Darla would go back in the living room and she'd talk about her homeschooling plans. But Jennifer had what might be the beginning of hives breaking out on her arms. Who knew what she had already eaten? Besides, she could imagine Darla laughing at her. *You're nuts*, she'd say. *I can't wait until they're both out of here.*

"She's a baby magnet," Darla said, gesturing toward Jennifer. "Watch out for that one."

"Ha," Beth said, vaguely baffled as she often was by Darla. Was she supposed to already start worrying about her seven-year-old dating one day, getting pregnant?

Call me later, Darla mouthed silently. Then Beth remembered she had told her last week about Keith leaving. Now she would be expected to provide regular updates. The thought exhausted her.

Beth held onto her daughter's hand and walked her across the street, readying herself for the contrast. Darla's house always felt like a party was under way or one might start up any minute. Even when Beth tried leaving music on, something about her own house always felt lacking and empty.

"I'm thinking we should do Spanish or French or Italian," she said, already trying to fill in the silence as they opened the front door. "What do you think, honey? Japanese? Chinese?"

"I'm not really hungry yet. We had a snack."

A snack, she thought. *Of course you had a snack.* Beth had recently read an article in a parenting magazine that suggested that kids with food allergies actually should be exposed a little to their trigger foods, that they might begin to develop immunity. But that was supposed to be under medical supervision. Still, she decided not to ask what kind of snack, whether it had eggs or cheese or nuts or chocolate in it. They were okay this time. The hives were sparse, already fading. "I mean the language, honey. I meant our categories. I read that kids your age are just sponges for foreign languages."

Jennifer shrugged. "I'm going upstairs to play," she said.

Beth opened the refrigerator and stared at its contents as if someone else had done the grocery shopping without consulting her. Oranges, all those tomatoes, goat cheese, soy milk. She had no idea what she might put together to make a meal. How would she ever put together a lesson plan? What had David said about not planning, letting the day reveal its own plan?

She picked up the phone to call him, put it back down, and then picked it up again. Hadn't he given her his number, said to call anytime? When a woman answered the phone, Beth almost hung up. Instead, she stayed silent.

"Who is this?" she heard.

"I'm sorry. Maybe I have the wrong number. I was looking for David?"

"Is this about homeschooling?" the woman asked.

"Sort of," Beth said. "Yes."

"Because he has an email address for that," the woman said. "Shoot him an email. I'm sure he'll get back to you when they get back from that godawful restaurant."

"Restaurant?"

"If you can call it that. It's all you can eat. More like a trough. The ducklings love it, though."

"Ducklings?"

"My girls."

"Oh, right," she said. "Homers night out. How did I forget? Thank you. Thank you very much." She closed the refrigerator, relieved that she wouldn't have to wait any longer for the perfect meal to reveal itself. "Who wants to go out for dinner?" she called up the stairs. "Who's ready to try something new?"

PHYSICS

"Are you sure we pay half price? I mean, it's not like we actually joined their club yet," Winter whispered.

"Don't worry so much," Patterson said, picking up four trays for his family and handing them out. "Make good decisions, boys, or we're leaving," he said. "I want to see some vegetables on those plates."

A man Patterson had emailed the day before for information about homeschooling had mentioned homeschooler's half-price night at the restaurant. He figured it might be a good introduction for Winter, that she'd stop looking at him so suspiciously if she met a few other homeschoolers.

But now that they were here, he had no idea how to pick the homeschoolers out from the rest of the buffet eaters. The restaurant was packed but oddly quiet, with everyone concentrating on shoveling in as much food as possible.

"Can we get root beer, Dad?" the boys asked when they got to the end of the buffet.

"Four waters," he told the girl at the checkout.

"Homeschooler discount?" she asked, already tapping her finger-nails, which had the same long, flat-tipped extensions that Winter wore, against the computer screen.

He nodded quickly before Winter had a chance to start rambling on about how they weren't really homeschoolers yet.

"Where are we supposed to sit?" she asked. "Is there a special homeschool section?"

Patterson didn't see one. The only thing a quick survey of the room let him know was that Winter was probably the prettiest woman in the restaurant and certainly the thinnest. Once again, he reminded himself that he was lucky to have her for his wife.

A bearded man at the head of a long table waved them over. "Patterson?" he asked.

He nodded.

"I saved you some seats."

"You're David?" he asked. He wasn't sure what he'd expected, but now that he saw David, he knew he hadn't expected a beard or T-shirt. "This place is packed."

"The same thing happens every month," David said. "Cheap food. Mostly one-income families. It's a deadly combination. Hard to turn down."

Patterson balanced his tray of food on one arm and reached out to shake David's hand. Although he hadn't bothered to stand, at least David had the manners to reach his hand out. "A pleasure," Patterson said. "Thanks for thinking of us."

"Don't mention it," David said, hunching back over his food.

"This is Aiden, and this is Nolan," Winter said, pointing out each boy. "Aiden has the slightly longer chin. Show them your profile, honey," she said.

Both boys turned sideways and stuck their chins out.

Patterson felt himself cringe. He didn't know why Winter had to do this every time someone new met the boys. Was she always this way? Why did it really matter if anyone besides them could tell Aiden and Nolan apart? The truth was that when he had a few beers, he didn't always get them right himself.

"Boys," Winter said. "What do we say when we meet new people?"

"Nice to meet you," they said in unison.

They took the four empty seats, and Patterson tried catching the eyes of the other children at the table, but three of them were hunched

over, intent on scooping up each last piece of pasta. A little girl whose
mother was cutting her plain chicken breast into tiny pieces looked
back at him.

"I'm Beth," the woman said. "And this is Jennifer. Forgive me in
advance for not remembering all your names."

"Oh. You all aren't together then?" Winter said, opening the boys'
napkins and spreading them across their laps.

"Together?" Beth said.

Patterson could have sworn she blushed. Who did that anymore?

"Oh, no. We're just friends."

"We're new to this," Winter said.

"We are, too," Beth said.

"We're going for the muffins now," the largest child said to David.
The two slightly smaller children followed behind her. Girls. They had
straggly long hair, small waists, and big bottoms. Patterson was pretty
sure they were girls.

"My wife can't stand it, but the kids love this place. If it was up to
her, we'd all go out for nothing but sushi," David said.

"Oh, I just love sushi," Winter said. "Yellowtail, eel, you name it."

"The thing is," David said, chewing vigorously while he talked,
"children don't just change our world. They *are* our world."

Patterson suddenly felt claustrophobic and reached up to loosen his
tie before realizing he wasn't wearing one. He opened the top button
on his shirt and pulled out his chair and stood up. What was wrong
with him? Here he was sitting with a man who had just said aloud
exactly what he believed, and all he wanted to do was flee. "I think I'll
go see what I missed the first time around," he said.

He walked past a round table where a family sat holding hands,
their heads bent in prayer over their full plates. It embarrassed him,
the public display of religion, the same way it had on the beach when
he tried praying with the Christian Surfers. *Get a room*, he thought
inanely.

Patterson made his way to the buffet's miniature-muffin section,
where David's three girls were filling up their trays. Why couldn't his
kids have some fun, too? In the dessert section, he took two chocolate
puddings with whipped cream and brought them back for the boys.

"We like vanilla," Aiden said.

"We wanted to get it ourselves," Nolan said.

"Say thank you to your father," Winter said.

Across the table the three girls were building towers made out of tens of miniature muffins.

"Aren't they creative?" David said. "Living physics. Which one will fall over first, the blueberry or the banana nut? Does the density the nuts provide make a difference or not?"

"That one won't fall," Jennifer said, speaking for the first time since Patterson had arrived. She pointed at the middle girl's tower.

"Good call, Jen," David said. "Look, boys, at how Emily made a support base first with those leftover mashed potatoes."

"Are they really going to eat all those muffins?" Patterson asked.

The biggest girl popped a miniature chocolate chip muffin in her mouth whole and glared at him.

David shrugged. "Playing with your food. It's what homeschool's all about for us."

Patterson felt his eyebrows rise. It wasn't what he had in mind. "There are children starving in Africa," he said.

"Absolutely. And they'd still be starving if the girls stopped building muffin towers. It's the whole way we've raped their land. Their whole continent. Not to mention huge swatches of our own country. Nothing but acres and acres of cheap, tasteless corn. Subsistence farming is the only answer."

"Wipe your mouth, son," Patterson said to Nolan. "You've got chocolate on your face."

Beth reached for a napkin and wiped her daughter's face at the same time, smiling meekly at him. He noticed that her fingernails were short and curved, and even though she wasn't thin, her fingers looked somehow longer and leaner than Winter's, with their fake square edges. He imagined how they'd feel scraping down his back.

"I want your number," he said, more abruptly than he intended.

"Excuse me?"

"For my wife. I think you two should network with each other."

"Oh, good idea," Beth said.

Winter handed Beth her cell phone. "Just type it in for me."

"Networking," David said, his mouth full of something red and slimy now. Jello. "That's fantastic."

Patterson glanced at his wife's phone as Beth handed it back, quickly memorizing the number she'd typed on the screen. Something about this woman made him feel simultaneously protective and reckless. He'd never cheated on Winter before, but now he felt like he was capable of sneaking behind his wife's back, even right in front of her.

Winter's plate was still full of bare lettuce she had cut into small pieces and was quietly chewing, her mouth neatly closed. His wife suddenly reminded him of an efficient cow chewing her cud. He looked across at Beth just in time to see Jennifer slide a sugar packet off the table and slip it into her pants pocket. Was this little family so hard up for money that the girl had to steal condiments? He decided he had good reason to take a special interest in them.

"You suck!" the oldest of David's three girls shouted, and Patterson looked over to see her miniature-muffin tower tumbled over. Tiny muffins were strewn across the table, floating in half-empty bowls of clam chowder, and dotting plates smeared with congealed fettuccine alfredo.

"He did it," she said, pointing at Aiden.

"Aiden," Patterson said, "did you knock her tower over, son?"

Aiden shook his head.

"Now, honey," David said. "Maybe it was an accident."

"Nope. He did it, and he did it on purpose. With his spoon."

"I saw it, too," the middle girl said. "I'm a witness."

"I think it might have been the other one," the littlest girl said, narrowing her eyes at Nolan "That other boy that looks exactly the same."

"How about we just call it an accident and, as always, name gravity the ultimate bully," David said, popping one of the fallen muffins into his mouth. "Thirty-two feet per second."

"Per second, per second," the middle girl added.

"Right!"

"Ready to go, troops?" Patterson said, secretly pleased that one of his boys had knocked over the big girl's ridiculous, wasteful tower. "A pleasure," he said to David, this time not even bothering to stand up himself when he shook his hand.

"Call me when questions come up. They always do," David said.

"I think Winter and I can take it from here." He stood up. He felt the earth roll beneath him like the smooth push of a wave and knew he wasn't alone. He smiled at Beth and her daughter, the sugar-packet thief. He felt the sure pressure of a hand on his shoulder. "We'll be in touch," he said.

Then he turned to his wife and sons. "Put your spoons down, boys. Dinner's over."

EXTRA CURRICULA

It turned out that the goggle lady had a name. It was Eleanor, and she was ten years older than Keith, and once he got his hands on her, he couldn't keep them off.

After their swim lesson on arm movements—word of the day, *Scoop!*—Keith had managed to meet up with Eleanor in the lobby of the gym and walk her to her car. They made out leaning against the car door and, the next day, in the back row of the AMC movie theater and, later, in the handicapped dressing room at Target, the floor littered with piles of sweaters from the junior section that Eleanor had tried on and discarded. They hid, wrapped in a towel, under the pier at Seal Beach with lust-driven teenagers who were skipping school.

During their first week together, he left her only once to take Jennifer to a movie, which he slept through. Eleanor had so fully taken over his world that he missed a stair walking out of the lobby of her apartment building and nearly twisted his ankle. He was so far gone that, at the end of that week, he nearly forgot to shoot a Saturday afternoon wedding.

Eleanor and Keith were in bed together in her apartment, and he was painting each of her toenails a slightly different shade of pink when his assistant, Victor, called from the Long Beach Museum of Art.

"Where are you? Did I fuck up?"

"Oh, shit. No, it's my fault," Keith said. "I'll be right there. I've been sick."

This wasn't really a lie. Since he'd starting sleeping with Eleanor, the hours blurred just the way they did when he had the flu, and a quick glance in the mirror when he brushed his teeth in the morning revealed skin creased from sheets and gray from lack of sunlight.

"Go," Eleanor said, flicking her wet, shiny toes at him. "We can finish the other foot later."

Keith had had plenty of girlfriends before he married Beth, but he had never dated anyone like Eleanor. His other girlfriends had all chatted constantly about either dull or ludicrous future plans or ex-boyfriends, but Eleanor, who lived off alimony and a small inheritance, seemed to devote an infinite amount of energy to whatever was directly in front of her, and Keith happened to be in front of her at the moment.

And Eleanor was fearless about almost everything. She had given birth at home, backpacked alone through Turkey, had a lizard tattooed on the small of her back, and, once, had shot up heroin to see what the big deal was.

Only swimming terrified her. *Fuck you*, Eleanor said, when Keith confessed the truth—that he had stumbled into the lessons at the gym and had only kept going back to see her. *Must be nice*, she said.

Eleanor had three ex-husbands and a grown son who lived in Seattle. Who could leave tiny, perfect Eleanor? The only one in her life Keith could remotely understand was her cat, who followed her everywhere she went in the apartment.

Keith hadn't slept in his office since the first night he'd slept with Eleanor, a week before. He hadn't felt like this about anyone since eighth grade, when he fell so hard for a seventh grader who French-kissed him in the stairwells between classes that he failed algebra, had to repeat it his freshman year of high school, and was taken off the fast track to college.

Keith had fallen for Beth slowly over the two years they had dated, mistaking what turned out to be her silent, grinding angst for quiet contentment. He had assumed that this was mature love, something you didn't have to lose sleep and your job for, a daytime kind of feeling that was natural enough to transfer over to your children after they were born. In all the years he'd been married, Keith had never been late for work. It was Beth who missed appointments, but that was largely because their daughter consumed her. It had nothing to do with him.

"Get lost," Eleanor said, pulling him back into bed with her. Keith looked at the corner of the room where he'd piled all of his cameras and equipment yesterday so he wouldn't have to stop at home this morning. How much time did it really take to get to the museum from here? Ten minutes tops, he figured.

"Watch out, you'll mess up the pedicure," she said, lifting one small, pointed foot high into the air.

When Keith finally got to the wedding, the parking lot and all nearby street parking was taken up with catering trucks, limousines, and pricey cars. He pulled up in a red zone by a corner and quickly began to unload the station wagon. Getting a ticket was part of the cost of doing a wedding sometimes.

Keith looked at his watch. Although he'd planned to arrive a half an hour ago, the ceremony itself wouldn't start for another fifteen minutes if it ran on time, which wasn't usually the way things worked. The trick to showing up late was to meld right in, begin setting up without making any apologies.

Keith found Victor smoking on the sidewalk in front of the museum. "Relax," Keith said, handing him two bags of equipment. "We're doing the posed shots for this one after the ceremony." This was the new thing, and Keith supposed everyone was more relaxed not having to get to the wedding so early. But even if it was easier, it felt slightly wrong to him, in a similar way that those birthday parties Jennifer went to felt wrong when the birthday girl didn't open her presents until after everyone had left.

"Might have been nice if you told me that," Victor said. He stubbed out his cigarette and opened his mouth and sprayed it with his signature breath freshener, which smelled like a cross between eucalyptus and formaldehyde. The first time Keith had seen him do this, he'd assumed Victor had asthma and turned away slightly so he wouldn't appear intrusive.

Keith didn't bother to answer. Victor had been his assistant nearly a year now, and although he was competent enough, the truth was, it was time to move on before Victor had worked for him long enough that he felt comfortable criticizing him regularly and expecting benefits or a raise. Maybe instead of placing an ad in the local paper, this time he would train a commercial-photography college student who needed a break. This was how Keith had gotten his start. The job didn't take much, just shoulders strong enough to carry the equipment and an ability to follow directions.

Weddings here always took place outside on the lawn between the two museum buildings, with the ocean as the backdrop. There were no heavy curtains and dark rooms to contend with, but the sun often felt so strong that Keith wouldn't have been surprised if one day a dropped empty wine glass ended up setting the grass on fire. Even if the brides shivered and had to force smiles, Keith preferred the overcast days, much better for shooting black and white.

Today was bright and hot, and as Victor set up, Keith circled the gazebo, testing out the angles the shadows would cast. Guests were still arriving, complaining loudly about the parking problem and then admiring the setting as soon as a server handed them a glass of wine. The bride and groom and their families, he knew from experience, were sequestered off in the small education building with the wedding planner and a justice of the peace.

Keith generally stayed away from that room. Sometimes things were delayed so long that he had no choice but to go back there and get an approximate start time. Once, he was asked to be the tie-breaker in an argument between a mother and bride about whether the bride's feet looked better in her white sandals with or without her toe ring. The bride had long, oddly shaped toes, and Keith found himself feeling momentarily nauseated as he stared at the gold toe ring and her gleaming, scrubbed feet. "I'd leave that one up to the bride," he said.

"Meet me at the wedding," Keith whispered into his cell phone during the reception. "You can be my second assistant. There's a million people. No one will even know you're here."

"Forget it," Eleanor said. "What would I wear?"

"Wear the light-up goggles. Wear the flowered bathing cap."

He slipped his phone in his pocket and went back to the candids. The trick was to concentrate, not to miss anyone because you never really knew, outside of the wedding party, who the bride deemed important.

He tried to keep a running mental list of everyone he'd already shot. Skinny man with aqua-blue tie, runny-nose teenage girl, twin boys in matching Sears suits, lesbian pair in tuxes, drunk man in green tie, sweaty-faced woman with heavy gold necklace. Big hat, suede sports coat, red platform sandals, turquoise necklace, smoker's cough, loud voice, backless dress. Every wedding he shot may as well have had the same guest list. And, in fact, there were often some actual repeats, especially in Long Beach, a deceptively large small town, where weddings had the tendency to feel like class reunions.

"Homeschool," a man said as Keith shot him patting the groom on the back as the wedding couple mingled, stopping to chat briefly with each guest. "We're taking back our children."

"That's brave," the bride said. "I don't know if I could do that."

"Children change everything," the man said, putting his arm around his wife and reaching with his other hand for a canapé from a server's silver tray. "The thing is that they don't just change our world. They *are* our world."

Keith shot one more picture of the homeschool man chewing. He was the kind of falsely confident guy Keith instantly disliked: clean-cut, vaguely military looking, the kind who, no matter how little money he made, always had a wife who was better looking than he was. Keith shot the wife smiling at the bride and took one last close-up of the asshole, so close you could see his pores and pieces of crab lodged between his front teeth.

Victor had loaded up another camera and was setting up a tripod so they'd be sure to catch the toast. The twin boys' suit jackets were now off, and their hands were reaching into the fountain. "Take one," one of the boys said. "I dare you, stupid."

Keith shot just as the boy soaked his entire long, white sleeve, reaching in for someone else's wish money.

While weddings didn't usually mean much more to Keith than hard work, these boys made him think of Jennifer. He guessed they were a year or two younger, but they were already taller than his daughter, whose growth rate hovered at the bottom of the chart at each yearly checkup. He had bought her a new doll stroller the last time he saw her to replace the one she told him had snapped apart in the Santa Anas, and he could almost imagine Jennifer sitting in it herself. She had so many allergies that Keith wondered sometimes if she had been scared off food entirely.

He and Beth had finally worked out a tentative schedule. As soon as the wedding was over, he would pick up Jennifer. He had intended to find an apartment by now, but getting involved with Eleanor had set him back. He had nowhere to take his daughter but out. To preempt her asking questions about where he was living, Keith always showed up with a plan. But he decided to let Jennifer choose the restaurant tonight, to take her somewhere she really wanted to eat. It would all taste so great that maybe she would forget she had so many allergies and would eat every bite and ask for dessert.

He knew it didn't make medical sense, but it seemed possible— even likely—to Keith that if he could get his daughter away from Beth's hovering presence, Jennifer might be able to eat like other kids, that it was her mother who was the problem, not milk or chocolate or eggs or nuts.

Two nights ago he had managed to leave Eleanor long enough to take Jennifer to a movie. *Are you sure your homework is done?* he'd asked her first. If she said it wasn't, instead of a movie, he imagined taking her to the coffeehouse where he met his clients, buying her a chocolate milk, and she'd do her first grade homework while the college students did theirs. Maybe he'd call Eleanor, and she'd stop over, and he'd manage somehow to keep his hands off her, pretend she was just a friend he'd run into unexpectedly.

But Jennifer had nodded. She was sure. *No more homework,* she said.

"I'm here. Now what?" Eleanor asked.

Keith turned around and looked at Eleanor in the viewfinder. She was wearing a low-cut green dress that, with her short hair and small features, made her look like Peter Pan but much sexier. He was surprised she had shown up but knew he shouldn't have been. He felt the way he always did when he saw Eleanor, like hiding her away somewhere, keeping her to himself. He shot a picture, and she smiled and he shot her again. "Take your clothes off," he whispered, and he shot a picture as she pulled a shoulder of her dress down to the side.

He finally put the camera down and looked around. What was he doing asking Eleanor to show up at this wedding? He had never brought anyone other than an assistant. He'd already lost track of his candids. Which ones had he already taken? The Birkenstocks, the pink satin miniskirt, the tiny rectangle-shaped glasses? It was too late to catch up with those now anyway. It was toast time.

"Here, carry this around and look official while I go help Victor," he said. He put the camera strap over Eleanor's head, letting his hands graze quickly over her breasts.

Keith helped Victor position the tripod by the head table, testing the shadows against the angle of the guest chairs. "I thought we weren't supposed to fraternize with the guests," Victor said, staring at Eleanor.

It was time. Keith could easily let Victor go. He swiveled the tripod and shot the toast makers, Eleanor loose on the lawn behind him.

"I saved the other one for later just like I promised," Eleanor said. She kicked her sandals off and arched her bare feet on Keith's dashboard, crumbling the parking ticket he had crammed there.

"You went to the wedding like that?" Keith asked.

"No one notices the hired help's toes," she said. "I got some great pictures of these wild twin boys. I made them stare off at the oil derricks and look miserable. Very Diane Arbus."

By the time Keith's cell phone rang, he was in bed with Eleanor, and the Chinese food delivery boy was leaning on the doorbell downstairs. It was tempting not to answer either, to throw the pillow over both of their heads and pretend that this was enough to drown everything out. But Eleanor was already digging through the clothes on the floor, searching for one of their wallets. Keith looked at the missed call number while Eleanor pulled on his shirt and paid for the food.

"I forgot my daughter," Keith said. "Shit, this is bad. This is really bad."

"I can't believe how much we ordered," Eleanor said. She was wearing his shirt as if it were a dress, had paid for the Chinese food wearing just that. He pulled it over her head, and there she was, naked.

"You still owe me the other foot," she said. Sitting cross-legged on her bed, she opened a steaming container and lifted out a piece of broccoli between two fingers as if her fingers were chopsticks. "Next time."

Keith pulled on his pants. It was eighth grade all over again. He was failing algebra and receiving tardy slips in every class. "I've got to run," he said. "You're ruining my life."

LIVING VOCABULARY

Jennifer was stuck with boys now, two loud mean boys a year younger than she was that she couldn't tell apart. The boys spent half their time whispering to each other about ways to get her and the other half pretending they were good. They called her mother Miss Beth, but Jennifer called their mother by her first name only, Winter. They were excellent liars, the kind of boys who, at a real school, the substitute always chose to hand back the corrected homework papers and take the attendance sheet down to the office. They tripped her and pretended to care when she fell. "Are you all right?" they asked loudly, so their mothers could hear. They filled her shoes with sand, stretched out gummy worms on her pillow, and set her alarm clock so it woke her at three in the morning. The only good part about Winter and the twins coming over every day was that her mother had begun tucking Jennifer into her own bed at night. Maybe she secretly felt the same way Jennifer did, tired and ready to be alone. But if this was true, she never let on to Jennifer.

"Aren't they cute?" her mother said while they sat on a bench at the playground watching the boys chase each other under and down slides while Winter shopped for school supplies. "I always wanted a twin when I was growing up."

"Not me," Jennifer said.

What she wanted was one baby brother like Jeremy. She'd push the baby around in the stroller, pretending she was the mother, or babysitter, or aunt.

"I hate them," she finally said one night while she soaked in the bathtub, her mother sitting on the vanity staring down at her. "I wish they never came over in the first place."

"Don't be silly," her mother said. "We're all just getting used to each other."

"I thought homeschool meant I got to stay home," Jennifer said, "with you."

"You are staying home with me. We're all staying home together, the five of us," her mother said. "It's more fun that way, don't you think?"

"I guess," Jennifer said, lying back down so her entire face was covered with water. *No*, she said underwater, and a big airy bubble floated over her face.

Jennifer waited for her father on the front lawn while her mother watched her from the living room window, snapping the shutters shut when he pulled up. Her father sent checks in the mail, and he didn't come into the house unless he had to because he was so late that Jennifer got bored waiting and went back inside. Her mother sometimes mixed up the time and forgot things, and now her father did, too.

Her father didn't know about the twins and how much she hated them. He didn't even know she was being homeschooled. Jennifer would have told him, but she had promised her mother that she'd wait until everything was all set up. Finalized, her mother said. Final.

It wasn't hard not to tell. It didn't even feel like lying most of the time. Her father barely asked her about school. He barely asked her about anything. He came late to pick her up, and all he ever talked about was his great new assistant, Eleanor, whom she was actually going to meet in person tonight.

"We're going to have dinner with Eleanor if that's okay with you, kiddo," he said as Jennifer slid into the back seat and buckled her seatbelt.

She didn't answer because she could tell this wasn't really a question. When her father lived with them, he didn't have plans, but now he had plans ready whenever he picked her up. They went to movies and played miniature golf, and one Saturday morning stood in line to take a dollar boat ride from one end of Long Beach to the other. Jennifer tried to take a souvenir from each place he took her. She held onto ticket stubs and a pink golf ball and a set of chopsticks still wrapped in their little white packet from a Chinese restaurant. The box under her bed was filling up.

"School was awful today," Jennifer said. "Twin boys. They harassed me all day long."

"They harassed you, huh?" Keith said. "That means they like you. It's what boys do."

Not these boys, she thought. *Harass, message, carnival, divide*, these were her vocabulary words today. Winter called it Living Vocabulary because Jennifer was supposed to try to use the words in actual sentences in conversations. Tonight she was supposed to tell her mother her sentences, and tomorrow she would have to repeat the same sentences to Winter.

Instead of one teacher, she now had two. They reminded Jennifer of the student teachers who came into Mrs. Miramir's first grade class twice a week, the way they always looked nervous and sometimes had to check printed-out directions when they tried to explain something new.

Her mother went along with things, but the assignments were mostly Winter's ideas. The twins were in kindergarten, so she said that their homeschool didn't really count yet. To make up for that, Winter came up with extra ideas to try on Jennifer.

"Aren't you going to ask me if I finished my homework?" Jennifer asked her father.

"Have you?"

She nodded. "Mostly anyway."

"I love this teacher," her father said. "Get it done in class. Leaves you time to be a kid when you get home."

Her father wasn't driving too fast, but he wasn't paying enough attention. The brakes squealed at a light that had been red for as long as Jennifer could see it.

"Sorry about that," he said.

"Why don't you ever come inside to pick me up anymore?" she asked. "Why do I have to wait on the lawn? Are you divorcing our house, too?"

"Oh, Jen," he said. "It's just your mom I'm divorcing."

"Why do you and Mom have to divide everything up?" *Harass, divide*, she was halfway done with using her vocabulary words, and she still had at least three hours to go before bedtime.

"It just seems like her house now. I guess it always did, really."

"It seems like my house to me," Jennifer said. "It seems like your house, too."

Keith made a turn. "Almost there," he said.

I hate you, she thought. *I hate the twins and I hate you and I hate your stupid assistant, Eleanor, even though I haven't met her yet.*

"How's the new doll stroller working out?"

"It's okay," Jennifer said even though she hated it, too. Her father had gotten her the wrong kind, one that couldn't go flat when her dolls wanted to sleep. *That's how you slept as a baby*, her mother said when she complained. *Perched up.* There were so many things wrong about Jennifer right from the beginning. She cried all the time and slept sitting up and needed special, expensive formula. She wondered, now that he'd left, how her father had managed to stay as long as he did.

"Here we are," her father said, pointing at a building.

Eleanor lived in an old house with fancy black bars on the windows and pointy peaks on top of the roof. It looked like a haunted castle out of one of Jennifer's Halloween books.

"The trick now is to find a parking space. Cool place, huh?" Keith said.

"It looks scary," she said. "Why don't you just call her, leave a message for her to come out." *Message*, she was almost there.

"We're having dinner at her place. Did you think we were going out? Eleanor's a terrific cook. Don't worry."

Jennifer touched her throat and breathed out. Nothing. She hadn't had asthma for weeks. Maybe she was allergic to her father living with them. Maybe he was right. It was her mother's and her house. Not his. "What if she makes something I'm allergic to? Does she know what I can't eat?"

"Don't be silly," her father said. "Of course she knows. I talk about you all the time."

Jennifer wondered what he said about her when he talked about her. Maybe he talked about how she was a good jump-roper or artist, but probably he talked about how she had asthma and was allergic to too many things and was too much trouble right from the beginning. Although her father told her he that he'd left her mother, not her, she knew the truth.

Her father circled the block in the car and then circled it again. It was never hard to park where she lived. She couldn't imagine not parking right in front of your own house. Jennifer felt sorry for Eleanor, who must be poor even if she had a big house because she lived on a crowded street and didn't have a driveway. She would try not to hate her and to eat what she made.

They finally parked and walked three blocks back to Eleanor's building. They walked into a lobby with an old couch and tall lamp in it and squeezed into an elevator so small that Jennifer thought if she reached her arms out far enough, she might be able to touch two walls.

"This isn't a house," Jennifer said.

"Ha," her father said. "That would be one big house."

When Jennifer had been in a real first grade class with Mrs. Miramir, she sometimes went to friends' houses to play after school. And some of them lived in apartments, too, but they had stairs, not elevators. The only elevators Jennifer had been in were shiny and public and belonged to doctors' offices.

Her father pulled the door shut by hand and then another metal door over it. "Going up?" he said, and he pushed the top button, number 5.

"Are you sure this is safe?" she asked. The elevator was made of heavy wood, and she wondered if it would crash right through to the basement.

"Don't be such a worrier. Live a little," he said.

As the elevator climbed, Jennifer stared straight ahead and not at her father, who had made her walk three blocks to a creaky elevator and told her to live a little.

The elevator opened outside on what felt like the roof of the building, and Jennifer smelled cooking. *This is where a witch would live*, she thought, *on the top of this creaky castle.* The food smelled like a stew, and Jennifer thought of a witch's brew, which would be full of eye of newt and a hair from a troll's head and maybe a horse's hoof and spider webs. Jennifer hoped it wasn't a witch's brew. She also hoped that it wasn't lasagna and that she wouldn't have to spend all dinner picking the cheese out of her piece.

"Come in, come in," Eleanor said, opening the door. She had a cat in her arms, but when Jennifer reached out to pet it, it meowed at her.

"Oh, she's even cuter than her pictures," Eleanor said, smiling at her dad, not her.

In Eleanor's apartment, huge, dark wooden masks with scary blank eyes and long noses hung on the wall in the living room, and none of the furniture had arms. Jennifer sat in a zebra-striped fuzzy chair and looked at her feet, which floated several inches above the floor.

"I'm going to go help Eleanor finish getting things ready," her dad said. "You okay here, honey?"

Jennifer nodded, but her father wasn't looking. He was already opening the little slatted doors that led into the kitchen. She sat in her chair and thought about the word *carnival* and how she might make a sentence using it. She walked around the room and looked at the pictures of people in black frames. One was of Eleanor when she was younger with a man who must have been the grown son her father had told her about, because he looked like Eleanor, only taller.

On a long table against a wall, she saw a bowl full of flat, black stones. She picked one up. It was smooth and cold. Jennifer stuck it in her pocket. A souvenir from the witch's house.

Jennifer walked over to the kitchen doors and peeked in between the slats. Eleanor was sitting on the kitchen counter with her legs wrapped around her father's waist. His hands had disappeared, one hand up under Eleanor's shirt, and the other hand down the back of her pants, and he was kissing her hard on the mouth. The cat that was curled on the kitchen counter next to Eleanor stared at Jennifer and meowed.

"*Carnival*," Jennifer said through the door, using her last living vocabulary word. "When will *a carnival* ever come to this boring town?"

"Shit," her father said, pulling his hands out of Eleanor's shirt and pants and backing up. "How long have you been standing there?"

Jennifer shrugged.

"Who's hungry?" Eleanor said, sliding down off the kitchen counter. The cat jumped down and planted itself next to Eleanor's leg. "How about you help me finish up dinner?"

"I don't think your mom needs to know about Eleanor, do you, honey?" her father said as they were driving home.

"Don't worry. I can keep a secret," Jennifer said.

"It's not a secret," he said. "It's just not the right time. She liked Victor, my old assistant. I'd have to explain what happened to him, and it's really not much of a story."

Jennifer nodded. It was too a secret, and she knew not to tell even if she wasn't supposed to call it that anymore.

Her stomach was already itchy and hot, and they had just finished eating minutes ago. Eleanor had made something called Chicken Marengo, and there was flat, flourless, eggless banana bread for dessert for Jennifer. But Jennifer had put a regular brownie on her plate, too, and no one said anything. She chewed the whole thing up fast while her father and Eleanor were looking at each other, not her.

"You surviving that chocolate?" Keith said now in the car.

Jennifer felt herself blush and nodded from the back seat.

"I thought it was getting to be psychosomatic. I had a feeling," Keith said, banging his fist on the steering wheel as if the man on the radio was telling him, not someone named Ricky in Covina, that he'd won tickets to something.

Jennifer's knees were growing warm now, too. Soon she'd be covered in itchy hives, but she could still taste the warm chocolate, and for now it was worth it.

"I told Eleanor how wonderful you were," her father said. "And

I could tell she liked you. Isn't she something, our little Eleanor? It's important to me that you like her. You did, didn't you?"

Eleanor was a pointy-nosed, short-haired witch who lived on top of a haunted house with a cat who followed her around and meowed at Jennifer, and all night her father had stared at Eleanor instead of her. Jennifer didn't bother nodding. It was getting dark now, and her father wouldn't see her even if he was looking in his rearview mirror.

He pulled up in front of her house. Jennifer kissed him quickly and got out of the car, went inside and shouted "I'm home," and then ran right up the stairs to her room. Hot from hives, she took off her clothes in the dark, pulled on a nightgown and got under her covers, afraid to look.

It made sense to her that she'd gotten hives in the witch's house. Maybe her dad was right, and it wasn't even the chocolate that caused them, and she wasn't really allergic. Maybe it was something witchy that Eleanor had put in the Chicken Marengo, like three whiskers from her own unfriendly cat.

When her mother knocked on the door, Jennifer told her she was already in bed, and her mother came in and gave her a kiss.

"Look what Patterson brought by," she said, turning on the lamp. "It's from the twins."

Jennifer looked at the piece of paper. The boys had drawn a stupid crayon picture of her between them, all three of them holding hands, the sun a big, fat yellow ball in the sky. Big fakers.

"See how much they like you," she said. "You really need to give them a chance. Did you have fun tonight with your father, honey?" she asked.

"Sure," Jennifer said. Then, before she forgot, she told her the four living vocabulary sentences. *They harassed me all day long*, Jennifer said, watching her mother's blank smile. *Why do you and Mom have to divide everything up?*

"Good job, honey," her mother said. "Winter will be impressed."

Jennifer wanted to impress a real teacher, her teacher, Mrs. Miramir, not the twins' mother with her matching sweatsuit outfits and ponytail and long, flat fingernails. "School wasn't really that boring, Mom," she said. "I take it back."

"My God," her mother said. "Look at you."

Jennifer felt it then, her face going hot with hives. It was like a fever that moved through her body, and the truth was she didn't completely mind it at first. Before the itching got really bad, it made her skin feel tight and tingly like a sunburn. It reminded her of summer, of coming home from the beach with her father, the trunk of the car filled with sand toys and orange towels and boogie boards. Her mother pulled back the sheet, and Jennifer watched her eyes fill up with tears.

"What did he feed you?" she said. She was already running down the hall. Jennifer could hear the click of the medicine cabinet door opening.

"It was Dad's assistant, Eleanor," Jennifer shouted back, somehow freer to tell her father's secret when she couldn't actually see her mother. "I thought they were carob brownies," Jennifer lied.

Her mother was back in the room now. Jennifer sat up and pulled her knees up to her chest so her skin was covered. She always felt contagious when she had allergies even though she knew that didn't make any sense. "Eleanor made vegan banana bread, too," she said, feeling bad about getting her in trouble now.

"So who's this Eleanor?" her mother asked. "What happened to Victor? I thought he was Dad's assistant."

Jennifer shrugged and opened her mouth, swallowed the cherry-flavored Benadryl syrup her mother poured into a special plastic spoon with the clear hollow handle that filled up and changed color. She swallowed quickly, in one gulp, so she wouldn't have to taste the fake cherry too long. So what if she had told about Eleanor and about the brownies? She didn't tell about the secret, important part, what she saw in the kitchen.

"Well, it's a good thing we don't have to worry about getting you to school in the morning," her mother said. "Did I tell you I'm filing the affidavit tomorrow? Patterson helped me finish it tonight. Now breathe. Let me listen and make sure this thing stopped at hives."

What's an affidavit? Jennifer thought about asking. But she was itchy and tired and didn't feel like talking or listening to her mother's answer or learning any new vocabulary words. Her mother got into bed next to her. She was still her mother, but she was skinnier now and she wasn't as soft. Jennifer missed her old mother, even though Mrs. Miramir had asked her at the beginning of the year if she was going to be a big sister. The side of her mother's face felt sharp when she rested her head against Jennifer's chest as if no skin separated her mother's cheek from Jennifer's heart. She breathed in and out as slowly as she could. Then they both stayed very still and listened out for the crisp catch of the beginning of an attack.

DACHSCHUNDS

David didn't normally make house calls, but Beth was one of his triple threats—no husband, no job, no homeschool support network—and she had him worried. He hadn't seen her since the dinner at Hometown Buffet four weeks ago. It was almost Christmas, a particularly loaded time for a triple threat, and she hadn't returned any of his emails or phone calls. Who knew what might have happened to her by now?

He had seen other triple threats not only bail on homeschooling but on their entire lives, selling everything and moving to Texas or Utah on a whim. Or worse. By the time he had chased down one woman, her husband had full custody, and she had retreated to a dark corner of her den and, as far as he could see, was living on a diet of red wine and Egg McMuffins.

His wife had taken a rare day of midweek leave. Deborah and the girls had some kind of exclusionary female-only day planned, and he found himself alone on a Wednesday. After catching up on emails and logging on to various websites to check up on his charities, he puttered around the house, neatening up the girls' projects and tightening hinges on kitchen cabinets that had become loose. After an hour or so of this, he felt slack and middle-aged and unmoored enough to simply get in his car and take off. He had saved Beth's address without paying any real attention to it, and now he decided visiting her might give him some purpose. He knew he should probably call first, but he had learned that there were distinct advantages to the surprise visit—no time for the new homeschooler to hide toy guns or Twinkie wrappers or to quiet screaming toddlers. David could get a real glimpse into a life and figure out how much he needed to insert himself. But as he drove toward the ocean, instead of feeling a sense of purpose kick in, he was gripped by an unexpected wave of jealousy.

Beth lived in the one neighborhood he had once imagined for Deborah and himself when they moved back to Long Beach, an established tree-lined area close to stores and the beach. It wasn't Santa Cruz, but it was the rare kind of Southern California neighborhood where people still walked to the post office and bank.

The neighborhood he and Deborah had been able to afford on one salary was lined on its outskirts with strip malls full of grocery stores and pizza chains, all within short driving distances of the ranch houses. Convenient, Deborah had commented as the realtor had driven them around, and David had nodded in somber agreement.

He thought about confiding to Deborah his jealousy when she got home later with the girls but quickly decided against it. If he got a job, they could live wherever they wanted, she would quickly point out, reminding him that homeschooling was his idea, and shutting him down. But David didn't want to stop homeschooling his daughters. All he wanted to do was air his feelings, something that had become increasingly impossible. He wasn't sure when he and Deborah had become adversaries, but their arguments had become so routine, it seemed to him that they had taken the place of actual conversation. Just that morning at breakfast, when he asked her if she wanted any honey butter with her toast, instead of saying *no thank you*, she'd raised an eyebrow and asked if it was too much to expect that they might have plain old regular butter in the house.

David was relieved to see that Beth's house wasn't one of the rambling 1920s-era mansions that lined these blocks or even a cookie-cutter remodeled Tuscan-something. Instead, she lived in a modest 1950s clapboard two-story with a peeling roof, the kind of house that would look equally at home in Oregon or Vermont.

When he knocked on the door, a chorus of barks answered. He'd pegged Beth as a cat person. He was usually right about these things, but now he decided he would have to reevaluate or at least recalculate. Instead of losing herself in red wine and McMuffins in the den, maybe Beth was a hardier variety of triple threat, the kind who planned a route of escape by loading her dogs in the back of her car and mapping out obscure hiking trails up the coast.

A man finally answered the door. Another surprise. "Don't I know you?" the man asked.

David did a quick inventory of people he had met in the homeschool world, always his first, and usually most, reliable point of reference. Definitely not an unschooler, or even a sympathizer. The man was wearing a suit and tie and looked like he used to be in the military. Maybe he was a Marine. That might explain the slightly salty smell mixed with aftershave. He was definitely the kind of guy who dropped next to the bed and did pushups in his briefs each morning before even peeing. "I got it. The twins," David said. "Hometown Buffet."

"Patterson," the man said. "You're that guy with all the girls. And ideas."

"David. I think I'm confused. Do you live here?"

"Here? Oh, no. I just stopped by to help out. With the dogs."

"Right," David said. "The dogs."

"A little busy now," Patterson said, blocking the doorway.

"That's okay. I came to see Beth."

"Suit yourself."

David followed him into the house, readying himself for what sounded like the onslaught of dogs that would greet him and was relieved they didn't seem to be in the house. He'd always been a little queasy about dogs and their massive need for affection. You never knew when one of them might jump on you, knock you down, and lick you in the face. Still, he wasn't completely immune to their charms. He'd once taken his daughters on a field trip to the pound and had had as much trouble leaving empty-handed as any of them.

They walked through the living room, where a tabletop Christmas tree was weighted down with ornaments, to the backyard. Beth's little girl was wearing a reindeer sweater and sitting crossed-legged on a glass table in the middle of the patio, throwing tennis balls for the dogs. Only one, a collie mix, David guessed, actually brought them back. A large white poodle sniffed at his leg and jumped up on him, sniffing aggressively at his pocket, which, he suddenly remembered, held a chunk of Katie's leftover chocolate cookie from yesterday's field trip to Mrs. Fields at the Cerritos Mall.

"Down, Charles!" Beth shouted. "Good boy."

David had been so preoccupied with the dogs, four of them at last count, and with the sight of Patterson in his suit, bending down to pick up piles of dog poop with tiny plastic bags, that he hadn't even noticed Beth. She didn't look nearly as terrible as he'd imagined she might. In fact, she looked a little better than the last time he saw her, although he couldn't figure out in what way exactly. She handed Jennifer a box of treats to dole out to the dogs in place of the now mostly scattered tennis balls.

"Are you interested in our doggie daycare?" she asked. "Because if you are, I have to tell you, we're still unofficial. It would be like your dog coming over for an extended playdate."

"So they're not all yours?"

"Don't I know you?" Beth asked.

"Homeschool. David."

"Oh, for Pete's sake. What's wrong with me? When did you get here? Never mind," she said. "I can't hear the doorbell with all these dogs out here. Maybe if that was the only thing they barked at, I'd stand a chance."

"Well, I'm leaving you with a clean playing field," Patterson said, walking up with several small, clear bags of dog poop hanging from his hands. "I'd better get back to the office before they notice I'm gone. You okay?" Still looking at Beth, he jerked his head in David's direction.

"Don't be silly," Beth said. "I'm fine. Jennifer, honey, you toss the dogs some more treats. I'm going to walk Patterson to the door."

"That's a lot of dogs you and your mom have to watch," David said as Beth disappeared inside the house.

"I'm used to it. They come every day," she said, "so they don't get lonely when their moms and dads are at work."

David nodded. He reached in his pocket for the piece of Katie's leftover cookie and tossed it to the poodle who had come back to sniff at him again.

"Dogs can't have chocolate," Jennifer said. "Like me."

"It was mostly sugar. He'll be okay. You know a lot about dogs, don't you? How long have you guys been doing this?" David said.

Jennifer shrugged. "I don't know. A week? That's seven days, right?"

"Right," David said. "Seven twenty-four-hour days exactly." David tried to decide which of his three daughters Jennifer reminded him of but came up blank. None of his daughters had ever seemed particularly worried about getting their facts right.

"We can't have milk either. I get hives and dogs get stomachaches. They're lactose sensitive."

"So how are we doing out here?" Beth was back, lifting her daughter off the table and putting her down, feet-first, on the ground between them.

"Aren't you hot in that sweater, honey?" David asked.

"No, I like it," Jennifer said. "I'm going in to read now before Winter gets here, okay?"

"Of course." Beth smiled at David. "I'm trying to let her make her own time-management decisions. She's already doing a better job of it than I ever did."

"Time management?" David said. "Sounds pretty corporate."

"Does it?" Beth asked, and David saw Jennifer's worried look cross Beth's face.

"I mean in a good way," he added.

A short, low-slung dog walked between Beth's feet, and she bent down to pick it up. "We were thinking about getting a dachshund ourselves," she said. "Fred's become kind of our trial dachshund, I guess."

Two blond boys pulled open the back gate and ran into the yard, which drew the dogs to the opening. "Stay!" a woman shouted, pulling the gate closed behind her. "Boys, how many times have I told you to close Miss Beth's gate! My word."

"Winter?" David asked.

"You're good," she said.

He shrugged. "It's a gift, I guess," he said, although the truth was, if Jennifer hadn't mentioned Winter's name only minutes before, he wouldn't have remembered it. She and Patterson had left quickly after eating at Hometown Buffet. He'd written them off as the kind of unimaginative family that looked briefly into homeschooling before sending their kids to a mediocre Christian school with a standardized curriculum and a prayer read over the loudspeaker each morning and before Friday-night football games.

"From the restaurant, right?" asked Winter.

"Your memory's not so bad either," David said.

He followed the women and boys inside to the living room. Beth shut the door behind them, and the dogs immediately started barking and scratching at the door.

"Winter's here!" Beth shouted up the stairs. "Whenever you're ready, honey."

"We're letting the kids work together part of the day even though the boys aren't exactly official yet, being kindergartners and all," Winter explained.

"Winter has so many great ideas," Beth said, looking vaguely apologetic.

"Today the kids are going to make their own pizzas for lunch in Miss Beth's kitchen," Winter said. "Right, boys?"

The boys stared at David. They were too quiet, pit bulls poised for a surprise attack. They made David nervous, but then, boys generally did. He wasn't the kind of man who'd always wanted a son, despite the fact that everyone assumed he was. Strangers would come up to him when the four of them were out as a family, Deborah clearly pregnant with their third. *Still trying for a boy*, they'd say. *Good for you, buddy!*

He remembered his fifth grade health teacher comparing girls' sexuality to an iron that had to be plugged in and slowly warmed up. Boys were gas stoves, she said. Just turn them on and they're fully lit.

While this analogy had caused him to squirm in his seat with embarrassment at the time, it was one of the odd elementary school lessons that had stuck, and he often found himself thinking about it as an adult. Boys were gas stoves, and this didn't just apply to their sexuality. They took off darting across streets, bit the edges off of pretzels to turn them into guns, and made spit balls out of credit card bills.

The boys he met through his homeschooling network gave him additional reasons to be glad he was homeschooling. They made fart jokes, talked incessantly about whatever video game they were playing, made slingshots out of banana peels, and seemed generally oblivious about whether anyone besides themselves had any interest in any of it. He couldn't imagine his daughters in classrooms full of them.

"They wouldn't be in the same grade at school, of course," Beth said, "but that's okay, right?"

"Multi-age groups. That's terrific," David said. Something about Beth made him feel like he had to offer her nearly constant reassurance. "That's what homeschooling's all about."

"David has a big turtle he keeps in the bathtub," Beth said to the twins.

"Tortoise," David said, instantly sorry he had corrected her.

"Oh, right," Beth said.

"They're the land ones."

"Cool," Winter said. "I'm working on a reptile unit. Maybe I can borrow him for it."

"Sure," David said, instantly regretting it. "I mean let's see how it works out." The barking made it hard for him to think. He didn't lend out his tortoise. It was an animal, not a book.

"Jenny and I saw an entire herd of tortoises once when we were in Joshua Tree," Beth said. "Maybe we could take the kids there. What would you boys think of that?"

Bale, David thought. *Bale of tortoises.*

"Let's ask Jennifer," one of the boys said.

"We'll go get her," the other said, and they took off running.

A door slammed above them, and he heard the squeak of a mattress being pounded by feet.

"Boys!" Winter shouted. "You better be getting Jenny. Stay out of Miss Beth's room."

"That's my cue," David said. "I just stopped by to say hello. I'm glad things are going so well."

"Oh, they are," Beth said.

David couldn't decide if this was a statement or a question. He studied Beth's face for a minute. *Eye shadow,* he thought, *that's what's different. She's wearing makeup.* "Call me if you need anything," he said.

By the time he got home, Deborah and the girls were back. The house was dark, the curtains drawn shut, but Deborah's car was parked in the driveway. After he left Beth's, he'd driven a few more blocks and then parked and taken a walk by the bay, trying to appreciate his time alone while plodding along in the sand, the sun in his eyes. He thought about the inner-city kids he'd donated the last of his meager retirement to so the lights could be kept on at their midnight basketball club in Fresno, how he had made lives better. But he felt small with envy, isolated and left out. Everyone seemed to be grouped up, his girls off without him. Beth's and Jennifer's lives completely entwined with this whole other family. And, here he was, alone and feeling sorry for himself.

And then, because he was feeling both unsettled and indulgent, he ordered a hamburger and fries at the kind of beach restaurant that catered to high school students and construction workers. He followed that up with a bad twilight movie at a multiplex, during which he ate a tub of greasy popcorn and went back for a chili dog. He was already regretting all of it. While they weren't complete vegetarians, he rarely cooked meat for his family, and when he did, he stuck to organic chicken. His stomach churned in the car all the way home. He missed his girls, but David braced himself before walking in. When Deborah was home, it seemed there was always something he'd done wrong that she had discovered in his absence, or something he was about to do wrong the moment he opened the front door. None of it amounted to much—leaving the girls' sneakers out back in the rain, recycling the newspaper before she'd read it, leaving his coat on the couch instead of hanging it up—but she treated each of these minor infractions as if they were evidence of some kind, or at least intentional betrayals. He knew what they needed was more time alone, just the two of them without domestic irritations or children, but it was the last thing he could imagine wanting. He imagined sitting across from Deborah at a dimly lit, expensive restaurant, searching for a topic that didn't have to do with the girls, the deep silence that had nothing to do with romance, everything to do with disappointment.

"Close your eyes!" Emily shouted when he opened the door.

David did as he was told. Were they having a surprise party for him? Maybe that's what they'd been doing all day, working on the decorations and presents. But why? His birthday wasn't for two months. Maybe Deborah and had finally *gotten it*, and this was their way of thanking him for everything he'd done for the girls. He hated to think of it as his sacrifices, but, after all, wasn't that part of homeschooling—giving up a piece of your own life so your children could more fully live theirs?

David heard giggling, and he felt little Katie's soft breath close to his ear. "Just one minute, Dad," she said.

"Lights!" his wife said.

"You can look now, Dad," Katie whispered.

David opened his eyes and took in his family. They looked freeze-dried, like waxed statues that vaguely resembled the people he had left only hours before. Deborah had highlighted her sandy hair with thick yellow and dark brown streaks. Madeline and Emily had shoulder-length hair that flipped out on the sides, and little Katie had long bangs that covered her eyebrows. "Do you like us?" she asked.

"Do I know you?" he said.

"We had makeovers," Madeline said. "At the saloon."

"I think the word would be *salon*," he said. "Unless they served you beer while they were doing it."

"Don't worry. I had a coupon," Deborah said. "It didn't cost nearly as much as it looks. I know how you feel about spending money on superficial things."

Was he supposed to be happy that his wife had been given a discount to make his children look like everyone else's children? Should he be relieved that he continued to spend their money on people who had real needs, real problems? Not that Deborah had any idea how much he'd spent on his causes. The truth was, he couldn't have used his own credit cards for a single haircut if he'd wanted to because they were both maxed out, the bills quickly shredded each month before Deborah could see them.

Or was he supposed to be happy that everything original about his children had been lopped off and smoothed away? David felt as if his family had been hijacked from him.

"I've got a stomachache," he said, although in truth, his stomach-ache had dissipated, and what he had now, a toxic headache of doubt and remorse, felt much worse. "I'm going to go lie down for a while."

"Don't mind him, girls," he heard Deborah say as he walked to their room. "Your dad's a bit of a control freak. He never was any good with surprises."

Was this true? Hadn't he been waiting for his own surprise party for years? None of his girls followed him as he walked away without even bothering to make eye contact with his wife. They were quiet, even Emily, whom he'd never known to be stunned into silence. He felt like a creep, a needy, pouty man who'd be better off at work complaining to his coworkers about his wife than home trying to raise inquisitive, happy children.

He lay down on his bed and stared at the ceiling. It was covered in a horrible bumpy texture he'd never liked. Once, he'd opened his eyes and stared up at the ceiling at what, he later figured out, may well have been the exact moment Emily was conceived. Deborah was on top of him, shuddering and saying this was it, she just knew it, baby number two, and all he was thinking about was ripping out the damn ceiling.

Cottage cheese, their realtor had called it.

Popcorn ceiling, the seller's realtor responded, as if it were some-thing festive. Very popular in the seventies.

Whatever it was called, David had intended to get rid of it years ago, but he'd planned to have it tested first to see if it was made of asbestos. This was the responsible way to approach things, but now he felt impatient. Maybe Deborah was right. He prided himself on being flexible, but he was actually overly careful, a control freak, unable to adjust to something as inconsequential as new haircuts on his own wife and children.

He stood on the bed and poked at the ceiling with his latest bedside book, a deeply discounted hardcover diatribe against capitalism. No-thing budged. He licked his finger and rubbed it over the bumpy texture, popped his finger in his mouth and licked it again. His ceiling tasted sweet and tart like the candy cigarettes he pretended to smoke as a child. He felt sick with remorse and a vague sense of nostalgia.

Tomorrow he'd get out some real tools and begin chipping away at it. He'd start his own makeover right here in the bedroom. What did they know? He was full of surprises.

TRAFFIC ENGINEERING

Patterson was beginning to wonder if he was really a better risk than a big-rig driver who hauled Little Debbies from New Jersey to Oregon. He got to work late and left in the middle of each day. He found himself on the freeway some days for more hours than he was actually in the office. When he was at work, he spent his time evaluating risks, imposing additional conditions and higher premiums on standard life insurance policies for ex-smokers, skydivers, long-distance truckers, the obese. He was easily insurable himself, because he'd never taken the kinds of risks that increased premiums and, until recently, couldn't even imagine wanting to gamble with his life.

Sometimes he invented appointments with clients. But he knew he'd get caught eventually, so he made up dentist appointments and eye exams and even a colonoscopy and, of course, multiple follow-ups. And each time, he ended up in the exact same place, parked in front of Beth Wheeler's house.

While Beth's house was only a mile from his own, he never once stopped in and surprised Winter with a midday visit. In fact, the one time he had misjudged his wife's plans for the day and found her minivan still parked after their normal "school day" had ended in what he'd come to privately consider his spot, he'd kept driving. He'd headed right back to work without seeing any of them.

He found his thoughts drifting toward Beth more than they had ever drifted toward Winter. And while most of his fantasies involved rescuing Beth from various mistakes, they always ended in grateful embraces and continued into more complicated embraces that could no longer be classified as solely grateful.

Each morning when Patterson surfed before work, God's hand planted firmly on his shoulder this one time of day, he asked for reassurance that he was doing the right thing watching out for this woman who'd been sent into his life. That thinking about another woman wasn't a betrayal of his wife. After all, here Beth was, left all alone with her child. Didn't she need a man in her life? Didn't her daughter?

Technically, of course, Jennifer still had a father. But as far as Patterson was concerned, Keith barely fit the definition. He was a coward who'd slinked away from his wife and daughter. And what kind of father could a coward be? According to Winter, the man wouldn't even walk across his own front lawn to pick up his daughter. Instead, he pulled up by the curb and waited, too meek to even honk his horn. The girl had begun to stall for longer periods each time her father came to get her, Winter said. At night over dinner, Winter rattled on, repeating her advice to Beth: *Let him wait. What more important business could he have than to wait for his own daughter? Let him sit out there as long as Jennifer makes him.*

Patterson could imagine his wife giving Beth this advice. Another woman might have felt vaguely sympathetic for the ex-husband, a man whose daughter was slipping away from him. But he was not surprised that Winter despised Keith almost as much as he did for taking the coward's way out and leaving when his marriage got tough. You couldn't be a part-time parent. Winter and he agreed on that.

In fact, Patterson and Winter disagreed about very little. They never squabbled in public and, in fact, seldom argued at home. When they did, their fights were benign and dull. They disagreed about whether the AC should be set at seventy-two or seventy-four in the summer. She gave the boys cookies with their milk before bedtime even though he believed the sugar wired them up. He believed in a weekly deep soaking, while she insisted on watering their yard lightly every other day.

Unlike some of their neighbors, neither of them ever slammed the front door and stormed off down the block or peeled out in a car. They were an ideal match and had two matching sons to prove it, the twins a fifty/fifty blend of both of them, with their mother's lean frame and straight, white teeth and Patterson's low forehead and solid chin.

Sure, sometimes, when they were given too much freedom, the boys caused trouble. Left to their own devices, they had shooting wars in the bathroom before going to bed, and their urine didn't always hit the toilet. They stole a watermelon from the neighbor's garden and played catch with it until one of them missed and it splattered on the sidewalk. They found a lizard in the yard and snuck it into their bedroom, where one morning Winter found it dissembled in dried-out little sections when she was vacuuming under their bunk bed. But they were basically good boys. They just needed supervision and the occasional time-out or swat on the bottom. So why was he making up lies at work and sneaking out to see a disorganized, bumbling woman who was a good twenty pounds overweight to boot?

Southern California's freeways were always a potentially messy bet at 1 p.m. on a weekday. Technically, morning rush hour should have been long over and evening rush hour not yet begun, but the 22 or the 405 north might be snagged from any number of bizarre crises. Once, Patterson found himself stuck in a thirty-minute delay because a center lane had been shut down by a child's portable toilet sitting in the middle of the freeway. Another time, he'd almost missed a meeting just a single freeway exit south because a heavy Santa Ana gust had shaken loose a truck bed full of purple dinosaur piñatas. At least the holiday season was behind them now, when cars piled up routinely at each freeway exit that fed into a mall.

Just thinking about the freeways used to be enough to keep him from venturing out even as far as the Olive Garden in Irvine for an occasional lunch with colleagues. But Beth had changed all that, and here he was, sitting behind the wheel on the 405 north, his workday interrupted once again much too quickly after it had begun.

Getting back to Long Beach was easy this afternoon despite a lingering fog, and he was grateful for the lack of obstructions, so grateful that for once he decided to drive by his own house first. Winter's minivan was parked in the driveway, and he imagined his boys napping inside the house.

Maybe this would be one of those days when the cloud cover didn't blow off at all, a sign that days of rain were on the way. The thought filled Patterson with panic. Would he surf in the rain? How would he make his trip back and forth to Beth's house mid-afternoon? Nothing slowed the freeways more reliably than rain, Southern California's equivalent of snow.

Patterson parked in front of Beth's house, opened his glove compartment, took out a bottle of aftershave, and slapped some on his cheeks. He walked across the neglected lawn, which was somehow both browning and overgrown, and knocked three times on the front door in rapid succession. He thought of this knock as their private code, although he had no idea if Beth even acknowledged the difference between his knock and anyone else's. He also didn't know if she thought it was unusual that he stopped by to visit her at least once nearly every day, if they were complicit in their secrecy or if there was nothing truly secret about any of it.

"Oh, I'm so glad it's you," Beth said, opening the door wide.

"Who else would it be?" Who else visited her without calling first anyway? Did she even have a deadbolt? A chain? He should install a peephole in the door at least.

"Who's left?" Beth said. "First it was the dog police or whatever they're called. Apparently an anonymous complaint by a neighbor. I had to call each one of the owners at work and have them come get their dogs before he took them all away in that padded truck. The man glared at me the whole time, too, as if I was committing a major crime."

"Whoa," Patterson said, looking around. "They're all gone?"

Beth nodded, and he followed her out to the empty yard, small pits dug under the lemon tree by the dogs, chewed-up tennis balls scattered around the grass. For a minute he wondered if they'd taken Jennifer, too, although of course this made no sense. "Where's Jennifer?" he asked.

"She's been upstairs ever since Fred's owners came and got him," Beth said. "She won't open her door. You know how she likes to disappear."

He nodded. He remembered when he first met Beth and Jennifer at Hometown Buffet, what a contrast Jennifer's quiet little presence had been from the three loud sisters, with their dirty fingernails and messy, overloaded plates of food. Over the past few months, he'd heard Jennifer talk, of course, but it seemed to him that she was happiest alone. She'd disappear to her room and later appear in the kitchen or living room or backyard, silent and waiting. Sometimes he wished his boys would be quiet long enough for him to wonder where they were.

"Maybe we should check on her," he said, remembering his self-assigned role of concerned male figure. "Make sure she's okay."

Patterson climbed the stairs with Beth and pushed the door open just wide enough to see Jennifer wearing her Christmas sweater and shorts, sleeping on top of her flowered bedspread. He pulled the door shut and turned to Beth. "Looks like she's napping."

"Hives," Beth whispered. "Under that sweater she's dotted in hives. From the dogs. She could have had an asthma attack. She didn't want to tell me because she wanted to keep the dogs, but I saw them. I knew all along. What kind of mother am I anyway to pretend I didn't know about them? Jesus."

She was crying now, and Patterson was so close to her in the hallway that he couldn't pretend not to notice. She was thinner than when he'd first met her. He could see her clavicle lightly outlined through her T-shirt. Did she think she needed to lose weight, that she wasn't beautiful the way she was, that the extra twenty pounds had caused her husband to leave? He wanted to tell Beth that her husband was dead wrong, whatever his reasons were, that he wasn't just an asshole but a crazy asshole. He could smell Beth's breath, toothpaste and something else. Red wine, maybe? But instead of leaning toward her, he felt himself backing away, his shoulder hitting up against a picture on the wall. He heard a knock on the front door, a sound he may as well have made himself by pounding his head into the wall.

"Be right there!" Beth said, leaving him in the hallway, running down the stairs as if grateful for an excuse to get away from him. Maybe he'd been right to back off. He would try praying with the Christian Surfers again, take his wife to San Francisco for a weekend, get his head back into the game at work. He heard Beth open the door without asking who it was first. He would install a peephole, a deadbolt, a thick brass chain. "So glad you're here," she said.

Patterson heard his boys clamoring in, one of them kicking something heavy—a stone? a hockey puck?—across the living room floor. Did all boys do this? Didn't any of them ever just walk into a house, take a seat on the couch?

"Dad!" the boys yelled when he came down the stairs. They ran to him and he put his arms out wide and let them knock him down onto a stair with their amped-up energy.

"Whoa," Patterson said.

"You called him, too?" Winter asked.

Patterson looked up at his wife, her hair clean and gleaming, pulled back in a tight ponytail. Tiny gold hoops shined against her earlobes.

Beth shrugged. "It all happened so fast. I didn't know what to do."

And Patterson knew then that next time he wouldn't back away, that they were full of shared secrets. He and Beth were in it together.

"Well, good idea," Winter said. "Boys, go clean up the yard while the grown-ups talk about what comes next."

EXPERIMENTS IN PROPULSION

They whipped around Jennifer, the homeschool girls in their stretchy pants, their long, smooth hair flying out behind them. The boys wore jeans and sweatshirts and acted like they were walking down the street, like they couldn't care less. But they all knew how to skate. Every single one of the homeschoolers. A few of the littlest girls wore earmuffs and short, shiny skirts with flesh-colored tights, which at first Jennifer mistook for actual skin. Before one of them skated by so close to her she could see a snag in her tights, she'd been mystified by their outfits, wondering why these girls didn't seem nearly as cold as she was.

Jennifer held tight to the side of the rink. Her hands were cold, and she longed to stuff them both deep into her jacket pockets, but she was afraid to let go of the side, so she only stuffed one in. Her ears were cold, too, and so were her feet. She'd watched other homeschool girls toss off their flip-flops and pull on thick knee socks at the skate-rental benches, but she had only the ankle tennis socks she was wearing. She wished she'd asked for mittens and a hat for Christmas, along with the pink minivan for her Barbies. This was where winter was hidden in Southern California, it turned out, right here inside the Lakewood Ice Palace.

Some of the skaters glided backward and smiled at her as they passed, but most ignored her entirely, which was just fine with her. Her mother sat in the bleachers, sipping coffee and occasionally waving at her. She wished her mother would ignore her, too, but she had a pair of rented skates in the seat beside her, and when she was done with her coffee, she told Jennifer she planned to put them on and get out there and see what she remembered. Jennifer wished that Mrs. Miramir could see her mother now, that she wouldn't wonder if she were having another baby anymore. It seemed to Jennifer that her mother had been working at disappearing. Every day she grew smaller. But every day, she was still right here, watching Jennifer's every move.

As far as she was concerned, homeschool was all about someone watching you every second. She wanted to disappear into the back row of her first grade classroom, where her teacher mixed her up with a girl named Melissa because they were both good and quiet. She didn't want to discuss things she didn't understand with grown-ups, like whether the electoral college was a fair system or not. She just wanted to raise her hand when she absolutely knew the answer for certain and had something to say.

When Jennifer had agreed to come ice skating, she had imagined disappearing, fading in with the crowd, but she had to hold on to the side and no one else did, so she couldn't blend in at all. She'd thought she'd be one of the girls gliding past at Wednesday Homeschool Skate Day, that the skates themselves would somehow magically teach her to use them. She had skated only one other time in her life, visiting her grandmother in Pennsylvania two winters ago. Her father had lifted her onto his shoulders while he skated on the pond, and when he put her down, she remembered balancing easily on her double glider ice skates, the kind that snapped right onto your sneakers. But these skates were nothing like those. These had to be laced up tight and high, and if she didn't concentrate on them every second, her ankles flipped out to the side like she was a big baby who didn't even know how to stand up straight.

The man with the three boy-girls skated by her backward, wearing jeans and a thick woolly sweater. Except for the beard part, Jennifer wished he were her father and would lift her high up in the air where she could forget about how cold she was and how much her ankles hurt and how much she didn't know about ice skating. She'd seen his girls leaning over the vending machine when her mother was helping her lace up her skates, arguing over what to buy with their quarters. So far, at least, she hadn't seen them on the ice.

The only other good part of the day was the fact that the twins hadn't shown up yet. She glanced up at her mother, who was leaning down, probably lacing up a skate now that her coffee was finished. She wanted her to get out here and take her hand. She always talked about growing up with snow. Couldn't she teach her how to skate?

In the center of the ring, a big girl, an almost teenager, with blond princess hair, was spinning around on one foot, her other leg behind her, the toe of her skate pointed at the back of her head. Jennifer inched along, watching her. If she could have taken her hand off the side of the rink without falling, she would have applauded when the girl finished her final spin, but she would have been the only one.

"Pretty impressive, huh?" she heard, and she turned her head forward. Standing right in front of her was David, the backwards skating man who wasn't her father, who wouldn't pick her up and whisk her around in the air like she was a princess, too.

"Ursala's being groomed for better things. Homeschooling's all about more skate time for that girl. Like those child actors whose mothers homeschool them just so they don't miss cattle calls. Diversity is what it's all about, though, right?"

It seemed to Jennifer that he always talked this way, in riddles she wasn't sure if she was supposed to get or not. "Where are your kids?" Jennifer asked.

David shrugged. "They'll get here. Sometimes it takes them a while to get acclimated. We haven't gotten out much lately. The girls have been helping me with a few home-improvement projects."

Jennifer nodded. She imagined the girls were still by the candy machine, seeing how much they could buy with all their quarters, sticking their fingers into the change part to see if any money was stuck in there, arguing over who got what.

"I don't know how to skate," Jennifer said, and before she even suspected she was feeling sad, she began to cry. She hated when this happened, when there was no time to suck things back in. Loud music blared out of the speakers and bright lights flashed across the ice. She hoped David was too distracted to notice her tears. "Here, let me show you," he said.

David put out his hands, and she realized she was supposed to hold onto them while he skated backward. They were large and the knuckles were hairy like his face, but she reached out for his hands anyway. And when David pulled her, Jennifer's feet finally moved the way she had hoped they would when she put on the rented skates. He wasn't her dad, but he was helping her, and she decided to go on and let him keep doing it. Even if his knuckles were hairy and she had never known a man with a beard before, this was definitely better than taking tiny steps and holding onto the side of the rink for the rest of the morning.

Jennifer wanted to show her mother how she was catching on now that David was helping her, but when she looked up at the place in the bleachers where she had been sitting, her spot was empty.

"That's it," David said. "Look how fast you're getting it. See, there's nothing to be upset about."

Why did adults always do this? she wondered. Why did they have to bring up the fact that you'd been upset when you weren't anymore? It just messed up everything good and made Jennifer feel confused, like she should be holding onto her old feelings at least as long as everyone else was.

"Dad!" someone yelled.

For a moment, even though she knew this made no sense, Jennifer thought her own father was here, that someone had spotted him. She turned her head and felt her balance slip. David pulled her up before she fell.

The boy-girls were out on the ice now, all three of them skating up to them. One of the girls had shouted to David. The middle one, Emily, the one who was her age and had wanted Jennifer to hold a bug in their vegetable garden, looped her arm through David's and skated forward while he skated backward. The other two skated next to Jennifer, so close she thought they'd run her into the wall.

They could all skate, even the four-year-old. They were all wearing boys' black skates and ugly plaid knee socks, pulled up over their jeans. Jennifer saw a candy bar wrapper sticking out of the biggest girl's jacket pocket. They had all had haircuts and now their hair was growing in, and they had bangs in their eyes. The oldest one had three braids with some kind of berries tied to the end of each. Emily had sprayed the roots of her hair purple. Jennifer wondered if you could wash it out with regular shampoo or if you just had to wait for it to grow out.

"How come you can't skate?" the youngest one asked. Katie. Jennifer remembered all their names, which were regular girl names, not names like Sydnie or Emerson or Bobbie, that could be for either. Katie was chewing a fat wad of blue gum. She could see it in her mouth when she talked.

"I've got to go find my mom now," she said, shaking loose David's hands and grabbing onto the wall before she slipped, the ice once again foreign and dangerous.

"Come back and skate with us again," David said as he glided backward away from her. But none of his girls said anything, even Emily, and she knew they didn't want her to come back. They were all holding hands now, the four of them. They were taking up a long space and skating fast, the oldest one and David going backward. It looked like they were on their way somewhere fun, and they were late.

She hobbled over to the exit and climbed up out of the rink, feeling only slightly more stable on land in her skates. She sat on the ground and unlaced them, shook her feet free, and carried the skates over to the bench, hiding them underneath. Her sneakers were under there somewhere, too, but Jennifer didn't bother looking for them in the jumble of homeschoolers' shoes. She'd wait until it was time to leave. For now, it felt good to walk around with just her tennis socks covering her sore feet.

She didn't want the blue gum the girl had, but she wanted something from the candy machine. Even though she knew she'd break out in hives, she wanted chocolate, had wanted more chocolate ever since she'd had the brownies at the apartment of Eleanor the Witch. They tasted way better than the dusty carob brownies her mother made, and she couldn't stop thinking about them. Her mother had all of their money in her pockets. Jennifer reached deep into hers just in case but came up empty.

Her mother was here somewhere, but she didn't know this place and she didn't know where to look. She had to go to the bathroom anyway. Maybe her mother was up there. She'd seen a sign pointing up the stairs when they'd walked in and she followed it now. Her feet felt cold through her socks on the cement of the stairs, and she'd wished she'd looked harder for her sneakers, but she was already halfway up and she decided to keep going.

Instead of a regular sign, the ladies' room was marked with a drawing of a girl wearing ice skates and the kind of short skirt some of the little girls wore. Jennifer pushed open the door. The air in the bathroom was cloudy with smoke, and she began to back up. The bathroom was on fire and she would call 911 or find a manager, but before she could do any of those things, she heard a toilet flush and a girl came out of a stall. The girl blew smoke out of her nose and then spit on her cigarette and tossed it in the sink. The girl reached in her pocket and sprayed her mouth with something, then stuffed it back in her pants. "What are you staring at?" she said. "If you tell my coach or my tutors, I'll kill you."

The girl walked by Jennifer. She was wearing suede ankle boots with furry trim, and her hair was curly and blond and fell all the way down her back. She walked like she was balancing a book on her head. Jennifer decided at that moment that this was how she would most like to walk, and she remembered then where she'd seen this girl before. She was the one in the center of the rink, the girl someone should have applauded when she had finished all her spinning.

"I remember you. You're the really good skater," Jennifer said.

"Okay," the girl said.

"Your name's Ursala," Jennifer said.

"What are you, a little stalker?"

Jennifer didn't know what a stalker was, but the word sounded mean coming out of Ursala's mouth. "No," Jennifer said. "I'm a home-schooler. Like you."

"No shit," Ursala said. "Well, hope you're having fun with that."

Jennifer wanted to tell Ursala that she wasn't having fun, that she'd rather be in school, but Ursala had already opened the door and was gone.

Ursala had left a thin pink barrette on the side of the sink. Jennifer picked it up and smelled it—smoke and violets or roses or some kind of flowers that grew in a frontyard she passed when her mother used to walk her to school. When she used to go to school. She shoved the barrette deep into a front pocket of her jeans. A souvenir of Ursala.

"Mom?" Jennifer said, although she was pretty sure there was no one else in the bathroom. All she had wanted for days was to be left alone, and now that she finally was, she wanted her mother. She wanted her so much she felt as if she was going to cry again for the second time in the same afternoon at the Lakewood Ice Palace.

She tried calling *Mom* again, and then she ran back down the stairs, calling *Mom* the whole way. She knew she was being a big baby right here at the Ice Palace. She finally stopped herself by touching the base of her throat and listening for a wheeze, making herself slow down before one had a chance to catch in her throat and start. No one was on the bench putting on or taking off skates, so she walked over in her socks to the opening in the rink and looked out. They were all out there, all the homeschoolers, and she finally spotted her mother. Aiden or Nolan held her hands. Her mother wasn't as good a skater as Jennifer had hoped, but she wasn't holding onto the side either. She skated in a straight line, her feet moving too much, like she was walking, instead of gliding. Patterson was right behind her with the other twin. Her mother had said she didn't know if the twins were going to make it to the skating rink or not, but here they were, the way they always were.

Sometimes Patterson filled in for Winter, who was home getting the new business going. At least he didn't pretend to be a teacher. At least he didn't make her sit with the boys and write journal entries about everything they learned by making applesauce from scratch. At least he didn't read them books about the Civil War and then leave her stuck pretending to be a runaway slave while the boys pretended to shoot her and each other in the backyard for the rest of the day, arguing over who got to be the North and who got to be the South.

"There you are!" her mother shouted. She let go of the twin, who skated off toward Patterson. He had a twin on either side of him now. When they skated by, Patterson nodded his head at Jennifer in his regular official-seeming way, and the twin closest to her threw a small chunk of ice at her so quickly that only she could see it fly through the air before landing on the side of her neck.

If she worked on it, she was pretty sure she could figure out how to tell the twins apart. Winter said Aiden had a longer chin, but that wasn't it. There was something else about the shape of their faces or the way their eyebrows curved, but she didn't want to waste her time bothering to try. What she wanted was for them to leave her life as quickly as they had appeared. What she wanted was for her dad to come home and to go back to school, and if that wasn't going to happen, she at least wanted to have her mother back to herself again.

Her mother skated up to the entrance to the rink with her small steps and stopped herself by putting her hands around Jennifer's waist. "I was beginning to wonder what had happened to you."

"I couldn't find you," Jennifer said. "I thought you left."

"Don't be silly," her mother said. "I was right here. Why's your neck red? That's not a hive, is it?"

"No," Jennifer said, touching the spot where one of the twins had hit her with ice. It felt hot and red like a hive, and Jennifer wished she had lied and said it was a hive and she was allergic to the Ice Palace and they had to go. Now. "I don't think so," she said. "Maybe."

"Good. Come skate with me." Her mother lifted her up and pulled her out onto the ice.

"I don't have my skates on," Jennifer said, remembering a moment too late, feeling the ice through her socks. They both looked down at her feet.

"Where are they?" her mother said.

Jennifer shrugged. "I was skating too much. I felt like I was getting wheezy." She stood on her mother's feet and leaned back into her and looked out to the center of the rink. Ursala was back out there again. This time she was jumping instead of spinning, her coach clapping to tell her when to jump. She saw Ursala's hair covering part of her face, and she stuck her hand in her pocket to feel the barrette.

"Poor girl," her mother said. "She's here six hours a day, I hear. Her parents have to work nonstop to pay for all this. She has tutors for everything."

Jennifer nodded and leaned back into her mother. She was thinking how lucky Ursala was, how she'd like a real tutor if she had to be homeschooled, and how, what she'd really like, was to leap like that, straight through the air.

In the lobby, her mother studied the snack machine. "You can have the yogurt-covered raisins, I think."

"Never mind," Jennifer said. She hated all her allergies and the way she could never just pick something that looked good. "I'll wait for lunch."

It was break time now, and a line for the snack machine had formed behind them. Jennifer could hear change shifting, someone's nickel or penny dropping on the ground. She stepped out of line. The boy-girls were behind her with their dad, who was doling out quarters. Jennifer heard quarters clang and bounce on the concrete floor as the girls pushed each other out of the way so they could be the next in line.

"My turn," little Katie said, winning and cramming her quarters into the machine. "I like that one, don't I, Dad?" she said, pointing to a bag of chocolate-covered peanuts.

"At least there's nuts in them," David said to her mother or her or maybe even to Katie. It was hard to tell. "At least we're talking a modicum of protein."

"I can't eat peanuts," Jennifer said even though she knew the chocolate-covered peanuts weren't for her.

David wrinkled his forehead like he was thinking about what he could say next.

"She could have had the yogurt raisins," her mother said.

"Oh, right," David said. "Good choice!"

"But she didn't want them," her mother said.

"I'm ready to go home," Jennifer said.

"Wait. Here comes the Zamboni," her mother said.

She looked out at the rink, where a tractorlike truck rolled over everything, smoothing it down.

"Did you know that machine was named after Frank Zamboni, who invented it in the 1940s for his rink right here in Southern California?" David said.

Jennifer didn't know this, but she knew from David's tone that she was back in school again, right here at the Lakewood Ice Palace. "Why doesn't the ice melt?" she asked, but David had already turned away,

back toward the boy-girls, who were pushing buttons and reaching
into the bottom of the machine and fighting over their candy.

"I don't know, but I'll find out for you," her mother said. "Or we
can look it up together when we get home. How's that?"

"It's okay," she said, sorry the way she always was lately when
she accidentally asked a question. "I don't really want to know that
much." In Pennsylvania, where she had skated on the pond near her
grandmother's house, her father hadn't tried to teach her anything.
He'd lifted her up and skated around with her on his shoulders, and
her lungs had filled with air that was so cold and thin, she thought she
might float if she leaned backward and fell off.

She walked with her mother closer to the rink. She looked around
for Ursala but she was gone now. She turned and saw David and the
boy-girls grabbing their shoes and scarves and leaving, too, arguing
about who got to sit in which seat in the car. But Patterson and the
twins were still here. She knew Patterson was standing near her. He
smelled the way he always did, like the ocean mixed with some kind of
cologne that smelled like the color light blue if light blue was allowed
to have a smell. Her dad never smelled this way, and Jennifer thought it
was wrong that Patterson did, that men should just use plain soap, that
they shouldn't put on extra things after they showered.

Jennifer kept looking straight ahead, pretending she really cared
about the Zamboni and how it worked. "Can we go now?" she asked
her mother, but it was Patterson who answered this time.

"How about we stop for lunch on the way home, ladies?" he said.
"My treat."

She wanted to say *no*, to shout *NO*, but her mother was already
saying how nice it would be not to have to cook. What she really wanted
was to go to the school cafeteria for lunch and sit with her class and
eat her fruit cup and drink her orange juice from its little sealed cup.

"We're hungry," one of the twins said.

"Are you boys ladies?" Patterson asked. "I asked the ladies, not
the men."

Jennifer wondered if he couldn't tell them apart either, if that's why
he didn't usually call them by name, if he also thought it wasn't worth
bothering to try.

She felt the red spot on the side of her neck. It wasn't hot anymore, but it felt sore when she touched it, and she hoped there'd be a bruise she could show her father when she saw him. From the twins, she'd say. One of the awful boys I told you about.

One of the twins had made another snowball out of scraps of ice he had collected from the rink. When no one else was looking, he threw it in the air, and Jennifer watched it fly up above her.

She put her hands over the back of her head and ducked. *I hate you*, she thought.

"Catch," he said.

THE METRIC SYSTEM

Beth didn't quite recognize her own house. Lamps she rarely used were lit in corners of the living room. Jasmine-and-lavender-scented candles to promote calm and serenity—Winter's theory was that serene people spent money more freely—burned on the fireplace mantle. Soft classical music played throughout the downstairs on portable speakers, and the kitchen smelled like pear tarts and Gruyère and macadamia soufflé.

Beth had planned to learn to cook, had assumed that when Jennifer started preschool she would take a cooking class or two. She'd even gone so far as picking up brochures for drop-in classes offered at a kitchen store just a few miles away, but, like so much she'd intended to do, she'd never gotten around to actually doing it. She couldn't get herself organized enough to get there at the right time, which always seemed to fall somewhere between preschool pickup and nap. Ultimately, though, it was Jennifer's food allergies that had dissuaded her from signing up for a class. The increasingly limited list of ingredients didn't offer much in the way of inspiration.

This may have been Beth's house, but she was only the hostess today. Winter was the Consultant, she explained, the one who'd run the Cooking Show, the one who'd actually make the food and demonstrate the overpriced cookware to the women they had invited to lunch.

"Your job is to open up your home and Meet and Greet," she told Beth in a way that sounded vaguely ironic but wasn't. Irony wasn't a quality Winter possessed. She was neat, organized, and occasionally bitchy. She laughed at YouTube videos of cats drinking out of toilets. She made the twins put Miss and Mister in front of adults' first names. If Beth needed a dose of irony, she walked across the street to see Darla. Over the past few months, though, she'd come to appreciate both the crisp certainty of Winter's reactions and the familiar feeling of being free to drift along in their wake.

Winter had an elaborate business plan all laid out that promised them commissions of $400 to $500 a month each if they held just two Cooking Shows a week. "We're in this together," she told Beth as she slid her business plan back into its clear folder the night before. "Professional, personal, and financial independence. That's where we're headed."

According to Winter, their goal for today wasn't just to sell kitchen products but to find other hostesses who would let them have parties at their homes. The new hostesses then would become Consultants themselves one day and eventually earn them additional commissions on all their sales.

"It's moms helping moms. What could make more sense?" Winter said when Beth questioned exactly how the plan worked. "And it all happens right in our homes."

She nodded even though when Winter used the word *home* in this way it made her feel inexplicably queasy.

"Look at Mary Kay today. She's loaded, and she started with nothing. Absolutely zero when she had her first makeup party in her home."

It had all made sense for a single moment a week ago. Beth designed the invitation on the computer while Winter worked on the guest list and the children looked over her shoulder and offered suggestions on layout.

She'd thought for that optimistic, isolated moment that maybe everything was coming together now. Here she was, using her work experience in promotions to start a home business that not only could help support Jennifer but could educate the children about all kinds of things. Who knew how many possible lessons they could all glean from this? Already, the children were learning new computer skills as she showed them which buttons to push to enlarge words and center headings.

But that moment had quickly passed. It was mid-January, and it became impossible for Beth to ignore the fact that they had missed the all-important holiday gift-buying season. As Winter had continued to explain the business, Beth's limited experience in promotions had fortified her with enough knowledge to realize that, at best, this was little more than a pyramid scheme. And they were likely to stay at the bottom of the pyramid or, more likely, be squished beneath it with their expensive Starter Package. But, by the time she had come to this realization, the invitations were in the mail.

Today, for the party, Beth wore her good black jeans, pants that finally fit loosely enough that she could sit down without taking a deep breath first. But she was still far from comfortable. She sipped at what had become a fairly regular glass of mid-afternoon red wine.

She missed the dogs. No matter how many scented candles Winter burned, the house still smelled of them. The dogs ruined her lawn and gave Jennifer hives. Still, dog daycare didn't require her to dress up in "hostess" clothes, and no one expected her to sell the dogs anything. But the dogs were out of the question now that the mystery neighbor had complained. And Keith's promises to keep paying for everything the way he always had already had proved spotty. So here Beth was, hosting the first party she'd had in her house in years.

At first the children had helped them try out recipes for the Cooking Show, measuring out teaspoons of honey, sifting flour, and converting cups to liters in an impromptu math lesson. But Winter had grown impatient with their spills and slow math, and Beth had ended up taking all three to the park that morning to do nothing more educational than climb on the monkey bars. Now Jennifer was across the street at Darla's house, and Winter had hired an actual babysitter for the twins, explaining to Beth in what felt like an unnecessarily patronizing tone that she could deduct this as a business expense.

Beth walked around now, sipping her wine, fluffing couch pillows, and waiting for the first guests to arrive. Over half of the women they invited they'd never met. David had passed on the names and addresses of other homeschooling mothers he thought liked to cook. He planned to stop in himself to order a new ice-cream scoop. When Beth tried to imagine Keith at a party like this, surrounded by women in the middle of the day, all she could imagine was him making an excuse to leave, taking his photography equipment and backing out the door as quickly as possible.

She tried not to imagine Patterson here. As it was, Patterson was taking up an increasingly large part of her thoughts. She felt guilty and increasingly impatient and skittish when she found herself alone with him.

The last time had been at the Lakewood Ice Palace two weeks before, when the twins had shot off ahead, slamming into the ice and walls before coming back to grab their hands, and Jennifer had disappeared upstairs to the bathroom. Beth had skated alone next to Patterson. "A man would have to be nuts to leave you," he'd said, the tips of his fingers planted lightly, and only for an instant, on the base of her back as they both turned a corner, Sheena Easton singing, an oldie about her baby taking the morning train.

Thinking about this now caused her stomach to twist up. Not telling Keith about homeschooling had that effect, too. So did worrying about money, a subject she realized only now she had left previously to Keith. For the first time since she'd given birth to Jennifer, she was losing weight. She tried on clothes shoved far back in her closet and pulled up zippers that wouldn't have budged a month ago. Her wedding band loosened enough so she could slide it off easily. And she did, storing it in a Ziplock bag with the credit cards she tried to avoid using.

She also avoided looking Winter in the eye.

This wasn't hard, since Winter was now focused almost obsessively on establishing a homeschooling curriculum for kindergarten and grade one and starting up their new business. She didn't even notice when her gas tank was close to empty or her cell phone's battery was dying. Just the day before, as the five of them took off for the Santa Ana Zoo in Winter's van, Beth found herself in the unusual position of reminding Winter about her boys' nearly forgotten dental appointment, after reading the sticky note attached to Winter's dashboard.

Patterson had told them he'd try to stop by on his lunch hour and lend a hand if they needed him, but today was really Winter's. He would or wouldn't stop by, and all Beth had to do was open the door and Meet and Greet. She still hadn't told Darla that she was officially homeschooling Jennifer, but she'd told her that Keith wasn't coming back, and Darla had agreed to watch Jennifer in the middle of the day today. Beth had planned to leave Jennifer with the babysitter Winter had hired to watch the boys, but she begged to go to Darla's instead. Jennifer often stayed home sick, and Darla hadn't asked any questions when Beth had walked her across the street earlier.

Little Jeremy had run up to Jennifer, the front of his shorts wet from one of his regular accidents. It seemed to Beth that Darla's nonchalant method of potty training resulted in far too many extra loads of laundry.

Jennifer bent down and whispered to him. "It's just the two of us until Lauren gets out of kindergarten." Then she took Jeremy's hand and let him lead her to his room.

"I just love that girl," Darla said. "How can you not love her?"

"I do love her," Beth said, and then she realized, of course, Darla was only being kind, not challenging her.

"Someone's looking hot," Darla said. "New jeans?"

"Oh, no. Not really, anyway," Beth said. "Stop over later if you want. For dessert. Maybe I'll buy you a spatula."

"Ha," Darla said. "Just what I need. Another spatula. You kids have fun with your little luncheon. We're happy eating play-dough burgers over here."

Now people were finally starting to arrive, and Beth saw how drastically Winter had misjudged the afternoon. No amount of mood lighting and soft music could change the fact that the homeschool moms all had their children with them. Of course they did. Why hadn't they thought of that? What else would they do with them?

She held open the door for first one group and then another. She smiled weakly and forgot everyone's name as they introduced themselves. She knew she should be taking charge, offering iced tea, telling the moms where to put their purses and diaper bags, that this was part of Meet and Greet, but the magnitude of Winter's miscalculation had left her temporarily voiceless.

A toddler had already stuffed a handful of mints in his mouth and spit them back out into the other hand before Winter walked in and whisked away the mint tray Beth had centered on the coffee table only moments earlier.

"Welcome, ladies!" Winter said, ignoring the throngs of children. Her cheeks were red and splotchy from the heat of the kitchen or anger, Beth wasn't sure which. She wondered suddenly if this was the way Winter's face colored when she was in bed with Patterson. She hoped passion made her splotchy and unattractive.

A boy threw a rubber ball up the stairs and watched it bounce down, caught it, and tossed it up again. Beth watched Winter glare at him, her own boys off with their paid babysitter.

"Thanks for coming to our cooking show and luncheon, ladies!" Winter said, ushering everyone into the kitchen. Some of the children held onto their mothers' skirts and followed along, but a few stayed behind. Two ten-year-old girls sat down across from each other in the middle of Beth's living room floor.

"Did you bring your string?" one girl asked the other, and within moments they were busy moving tied loops of string around in their hands, holding up surprising shapes and talking all the while.

"Do you know witches' broom?"

"Apache door?"

"Cat's cradle?"

"Jacob's ladder?"

Beth felt dizzy, like she was catching the flu or had downed her wine too quickly. She sat down on the couch next to a woman who was nursing a baby and texting and felt the soles of the baby's bare feet bump up against the side of her shirt. The baby kicked like he wanted

Beth to get out of the way.

"This is my house," Beth said.

The woman nursing the baby looked up from her phone and smiled at her. "They're doing math," she said, nodding in the direction of the girls making string figures. "Tactile learning."

"Of course," Beth said. "I thought so." But the truth was she hadn't been thinking anything like that at all. Would Jennifer like doing this? Was this something she should be teaching her?

"And they learn how to think systematically," the woman said, switching the baby to her other breast.

"Are they both yours?" she asked.

The woman shook her head. "The one making the banana tree is mine. It's quite an advanced piece of string work, really."

She looked at the complicated geometric shapes both girls held up in front of them. Which one was the banana tree? She had no idea. Before she could ask the woman on the couch, the girls were twisting their strings again.

"Six eyes," one of the girls said, holding up her design.

"Salt cave," the other one said, still twisting the string in her hands. "Can we go check out the food now, Mom?"

The woman continued texting and nodded, and both girls jumped up, shoving their string pieces into their back pockets.

"I'm sorry. We're not planning on buying anything," the woman said, looking up from her phone. "It's just nice to get out once in a while. I mean I would if I could, but we're on a strict budget," she added.

"Of course," Beth said. It seemed that nearly every homeschool family she'd met was on a strict budget. They showed up in droves for Free Movie Monday Morning at the Cineplex, bags of home-popped corn and thermoses of lemonade shoved deep into their children's backpacks. They cruised Costco at lunchtime, children running through the aisles while their mothers lined up for the samples of taquitos and chicken-apple sausages and coffee cake. Like Beth, they found discounts online and in newspapers and clipped coupons; they knew when Cold Stone was giving away free scoops of ice cream to their first 100 customers; they knew that Babette Bakery marked its pastries half price fifteen minutes before closing; and they knew which nights kids ate free at Denny's and Super Mex and Lucille's.

They all seemed to be on budgets except David, who sent her emails routinely about multiple charities he helped support. She pictured his girls pushing each other, in line behind them for the candy machine at the Lakewood Ice Palace, their chubby hands full of so many quarters they couldn't help but drop them.

Only a few months ago Beth had donated the television to Goodwill, but she knew now she should have listed it on Craigslist and tried to sell it instead. The baby on the couch next to her slurped loudly as he nursed and kicked Beth again in the side. Clearly, they weren't going to be making any money today.

"We're submitting our résumés to *Homeschool Help*. They don't pay directly, but I hear you get lots of prizes if they pick you. And it can lead to endorsements, of course. There's always that."

"Excuse me?" Beth said.

"You know, that new cable show. It's like that nanny show but for homeschoolers. They send some expert to help you with lesson plans, organization, creative projects, yada, yada."

Beth watched her shift the baby to her lap, efficiently hook up her bra and pull down her shirt.

"But you don't seem to need help," she said.

"Who doesn't need help?"

Winter, she thought. But then she considered the fact that she might be very wrong. Meet and Greet had been over for thirty minutes and she knew she should go into the kitchen to see if Winter needed help.

And Beth had meant to walk through the house into the kitchen, but she walked out the front door instead. It was January now, nearly three months since Keith had left, and she needed a sweater but didn't want to go back inside and look for one.

She had lived in this house for ten years but, except for Darla, barely knew any of her neighbors. Ever since she'd been forced to shut down her dog-sitting business, Beth had wondered if she and Keith should have been friendlier. But in truth, it just wasn't that kind of street. Except for Darla, the neighbors barely made eye contact.

If her arms hadn't been folded over her chest to keep herself warm, she would have waved at David as he pulled up in his Volvo wagon. Although his competence could make her feel defensive, he did have a certain rational male quality that she found herself longing for suddenly. Even without a degree in marketing, what man thought he could make a living hosting "cooking shows" in his friends' homes?

The three boy-girls got out of the car while David was still edging in closer to the curb, the smallest one climbing over the seat first and going out the front door. They walked out wearing white hard hats and loose khaki overall shorts without shirts underneath, opened her front door, and went inside.

"They are way into the construction zone," David said. "I had to bribe them with a free lunch to get them away from the demolition site."

"Demolition site?"

"Today, the bathroom. My girls and I are remodeling. It was time even though Iggy did not appreciate being displaced, but it couldn't be helped. Besides, it's only temporary. We're betting he's going to love the new soaking tub."

"Iggy?"

"Our tortoise?"

"Oh, right. I remember. Tortoise."

"I'd better go see what the girls are up to in there," David said. "Coming?"

"In a minute," Beth said. "I'm just going to get a little more air."

"Sounds rough. Everything okay in there?" He stared at her in a way that let her know "in there" meant more than inside her house. She knew he meant well, but his attempts to check up on her were exhausting.

"Oh, no. It's fine. I'll be in soon."

Beth watched him walk inside, realizing that the free lunch he'd promised his children was being cooked in her kitchen right now.

Standing in front of her house, she could hear the party under way inside and peals of toddler laughter coming from Darla's house across the street. The street was lined with minivans. She read a small round sticker affixed to a back windshield of a van that blocked her driveway. *Presidential Prayer Team.* She'd parked her own car in the driveway that morning to leave more room on the street, and now she couldn't get out.

Science 2 U: Science for the Homeschooled Child was etched across the back window of another car. They weren't real guests, but her house finally sounded like Darla's, as if they both were hosting perpetual parties. She didn't feel as if she'd really be missed at either one of them. When she saw Patterson's car coming down the street, she realized that she'd been waiting for him to pull up. They'd made no plan, and she had no reason to believe he would even show up today, but she saw now that she had counted on it anyway.

She opened the passenger door and got in before he had a chance to get out. "Can we get out of here?" she asked, not looking at him. She pulled the door closed and buckled her seat belt before he had a chance to answer. She breathed in the salt air he carried with him and the now-familiar scent of his aftershave. She looked out the passenger window and caught a glimpse through Darla's big living room window of her daughter laughing and chasing after Jeremy. *Be careful about your asthma*, she thought.

"Is that okay," she said, "if we just go? Somewhere."

He didn't answer, and she wondered if she'd really asked. In the past, with Keith, there had always been so much she hadn't said. But after a minute, she heard his car key click back into place and the car start up. And she knew then if he was willing to drive, she was willing to let him take her just about anywhere.

AMPHIBIANS

He had gotten through Christmas and New Year's. Keith lived in his office, showered at the gym, and spent the night with Eleanor whenever she invited him, but the new year made it harder to avoid the obvious, that it was time to find an actual place to live.

Keith sat on a bench scrolling on his phone through apartments for rent on craigslist and watching his daughter play on a ship docked on dry land at the aquarium. He smiled in her direction periodically as she turned the ship's wheel and pretended to head out to sea.

Watching Jennifer from this remove reminded him of Sunday mornings when she was younger. At their neighborhood playground, he'd sit on a bench glancing up from his newspaper to smile at her while other parents shouted at their kids not to throw sand and to give back that stick right this instant. Noisy childhood chaos blooming around her, Jennifer would remain alone under the slide, piling sand into a bucket and pouring it out again. Sometimes Keith would bring his camera and snap photos of her, impressed with her intense focus and ability for solitary play.

Keith was relieved now to see that his daughter still possessed this same independent spirit, that she was able to keep herself entertained on the moored ship with not much more than her imagination for company. Maybe she'd be an artist one day, a photographer or a painter.

The only problem was, he hadn't been watching his daughter at all. Instead, he'd been watching another man's daughter. The girl he'd been watching looked very much like Jennifer but wasn't. He saw that when she finally turned around and gave someone else the wheel. Her face was all wrong, eyes closer together, too big of a smile. He'd had this problem at weddings, winding up with way too many pictures of an unimportant child when he thought he'd been shooting the ring bearer dancing with the flower girl, when actually the real ring bearer was asleep across two folding chairs. But he'd never had this problem keeping track of his own child. Eleanor had done this to him, he was sure. He couldn't focus on anything anymore.

Jennifer was lost, and he was the one who lost her. He hadn't lost her just in the metaphorical way he was worried about when he first moved out of the house three months ago. He'd literally lost her, for ten whole minutes, maybe longer now. He remembered how she used to hide when she was younger, how Beth would call him sobbing so loudly that Jennifer would finally creep out of the back of the hall closet while Beth was on the phone, or slide out from under her bed and hug her.

There were too many places to hide in the aquarium. Doorways, dark hallways, stairwells. He shoved his phone in his pocket and stood up, ready to take off in several directions all at once. The place was packed with kids. They bent over the touch tanks of pettable sharks and stingrays. They shot water canons toward the docked boat. They shook their hands and hair and screamed in front of the huge fish mouth of the hot-air hand dryer. They ran up the stairs bound for the seals. They pushed each other as they waited in line to buy food for the lorikeets. None of them stood still. None of them was Jennifer.

The aquarium was huge and impossible to navigate quickly. Inside, long, dimly lit hallways led through the Pacific and Atlantic Oceans, the warm waters of the Caribbean. He would never find his daughter, and Beth would kill him.

Beth will kill me, he thought, knowing all the while how self-centered and distracting this thought was. *She'll never let me see Jennifer again.*

He took off up the stairs in the direction the most children seemed to be heading, tugging on their parents' hands, sitting on their shoulders. It was feeding time for the seals, someone was announcing somewhere. That's where they were all going, to watch the seals bark and dance and catch fish and swallow them down whole. His daughter was no bigger than a seal. Certainly, she weighed less.

He had no idea how many inches tall she was, how much she weighed. How could he report her missing? *She smells like soap*, he would tell the police. *Her hair is tangled at the ends where she doesn't pull the brush through all the way.*

When he picked up Jennifer at her mother's that morning, he'd had to wait so long out front that he'd finally gotten out of the car, gone to the door, and rang his own bell. Beth answered. She was thinner than he'd seen her in years. Another woman who looked vaguely familiar stood next to her. Who was she? They both wore jeans and buttoned-up shirts. Had his wife become a lesbian?

"Is Jen ready?" he asked.

They both looked at him long enough before speaking that he wondered if he'd gotten something wrong, that maybe he wasn't supposed to come this Sunday at all. Had they changed the day that week and he'd forgotten?

"She's still in the shower," Beth finally said. "Did you want to wait for her inside?"

He didn't, and he wasn't sure her question was actually an invitation. But he came inside anyway, sitting on the edge of the couch in the living room and smiling into the distance while the women disappeared into the kitchen. The house smelled vaguely of dog and of something burning. But if he went to check, he worried he'd seem like he was intruding or expected to be fed. Beth hadn't asked him for any help at all since he showed her how to fix the television months ago.

He picked up a piece of string tied into a loop lying next to a book called *Fun with String Figures*. He tried the first one, something called cat's cradle, labeled *Easy*, and quickly gave up as the string slipped off his fingers. Did his daughter actually know how to make these shapes? Maybe Beth did. The truth was, he had no idea what she did with the majority of her time before he left her, and certainly couldn't claim to know now.

"Bagel chip?" the other woman asked, holding a paper plate in front of him with slices of what appeared to be burnt bagel arranged on it. "They're all the same. Everything."

"Excuse me?" he said.

"Everything bagel chips," Beth said. "They're all everything."

Keith took a bite. "Good," he said even though they tasted bitter and burned. He chewed hard and smiled.

"We're thinking four bucks a pound," the other woman said. "High or low?"

"I have no idea."

"What would you pay?" she asked.

Keith looked at Beth, who stood next to the vaguely familiar woman. *Help me here*, he thought. She shrugged.

Jennifer finally came down the stairs, her wet hair hanging at her shoulders. She didn't look particularly surprised or happy to see him there, sitting on the couch. "Bye, Mom," she said. "Bye, Winter."

They found Jennifer at the turtles just as he was about to punch 911 into his cell phone. He had grabbed an employee to help him, a big, sunburned kid who had been assisting with the seal feeding, whose job it was to carry over the paint buckets full of mackerel. Keith couldn't tell if he was nauseated by fear or the kid's odor, but the first thing he did was vomit when he spotted Jennifer, her face edged up against the glass next to a turtle so huge it looked as if it could swallow her.

"Jesus," the kid said, staring down at the ground. "I better go get the bucket."

"I've been looking for you everywhere," Keith said, running over and grabbing her up. He wanted to shake her, but instead he held onto her tight. His mouth tasted of bile, and he looked over at the kid who had helped him, mopping up now and putting out a yellow *Wet Caution* sign. Keith wiped his mouth with the back of his hand. He knew he should apologize and thank the kid, maybe give him some kind of tip, but all he wanted to do was take Jennifer and get out of there.

"You smell bad," she said in his ear.

"I was sweating," Keith said, and he realized he was. He had soaked through his shirt. "I was sick," he said. *Sick with worry*, he thought, understanding the phrase for the first time. Is this how Beth felt every day as she listened for Jennifer's labored breathing, watched her skin for signs of hives? "Come on," he said. "Let's get out of here."

"I want to go to the gift shop first," Jennifer said. "I need a souvenir."

"Of today?" The stench of mackerel and vomit was more than enough of a souvenir for him. But he followed her, stayed only inches behind her as she walked into the gift shop. He felt people pull away from him as he hovered while Jennifer sorted through a big plastic bowl of aquatic-themed erasers.

"I want this one," she said, holding up a tiny version of the turtle that had floated behind the glass inches away from her face.

In the car, Jennifer sat in the back seat while Keith, his hands on the wheel, considered where to go. Absurdly, he thought about driving to a hospital. Or the police station. He still hadn't found an apartment he could afford.

When he didn't have his daughter with him, sleeping on the couch in his office or at Eleanor's apartment felt almost normal. But when Jennifer was around, it was harder to ignore the fact that he didn't have an actual home or enough money to rent one while he was still making the mortgage payments. He never felt as close to being homeless as when he was with his daughter. And now here he was, sitting behind the wheel of his run-down car, smelling of sweat and vomit, with nowhere to go.

"Do you know the difference between a tortoise and a turtle?" Jennifer said from the back seat.

"No, but I bet you do."

"A tortoise lives mostly on land."

"That's right," he said. He'd never been much of a student. In college he had flirted with the female faculty and pretended to be impressed with his male professors. But he had always gotten by. "Now I remember," he said. But he didn't. He looked in the rearview mirror and saw Jennifer squishing up her mouth skeptically at him. He'd always gotten by until now. He wasn't even fooling his seven-year-old daughter.

Keith's hands were planted on the steering wheel. He may as well have been steering the grounded boat at the aquarium. He backed up and pulled out of the aquarium's garage, finally deciding to make a right turn.

"Which would you rather be, Dad?" Jennifer asked, "a turtle or a tortoise?"

He thought about the huge turtle swimming in the tank by his daughter's face. "A tortoise," he said. "I'd rather be a tortoise. How about you?"

"A turtle," she said. "Did you know that some turtles can live for more than a month without food, and the green sea turtle can stay underwater for over five hours without coming up for air?"

"You're full of interesting facts now that you're a big first grader."

"Box turtles sometimes eat so much that they can't fit in their shells anymore."

He couldn't stop thinking about the woman at home, how he'd seen her somewhere before, how she and Beth dressed similarly, as if they were more than business partners. "So who's Winter exactly?"

"Mom's friend."

"Do you like her?"

"She's okay."

"She's kind of pretty, don't you think?" he asked.

"She's married already, Dad. You can't marry her."

"I wasn't planning to marry her. Where would you get that idea?"

"You said she was pretty."

"I just meant that in a general kind of way. She's not even my type."

This was not going at all the way he had intended. He sounded like an asshole and knew it. Jennifer went silent again in the back of the car. He glanced in the rearview mirror and saw her looking out the window.

"David has a tortoise named Iggy," she finally said, facing forward now. "Tortoises can live 150 years. You'd like him, I think."

"Who? Iggy or David?" Keith asked.

"Iggy," she said.

"Who's David?" Keith asked.

"Mom's friend," she said.

"Mom sure has a lot of friends these days." He heard himself sounding like an asshole again and stopped talking. How was it any of his business if his wife had started a new life? Hadn't he started one of his own? Wasn't that the whole point?

"Should we go out to lunch?" he asked. "Are you hungry yet?"

"Sort of, I guess," Jennifer said.

In his wallet was a folded, laminated list labeled with a bold headline: OFF-LIMITS FOODS. Jennifer had handed it to him when he picked her up several days after the dinner at Eleanor's. Keith didn't ask her why her mother had made the list then, after months of being separated. He didn't have to—at the bottom of the list, under *Any Kind of Nuts*, the words *Follow Exactly if You Want to See Jenny Again* were typed out as if they were simply another category to avoid.

At the restaurant, he ordered Jennifer the safest thing on the menu, egg beaters and potatoes, and pointed at a glossy picture of some kind of meaty special for himself. He'd felt lately that he needed extra protein. Although Eleanor was ten years older than he was, he'd worn himself out trying to keep up with her.

Thanks to the settlement from her marriage, which served as a kind of trust fund, Eleanor's days were organized around classes the way other people's were organized around work. Each day she had a different routine, a time frame to which she strictly adhered, as if it mattered. Although he was the one who actually worked, he felt like a slacker around Eleanor.

Her days were filled with quasi-self-improvement classes he never knew existed. She enrolled in a mosaic-making class with a spiritual bent and glued fragments of tile into the shape of a splintery-looking peace sign, which she hung above her living room couch. She took rock climbing on Tuesday mornings at a gym he'd once taken Jennifer to for a birthday party. She did belly dancing at a community center and regularly took two different types of yoga, one on a grassy park area near the bay and another in a blank, padded room kept at the temperature of a sauna. Today was her ice-skating day, followed by two hours of free skating. When he'd left her apartment that morning, she was pulling on leopard-print leggings.

He hadn't gone to a skating class yet. But he had tried nearly everything else with her. Except for the belly dancing, which seemed exclusively female. That, he'd watched from one of the folding chairs put out for spectators in a semicircle around the Parks and Rec gymnasium on Show Day, surrounded by well-dressed Middle Eastern men and several overweight white men. The lights were too bright on all of them. With the woman writhing in front of them, he felt as if he and a bunch of strangers were watching something vaguely pornographic together smack in the middle of the day, something he'd rather watch Eleanor do alone for him in her apartment bedroom.

But he'd taken her to her first session of cake decorating for dummies. Gone to the feng shui orientation. He'd even suffered through the free introductory Bikram yoga class, so he could scout the room for potential competition. Not that he was interested in any of these things. His sole purpose in showing up was to stare down the rare straight man who signed up to decorate cakes, arrange furniture, or stretch out in a suffocating hot room at 10:30 on a Wednesday morning.

Eleanor persevered in each of her classes until whatever she was trying suddenly made sense to her. "Watch this," she'd say, pushing furniture out of the way and balancing on one foot, her other leg raised high. He applauded her the way he did Jennifer. *Watch me, watch me, watch me.* This was something he knew how to do. The only thing she had failed at was swimming, still holding tight to her kickboard on their last day of class.

"How're your potatoes?" he asked. "You want some ketchup?"

"No thanks," Jennifer said. She had an eraser in each hand, the turtle-shaped eraser he had just bought her and an octopus-shaped eraser she must have already had. She moved the erasers toward and then quickly away from each other as if they were repelling each other.

"You know you scared the hell out of me back there," he said.

"Where?" she asked, looking behind her.

"At the aquarium. That's where."

"I thought you were right behind me," she said, putting down her erasers and stabbing a small piece of potato.

"The whole time?"

"Whatever," Jennifer said, chewing.

"I don't like that word."

"What word?"

"*Whatever.*"

"Whatever," she said.

"Ha, ha. Very funny." He looked around the room, hoping to share a kind of community of other fathers having a laugh with their daughters during a late brunch on a Sunday afternoon. He would have even taken a family or two. But all he saw were single men wearing sweatpants or the kind of thick, crisp jeans his mother used to order for him from the Sears catalog, and drinking free refills of coffee and concentrating too intently on a single page of the newspaper.

He looked at the bill and wished he'd stuck to the endless cup of coffee. He knew he ate out too often for his budget, but he didn't have a kitchen and justified the extra expense until he found an apartment. Eleanor alternated between cooking huge, elaborate meals—paella and Malaysian lamb and Moroccan chicken—and eating nothing at all. Sometimes, on the nights he stayed over, he opened her refrigerator in the morning and couldn't find an egg or a single slice of bread to toast.

This restaurant was in a quasi-business neighborhood, an odd place to be on a Sunday, but it was close to Keith's office and the gym. With his meaty breakfast now finished, all he wanted to do was brush his teeth, get more clothes from his office, and take a shower in the locker room.

Instead, he said to Jennifer, "How would you feel about going ice skating this afternoon?"

"I don't know how to ice skate."

"I can teach you."

"Really?"

He smiled at his daughter. When she looked at him this way, he felt like her father again, not like some remote uncle.

"Absolutely."

He was relieved to spot Eleanor's toylike car in the parking lot at the Lakewood Ice Palace. She had given him no reason to suspect she was cheating on him, but Keith felt the persistent low-level buzz of worry anyway. He'd witnessed her effect on men, waiters stumbling over their memorized lists of specials, security guards at gate-entry weddings who quizzed him for identification but waved them through when she drove. With her too-angular features, she wasn't beautiful, but she was sexy with a disarming pixie quality that threw men off. She might have been thirty or forty or twenty-five or fifty. The normal markers of age didn't seem to apply to her.

"I've been here before," Jennifer said, taking his hand as they walked through the parking lot of the Ice Palace.

"I don't think so," he said. The last time he remembered taking her skating was when they had visited her grandmother in Pennsylvania two years before. The shallow outdoor pond by her house was frozen solid, and he'd lifted his small daughter up on his shoulders and skated away. It was nothing like the Ice Palace, where Mariah Carey blared over speakers, and, periodically, pink and purple strobe lights flashed across the ice.

"With Mom," Jennifer said. "I was here with Mom."

"Oh, right," he said, reminded again about the whole world that existed for Jennifer that didn't include him.

"We forgot to bring hats and sweaters," she said as they carried their rented skates over to the benches.

"Who needs that stuff? We're indoors, aren't we?" He smiled at his daughter and leaned over to finish lacing up her shoes. He noticed that her pants weren't quite pants at all. They stopped short, just below her knees, and her skin was exposed over the top of her skates. He probably should have stopped by the house and picked up a sweater, had her put on real jeans, but he knew from Eleanor's schedule that there was only an hour left of free skate time left.

"Ready, Kiddo?"

"I guess," she said, looking down at her bare shins.

Keith took her hand and led her out onto the ice. Despite the number of people, it was easy to spot Eleanor in her leopard-skin leggings and black sweater, hands clasped behind her back as she skated. But Keith didn't shout out. Although he doubted she would believe he'd forgotten she'd be there, he had decided to act indifferent, the next best thing to surprised.

"That's Ursala," Jennifer said, pointing at the center of the rink, where a girl spun around backward. "She's always here."

"Pretty impressive," he said. "Now here's the trick. Don't walk. Glide."

"Like this?"

"Hey, you," Keith said as Eleanor completed a circle and caught up to them. "That's right, you had your lesson today, didn't you?"

"Just like we discussed this morning," she said. "Are you following me?"

Keith was pulling his daughter along next to him, but he could tell from the sound her skates made stumbling over the ice that she wasn't gliding. Did Eleanor sound irritated, or was he only imagining it? Sometimes, after he'd spent two or three nights in a row at her house, she said *time to go home now* and pushed him toward the door, but they always ended up making out in the hallway before he left.

He looked over and saw Jennifer moving on the ice as if she were just learning how to walk. "Glide!" he shouted louder than he intended, feeling all at once like the swim teacher at the health club. He gave her what he thought of as a little yank of encouragement, but instead of gliding, she ended up on the ground.

"Remember Eleanor, honey?" he said, pulling Jennifer up as skaters passed them by. "Look who's here."

Jennifer stared at Keith and then Eleanor and touched the base of her throat. "I'm ready to stop," she said.

"Are you sure?" he said. "Already?"

"Can I have money for the snack machine?" she asked.

He reached in his pocket and pulled out a handful of change. "Have at it. And come right back. I don't want to lose you again."

"If you want, after your snack I'll show you some of the moves we learned today in class," Eleanor shouted after her.

"Whatever," Jennifer said. She was holding onto the side and taking careful steps around the rink to the exit.

"I can show you now," Eleanor said to Keith. "Or I could just skate away from you. As if you didn't know I'd be here. Maybe I should file charges against you for stalking me."

"Whatever," he said.

"Look at that," she said.

Keith looked at the center of the rink where the girl Jennifer had pointed out earlier was spinning in circles on one skate, her other leg bent behind her back, but all he was thinking about was Eleanor. People who were mad didn't joke about filing charges, did they?

"Is that what you're going to show me?" he asked, pointing at the girl who was leaping now and somehow landing softly on one skate.

"Not quite yet."

"These skates are shit," he said. It was true. They were stiff and his ankles already hurt.

"You need to invest in a pair," she said, "if you intend to come here and stalk me regularly."

There it was again. He couldn't tell if she was teasing him or not, but he couldn't imagine leaving her alone anyway. She had white figure skates laced tight with gold laces. She wore fuzzy pink socks folded over the top of her skates. He knew her toenails were painted fire-engine red. Although he hadn't left his wife for her, he felt as if he had. He rested his hand on her lower back, let his fingers creep down until she grabbed his hand.

"Bad boy," she said. "And you smell almost bad enough for me to invite you over for a shower."

"Show me," he said, "what you learned in class today."

In the car on the way home, Jennifer was quiet in the back seat. Keith could hear her chewing on whatever she'd bought from the snack machine. "No chocolate or nuts, right?"

"Right."

"So, what was the most fun today, the aquarium or the skating rink?"

"I liked the turtles the most, I guess," Jennifer said. "Do you know that in the country of Louisiana some people eat turtles."

"I think that's a state."

"When I grow up, I'm going to protect turtles."

"That's a noble cause," he said. "It was a nice surprise running into Eleanor at the rink. Don't you think?"

Jennifer chewed and swallowed, then stuck another piece of candy in her mouth and chewed some more.

"She really likes you," Keith said.

"Next Sunday can we just do something normal like make cookies?" she said as he pulled up to the curb in front of her house.

"I don't have an oven," he said. "I don't even really have an apartment yet. You know that."

"Well can you get one for next time? Sometimes I just like to stay home."

Jennifer got out of the car, closed the door behind her, and ran across the front lawn without hugging him. When had this started, her leaving this way? The skin on the back of her shins was red where the tops of her skates had hit them. He honked the horn lightly three times, the closest he was going to come to kissing his daughter goodbye without running across the lawn himself and grabbing her. Had he already been replaced? By Winter? Or maybe his wife hadn't turned into a lesbian after all, and he had been replaced by someone else. The turtle man maybe? How had all of this happened so quickly?

Keith reached into the back seat and looked at the candy wrapper she had left behind, read the ingredients. *May contain traces of peanut or peanut oil. Shit.* Still, he knew from experience that *may* also meant *may not.* No one wanted to get sued.

He traced Jennifer's movement through the house by the lights that flashed on, the stairwell, the upstairs bathroom, her bedroom. He picked up his phone to text Eleanor. *You're the hottest thing on ice*, he typed but stopped himself before pushing *send*. He was behaving like a teenager or some kind of addict. If Eleanor didn't call him, he decided he wouldn't push things, that he'd sleep on the couch in his office tonight. Tomorrow he'd look for a real apartment, something small but with a kitchen. And big enough for a turtle—or a tortoise—tank.

ESCHRICHTIUS ROBUSTUS

When the garbage truck pulled up on Tuesday morning, David hid by the edge of the living room window and watched it. Two weeks ago, he had seen what he could have sworn was one of the garbage men leaning off the side of the truck and photographing his trash before the automatic arm was lowered down to pick it up. And, sure enough, last week he'd received a written notice on the front door, warning him in bold letters: ALL CONSTRUCTION MATERIALS ARE CONSIDERED HAZARDOUS WASTE.

This morning while he watched the garbage truck, the girls sat three in a row on the couch tracing the plight of SpongeBob. This cartoon was tedious and sloppily drawn, and lately David had noticed an odd moral or two hidden a bit too subversively for his taste in the plot, easy, mainstream ideas about the importance of sharing or being a good friend.

At least *SpongeBob* was less overtly pious than the DVD series of cartoons featuring New Testament–reciting vegetables that one of the Christian homeschool families had outgrown and handed down to his girls. They'd found the complete set at the bottom of a box filled with wooden puzzles and board games, and he couldn't help but feel the cartoons had been planted in a burst of missionary zeal.

The truth was that his girls were always subdued when the television was on no matter what the show was; they became more cats than ducklings. Occasionally he heard one of their hard hats tap against another as they shifted on the couch and stretched. Already this morning, they'd taken out the ceiling in the bathroom—David imagined exposed beams and a skylight opening up the plain rectangular space—and they were ready for a break.

Despite the warning from the city, he had filled their garbage cans with chunks of drywall once again. This time they were packed so high with debris that the attached lids not only didn't close, they bent back behind the cans, and one of the lids had come loose at a hinge and was hanging off one side. It wasn't that David meant to buck the warning blatantly. He had hoped to hide just a few materials under the regular garbage. But once again, he had underestimated the amount of demolition rubble.

It was surprisingly easy to knock down walls. Almost as easy as ripping out ceilings. He could not believe he hadn't done this before. He felt as if a huge secret had been kept from him. Certainly, this was as much his right as a homeowner as it was to plant beds of cauliflower and tomatoes in the backyard and to line a path to the front door with river rocks he and his girls had found on a trip to the San Bernardino mountains. Why hadn't he ever considered it before now?

For years David had mused about living off the grid entirely, right here in his suburban neighborhood in Long Beach. He read an article once about a Pasadena family that created a self-sustaining farm on less than a quarter of an acre. He imagined one day the girls and he growing all their food, maybe even keeping some chickens and a goat. Building their raised garden and planting vegetables always felt hopeful to him, like maybe he wasn't just dreaming about doing something meaningful and big with his life, with all their lives. Growing their small share of organic crops was something.

But the joys of gardening couldn't compare to the feeling that came from smashing through interior walls with a sledgehammer. David was certain he was smashing through something more urgent and important than drywall. Although he hesitated to name the metaphor, certain that it would diminish its significance, old rock lyrics pounded in his head as he worked, the Doors singing *Break on through to the other side*, the Eagles singing *Take it to the limit one more time*.

His girls were naturals at construction work. Although he constantly had to stay after them to wear their bike helmets, they put on their hard hats every morning when they got dressed, often brushing their teeth and eating their bowls of cereal that way. Which was probably a good idea, since none of them was ever quite sure when a wayward piece of ceiling or wall might crumble down around them.

David had big ideas about turning around their dark seventies tract home. If he was stuck living in Southern California, he decided he may as well make the most of the outdoors and the sun. He envisioned an airy, open floor plan with an arched entranceway and skylights. Using computer software, the girls and he had drafted several designs themselves, but Deborah barely looked at them, even when they laid them out, numbered, on the dining room table so she could vote for her favorite.

"They all look okay, I guess," she said. "A lot of things look good on paper, though." She kicked hard at a loose nail on the floor, and he heard it bounce several times before it landed in a heap of smashed drywall.

"But which one do you like best?" he asked, feeling uncomfortably like one of his girls, their three ducklings. *Pick me. Pick mine.*

"That one, I guess," she said, pointing at Katie's imaginative but nonsensical design that featured, among other things, a kitchen on the roof and trees growing in the living room.

Although he had to admit that his feelings were hurt that she refused to care, he wasn't particularly surprised by her lack of enthusiasm and tried not to take it personally. In retrospect, she'd never been much of a process person. She was indiscriminately impatient, it seemed to David.

When he met Deborah—both of them protesting loudly at the nuclear power plant in San Luis Obispo—he mistook her impatience for the same angry activism that he possessed. It wasn't until years later that he witnessed the same kind of impatience as she studied to pass the bar, angled to be promoted at work, waited for each pregnancy to end, and plotted to get their mortgage paid off before she retired. Then he realized he had misread her from the start.

But, despite her impatience, David hoped she'd feel differently when the house was finished, that she'd see that it was all just a temporary inconvenience, the disconnected washing machine, the exposed wire and pipe sticking out of the remainder of a wall that separated their kitchen and dining room, the fine white dust that floated throughout the house. And she'd agree with him: It had all been worth it.

This morning they got lucky. The truck had barely stopped when the lift came down and threw the trash into its bed. David stood up from his crouched position and felt his knees shift back into their sockets. The front of his thighs ached. He looked down at his legs. They were covered in bruises. He and his girls all were bruised. What they needed was a day off. A beach day in February. It fit in perfectly with his new plan to embrace Southern California, to stop pretending they really lived in Oregon or were only passing through on their way there. *They paved paradise and put up a parking lot.*

David tapped his girls on their hard hats. "Who wants to go to the beach today?"

Except for a couple in wetsuits sitting on a surfboard together beyond the breakers and an old man combing the sand with a metal detector, Seal Beach was practically deserted. This was something he loved about homeschooling, pulling into an empty parking lot midweek with his girls, giving an impromptu oceanography lesson when a particularly large wave broke around the posts of the pier. But most of all he loved sitting back in his sand chair and watching his girls in their swim trunks and T-shirts running free.

Katie had insisted on bringing her hard hat. Now, she held it out in front of her as she ran, filling it with air or some magical, invisible substance that she periodically shook free. Next year would have been her first locked-up year, if he sent his girls to school. Kindergarten. It was so structured now, he learned from his school visits with Madeline, that five-year-olds had to pass reading tests before being "promoted" to first grade.

He'd read somewhere that children shouldn't even be taught their letters until they'd lost their first teeth, but Katie had wanted to learn, so he'd showed her the accidental alphabet, found in telephone wires and the branches of trees. *Look at that perfect V,* he'd said to his Katie one day, pointing at the shape a girl made hanging by her knees and holding on by her hands at the monkey bars at their local playground. Sometimes he imagined opening the doors to their local elementary school, the one where their neighbors were so grateful to send their children, and shouting inside, *Go! Get out while you can!*

Whale-migration season should have been in full swing by now, so David sat up taller and looked out beyond the couple on the surfboard, keeping watch. When they got home, he decided he and the girls would get online and study the gray whales' route. *Eschrichtius robustus.* He had studied their migration habits briefly in an oceanography class he'd ended up dropping his first year of college and surprised himself by remembering their scientific name.

He knew the whales made their way down to Baja each year, but he couldn't remember if it was to mate or to give birth or both. How long was a whale pregnant? How large was her baby when it was born? He seemed to remember something about whale babies being called puppies, but he could have been wrong. And that would be okay. He was a student, too. There were tens, maybe hundreds, of questions they could look up together.

He decided the girls and he would stretch out a long sheet of the thin brown paper he bought by the ream and map out the route, what happened where and when. Without the wall separating the living room from the kitchen, they had plenty of room now. When they were finished coloring in everything, he'd tape it up throughout the entire house.

They needed a break from all the construction work, all of them. For one thing, he had exploited everything easily teachable about the project already. Katie experimented with throwing small and large rocks to create initial holes in walls they planned to tear down, and Madeline and Emily converted inches to centimeters as they measured the holes. He'd even taught Madeline how to measure circumference, something he hadn't planned to get to with her for at least another year. But she was good with math, his oldest daughter, and she caught on fast. Only eight and already she was ready for elementary geometry. David shuddered, imagining her boredom in school if she'd been stuck with multiplication and division, the most advanced boundaries of third grade math.

But the biggest problem with going back to their construction project was that David wasn't sure what to do now that he'd knocked out most of the walls and ceilings, despite the fact that he'd spent many late-night hours scouring construction-related websites. The problem was there seemed to be entire new vocabularies to learn before he could even begin to understand what to do. Words like *bearing point* and *gypsum* and *gypboard* and *rim joist* ran through his head as he tried to fall asleep each night. And they had no money to contract outside help or even buy all the supplies they needed to complete the work on their own. He had convinced Deborah that he could do it all by using their regular household budget. While not an outright lie, this had been a clear miscalculation. And having maxed out his credit cards and gone through his small 401K on charities, he had none of his own money left to cover his mistake.

The only budget they had for the project to start with was the small amount of money he made selling the homeschool mailing list he had compiled. And he had quickly depleted this fund buying sledgehammers, picks, hard hats, and their design software. He donated the list to the nonprofits, but he did charge fees to the few homeschool-related businesses he deemed legitimate. Selling the lists secretly wasn't something he was particularly proud of, but it was too hard to give up such a reliable way to make a small income of his own—money he didn't have to account for to Deborah.

Even the tearing down hadn't gone completely smoothly. David had accidentally begun knocking out what he thought now, after some reading, might be a bearing wall between the kitchen and the laundry room. All he knew at the time was that when he'd felt the ceiling begin to give above the hole, he'd quickly shoved a bookshelf into the new shape he'd made.

The fact that he was in too deep was not something he was eager to admit, not to his girls and especially not to his wife.

Without a loan, they had no means to hire outside labor to finish up the job. He thought about approaching his wife with this idea, priming her with the economic benefits of home improvement. But he couldn't bear to hear Deborah lecture him about the difficulties of a family of five living on one salary—even a good salary like the one she made, she'd be certain to point out.

David was so desperate that he'd even fantasized about a kind of modern TV miracle happening, a camera crew following a construction crew to clean up the mess. But preliminary research, which consisted almost exclusively of watching various home-improvement shows, told him that there was nothing needy or photogenic enough about their situation to get a producer's attention. At least one of his girls needed to be precociously talented in music or dance—or stuck, however temporarily, in a wheelchair—to make applying worth his time.

"Come swim with us!" Emily shouted, running up to David and shaking her wet hair in his face.

"Are you nuts?" he said. "The ocean temperature can't be much more than 60 degrees this time of year."

"Wimp!" she shouted, and then Katie was there, too, each girl gripping an arm and trying to pull him up from his chair.

"Okay, okay, you win," he said. He spotted Madeline, hunched over like an old woman, apparently inspired by the man with the metal detector, walking along the shoreline, bypassing perfectly good-looking shells. Maybe she was looking for loose change, too. He wondered briefly how much a metal detector would cost, if the girls and he combed the right beaches, maybe farther south, in La Jolla, perhaps they could land one good find—a Rolex would do it—that could buy him some help putting the house back together.

David looked out to sea just in case a whale happened to be swimming by so he could show the girls, get them ready for the project he had in mind. He could work with a dolphin or even a seal, but all he had so far was the couple on the surfboard.

Not that they wouldn't offer a certain kind of segue into a discussion on mating. They were wearing wetsuits and facing each other, kissing so intently that he doubted they even noticed the shouts as David and his two youngest girls ran into the water and dove under a frigid wave together.

"We know him, don't we, Dad?" Emily said as the three of them jumped up and down in the water, waiting for the next wave to dive under. "He's the GI Joe doll, right?"

"GI Joe doll?" And then he remembered. The man at Hometown Buffet who turned up later at Beth's house when he'd gone to check on her. He'd made up the name in the car on the way home from the restaurant way back in early fall, thinking he had this guy all figured out, certain they'd never see him again. He'd have to be careful about his assumptions from now on, or at least careful about sharing with his girls the private names he made up for people.

"Yeah, I think you're right, honey. But let's not call him that, okay? He may not appreciate it."

"I remember his real name," Katie said. "Pat-ter-son. Three syllables. I clapped it out when we got home. It's like Mad-e-line and Em-i-ly, but not Kat-ie."

"You are amazing, you know that?" David said.

"Amazing," Emily said, making a face at Katie just as a wave rose up in front of them.

"Duck!" he yelled, his mouth already full of salt water.

"Pat-ter-son!" little Katie shouted as she bounced in the water between waves. The man on the surfboard looked back at them, started to raise his hand in an almost wave, and then put it back down by his side.

Maybe it wasn't him. He pictured Patterson's twin boys, the way they pounded up the stairs at Beth's house, how one of them knocked down Madeline's muffin tower at Hometown Buffet. Could this man really have time to drift with his wife on a surfboard beyond the breakers in the middle of a weekday? David felt his legs going numb from the cold and wished he had a wetsuit. His two youngest daughters, apparently, were hardier than he was. "Time to get out, ducklings."

Back on the sand, David huddled in his chair, covered in a towel while all three of his girls built a drip castle. This time when he looked out to sea, he wasn't hoping to spot a gray whale or even a seal. He focused on the couple on the surfboard. Emily was right. The man was Patterson, but it was the woman David wasn't quite sure about. Her body curved in ways that didn't seem possible on a woman as skinny as he remembered Patterson's wife being. But, he reasoned, people probably looked different in wetsuits. He tried to imagine Deborah in one, an almost impossible feat but strangely appealing.

The old man with the metal detector was walking away from the ocean now, looking disappointed but resolved and official.

"I want lunch," Madeline said. "I think my blood sugar's getting low." Fed up with all their snacking between meals, he had given the girls an impromptu lesson on good nutrition a few weeks before, and he smiled at his clever daughter now, smart enough to use his lesson to manipulate her father.

They walked through town to their car, their arms piled with towels and buckets. Katie wore a bucket on her head, her hard hat full of sand she promised to play with only in the backyard. "I'm thirsty," she said. "Why can't you buy us soda?"

"No soda," David said. "It's bad for you." *And expensive*, he thought. He pointed out the sign in the window of a coffee shop for the Winter Polar Bear Plunge the weekend before.

"We could have done that," Emily said.

"We just did," David said.

"I didn't," Madeline said, frowning.

"That's because you didn't want to," he said.

"Because she's a wimp," Emily said.

"Because she gets to make her own choices," he said. "You all do."

"I'm a polar bear," Katie said.

"Polar bears don't wear buckets on their heads," Madeline said.

David had been here before, in that moment right before everything good about the day began to unravel. Yes, his girls had choices, but it was his job to lead, even if leading just meant changing the subject. "Is anyone else ready to go home and have lunch?"

"I can do veggie burgers or PBJs!" David shouted from the kitchen, although, with the wall torn through, there wasn't really any need to shout any more.

"Grilled cheese!"

"Tuna melts!"

"I want takeout!"

His girls shouted back at him from the now semi-wall-less rooms while the shower water ran. They'd tracked sand through the house and peeled off their bathing suits as they ran to the bathroom, fighting over who got to shower first. Instead of a written notice about overstuffing their garbage cans, this time they'd come home to an actual fine for $125 stuck in their door. He'd been so thrown off by the fine that he forgot to make his girls wash their feet off outside.

Deborah would complain about the sand first, ask about their adventures second—if she even got that far. Maybe this time, for once, she wouldn't notice the sand. The floor was already bumpy with sharp, small chunks of white debris that he couldn't seem to quite sweep or vacuum up completely.

He wouldn't allow himself to fully consider what he might have let loose in the house, possibly something insidious and toxic. He realized he should have researched so much more before starting. Shouldn't he be making his house "green" if he was disassembling it anyway? But even thinking about replacing light fixtures with low-energy fluorescent bulbs and installing solar panels seemed a frivolous extravagance when they didn't currently have a working washing machine.

A short break from the house had made it harder for David to face it when they returned. The thing had become impossible, a huge mess for which he knew he could only blame himself, although he felt more a victim than a culprit. Why had no one ever taught him anything about construction? How had he gotten this far in life knowing so little? His father had never been the kind of man to putter around with home projects on the weekend, preferring instead to play a round of golf or catch up on the pile of newspapers that built up during the week. Shouldn't a father be obligated to pass on some kind of knowledge of construction to his offspring? David didn't have to look further than the public school system to see the genesis of his own father's failure:

Children stuck at desks all day don't grow up with many real-world skills.

At this point in his life, David's network of friends was almost exclusively female, and while a few of them might know a bit more about construction than he did, the truth was, no matter how feminist he was in the overall sense of the word, he wasn't thrilled with the idea of going to women for this kind of help. He'd already had the disturbing experience of finally stumbling into a fairly useful website only to discover it was designed exclusively for females. When he scrolled over to the site's "Marketplace," he noticed that all of the hammers had pink handles and the Phillips head screwdrivers were distinguished by rhinestones embedded into the bases.

He decided seeing Patterson at the beach today was a sign of some kind. Wasn't Deborah always after him to make a male friend or two? He'd reach out to Patterson, a man who looked like he might know something about home repair, and ask for a little help. Maybe he could repay him in some way, teach him how to start an organic garden or help him better slog through the homeschool paperwork bureaucracy.

They had exchanged an email or two before he'd shown up with his family at Hometown Buffet. He let the refrigerator door close, walked into what remained of his office, got online, and quickly found it.

"Thought I spotted you on the beach today," he typed, "but I didn't want to bother you out there on your board. Looked like you two were having too much fun. Hope all is going well with the homeschooling. Let's catch up this way. I have a few questions I was hoping you might be able to help me out with." He read it over quickly, pushed *send*, and felt immediately grateful with relief.

While he didn't have any more money to give, he felt inexplicably wealthier and allowed himself to stay online long enough to surf through the sites of some of his most recent favorite causes. His screen filled with large-eyed children smiling at him with hideous cleft palates, street children in Brazil sleeping on sidewalks, a woman at a refuge camp in Darfur making rice huddled over a solar stove that he wished he had the money to buy for her.

David logged off his computer and shook the dust out of a big garbage bag he found in the corner of his office. Before he could clean up the world's mess, he would have to finish cleaning up his own. He began grabbing up all the dirty clothes he could find. If he couldn't send street children in Brazil new shoes, he could at least get his family's laundry done.

He would pick up takeout for the girls, and they'd eat it in the laundromat while they planned their whale-migration project. Maybe instead of one long drawing, they'd make an actual full-size whale out of wire and papier-mâché, or they'd make several smaller ones to scale that they could position along the actual route the whales took.

Why not take a drive next week down the coast, follow the migration in process, try to keep up with the whales? How fast did a whale swim compared to how fast their car might meander down Pacific Coast Highway? Would Madeline be able to come up with an equation? They could drive at night, use the stars to navigate. He'd been meaning to get them into astronomy this year. Maybe even Deborah would want to come along. They could camp or splurge on that hotel in Del Mar where they gave you hot chocolate chip cookies when you checked in. He felt rich with ideas.

And he definitely felt like celebrating, even if he couldn't pinpoint the occasion. "Takeout today!" he shouted to his girls.

"I want tacos!"

"Pizza!"

"You promised Chinese this time!"

"We'll just have to make three stops after you're all showered, then," he said, feeling nearly as aloft with possibility as he had when he smashed through his first ceiling. "Everyone can get what they want."

BRAIN CHEMISTRY

Beth felt like a teenager. Not like the teenager she had been, the neighborhood babysitter who took studying to get her driver's license seriously instead of cramming an hour before the test and who spent her free period reading to kids in special ed instead of smoking pot in the parking lot. More like the kind of teenager she'd secretly envied— the ones who crash dieted, shoplifted tubes of spermicide jelly from Rite-Aid, and pierced their eyebrows.

Although she didn't even really like him that much, Beth had had a single boyfriend, Paul, throughout her junior and senior years, and it had never occurred to her to cheat, especially with someone else's boyfriend. To Beth, her friends' complicated deceits, which involved keeping track of fake sleepovers and cribbing summaries of movies they didn't go to, took far too much energy. Instead, she dutifully let Paul feel her up after they'd been together three months, stopped pushing his hands out of her pants after six, and unceremoniously lost her virginity to him at the end of the summer between junior and senior years in his bedroom while his parents were celebrating their twenty-fifth anniversary at the Olive Garden in Doylestown.

But now, here she was, 37 years old and lying routinely. And the guilt was the best diet she'd ever tried.

Lying had left her with a perpetual knot in her chest that made eating even more of a challenge than it had been during the weeks after Keith left. She wondered if this was how the beginning of an asthma attack felt for her daughter, a fleshy, constricting fist lodged somewhere just above her lungs.

Each day, the fist wedged itself in tighter, and she reached farther back in her closet to find out-of-date clothes that fit. Fashion-wise, she was well into her twenties now, back to her first years of marriage.

For the first time in her life, not only was she losing weight easily, she was also keeping track of appointments. In addition to each day's actual schedule, she had what she thought of as her *shadow schedule* to account for, stories she made up to cover for the time she snuck away to be with Patterson.

It turned out that Beth's actual schedule was far more complicated now that she was homeschooling. Homeschooling meant that Pizza Night and Sports Shirt Day had been replaced with Homeschool Day at the Ice Palace, Homeschool Night at Hometown Buffet, Beach Clean-up third Wednesdays, and endless planning meetings with Winter, including Winter's regular Keep-on-Track Tuesdays.

Overall, it turned out that homeschooling required far more planning than Beth had ever imagined. And even though she tried her best to keep up with it all, she had moments when she felt a deep welling up of panic so insistent that she found herself checking her purse for her EpiPen in case she needed to jam it into her own thigh so she could breathe.

And then there was the issue of money.

When it became clear even to Winter that they were unlikely to make a living any time soon selling overpriced cookware at parties, Winter moved onto fresh bagel chips. That start-up was much cheaper—day-old bagels purchased at half price by the dozen—but they quickly ran into problems with the product. They were easy to overcook. There were the licensing issues to deal with before stores would even consider stocking their chips. Neither of their kitchens was anywhere close to meeting state standards. In California, it turned out, it was far easier to legally homeschool your child than it was to sell food to the public.

So they started again. Their newest employment required neither cooking nor start-up costs. "Life of the Party Life Planners," their business card read. The only license they needed was one they already had. Winter had taken an online course to become a notary when she was pregnant with the twins.

When Beth pointed out the possible confusion—whether they were planning lives or parties—Winter said the confusion was deliberate and pointed toward the bottom of the card. SHOULDN'T ALL BIG LIFE DECISIONS BE FOLLOWED WITH A PARTY TO CELEBRATE? And under that line, LEGAL NOTARY SERVICES.

They'd notarize mortgage documents and separation agreements and then organize lives and parties, a double niche, a triple niche, Winter explained. "Imagine the possibilities. Gotcha Adoption Day Celebrations. Fifty Is the New Thirty Birthday Parties. Drug-Free and Divine Dinners."

Beth longed to say *no. Count me out.* But if she said *no* to Winter, she would be saying *no* to Patterson having an excuse to stop by whenever he could, and she wasn't about to say no to that.

"Couldn't we do something a little less creative?" Beth had asked at their last Keep-on-Track Tuesday. "Something with a more regular income?"

"What suggestion do you have, then?" Winter asked, holding her pen in the air above her Keep-on-Track Tuesday notebook, ready to take dictation.

Beth missed the easy company of the dogs. After they were forced to disband their doggie daycare, she'd briefly imagined starting a dog-walking service instead. But with Jennifer home all day, she had no choice but to imagine her daughter walking with her, bouncing along happily, a leash in each hand, her belly, hidden under a sweater, covered in hives, a catch starting in her throat.

Without any viable ideas of her own to counter with, Beth could only point out the flaws in Winter's newest plan. Their first and biggest problem—as far as she could see—was getting the word out beyond the homeschool community. While they encountered plenty of people open to changing their lives and certainly many who liked to celebrate, homeschoolers were, for the most part, a frugal bunch.

It wasn't just that most of them lived on one salary—a lot of people did—but it seemed to Beth that homeschoolers lived a little too proudly that way. They bragged about ripping up credit card offers, paying cash for used cars, and making higher mortgage payments each month to reduce the principal.

"A few might need a notary occasionally, but none of them will pay us for ideas or party planning," she said. "They wouldn't even buy a melon scoop, remember?"

"Exactly," Winter said. "We need to get the word way out. Give some of those cards to Keith. He shoots expensive weddings. He knows people with money." She folded Beth's fingers over the cards.

I am sleeping with your husband, she thought. *How can you stand to touch me?*

When she'd disappeared for an hour during her own party, even then Winter hadn't suspected anything. Patterson had parked his car in the empty lot by Mother's Beach and they had sex right there in full daylight, their pants twisted at their feet in the back seat. They might as well have walked back into the house together instead of a carefully planned fifteen minutes apart.

Winter had the annoying self-confidence of someone who had always been popular.

"You can convince Keith," she said, letting go of Beth's hand. "Look, maybe I was a little wrong before about the dog-sitting and the bagel thing and the cooking shows. But there's no pyramid thingy or licensing with this one. We collect all the money. Period. Just tell Keith that the more we make, the less he has to give you each month. That'll give him incentive."

"I don't know," Beth said. "He's pretty protective of his clients." She thought about Patterson coming by to pick up papers that Winter needed to notarize, how if she managed to send Jennifer over to the neighbors to play, they could have a half hour alone. "I guess I can give it a try."

Now Keith was on his way over, and the business cards looked less likely to Beth than ever. His informal child-support payments were erratic, and she knew she should be more worried about making money than she was. Still, she had bigger concerns than getting him to believe in their business and give out business cards at weddings.

Five months had passed, and Beth had still managed to avoid telling Keith that Jennifer was being homeschooled. She'd only intended to keep it from him until she could make a decent argument and had the paperwork and details to support her. But too much time had elapsed now for it to be anything other than a betrayal.

Instead of disappearing into the kitchen or up into her own room while he waited for Jennifer while she dawdled in her room, this morning she'd offer him a cup of coffee or maybe a glass of wine and sit with him. Beth took out a bottle of red and two glasses and left them on the kitchen counter. It would be natural for their conversation to drift to Jennifer and school, and she'd explain it all so logically, he'd have no choice but to see what a committed mother she was to have made this choice.

She even imagined laughing with Keith about some of the people she'd met along the way—the *string* girls, who worked on their geometric designs nonstop and at a breakneck pace; the texting nursing mothers; the three *boy-girls*, as Jennifer called them. Beth might even mention Patterson and Winter and Nolan and Aiden. The "evil twins," she'd joke, explaining how they weren't really evil at all, just a little difficult. Most recently, they'd filled their pockets with pebbles at the beach and emptied them onto Jennifer's bedroom floor. After all these weeks and all of Winter's insistence on how easy they were to tell apart because of their different chins, Beth still mixed them up routinely.

She would render the whole family and her relationship with Patterson innocent in a single sentence. She imagined laughing with Keith now the way they'd seldom laughed when they were together. Why had she always been so serious back then?

Beth heard the shower start running upstairs. She'd told Jennifer to take a shower over an hour ago, but this is what she did, waited until it was almost time for her father to get her. It didn't take a degree in child psychology to see that she was punishing her father by making him wait.

This morning Beth felt almost sorry for Keith when she looked out the front window and saw him walking toward the house, his hand already poised into a weak fist, ready to knock on what used to be his own front door. Despite Jennifer's protests, they'd have to switch to evening baths—which Jennifer insisted were for babies—if she continued to keep this up much longer.

Beth opened the door before he had a chance to knock. "She's just gotten in the shower," she said. "Come on in."

He loosened his fist and reached up toward the top of his head as if he might have a hat to remove. He ran his palm over his hair instead, smoothing down unruly waves that shot right back out again. He looked less like an unkempt graduate student today, more like a man without a wife to remind him it was time for a haircut.

"Glass of wine?" Beth said.

"It's not even noon yet, is it?"

"What am I thinking? Coffee? I meant coffee."

"Sure, thanks."

In the kitchen, Beth quickly stowed the bottle of wine and glasses she'd left out. What *was* she thinking? Loosen up Keith and then tell him? Loosen up herself? She started a pot of coffee and poured milk into a pitcher as if she didn't know exactly how much of it he took in his coffee, and brought a tray out to the living room.

"You look different. Good, I mean," he said. "Not that you didn't look good before. You just look better now. Oh, shit. I should just shut up, shouldn't I."

"Probably," Beth said.

"I just meant to say you look good. Now I'll stop."

"Do you ever feel like there's a fist sort of shoved in above your lungs?"

Keith looked at her, then shook his head. "Not really. No."

When she'd finally gotten up her nerve to tell Darla she was homeschooling Jennifer, all Darla had done was laugh and say *better you than me*. Maybe Keith would laugh, too.

"Winter and I are starting a business," she said, hoping she was just warming up, getting to what she'd planned to talk about. "She wanted me to give these to you."

Beth handed him the stack of business cards from the coffee table. "She thought maybe you could pass them along to people you know from weddings."

"She's really special to you, huh?"

Beth shrugged. What was he getting at?

"I'm not sure I get it," he said, reading over the card.

Beth tried to remember how Winter told her to sell it. "Sweet Sixteen Quintuplet Birthdays, International Adoption Airport Celebrations. That kind of thing. All we need is for you to hand them out to people who actually have money to pay us."

"Okay," he said, drawing the word out into a question.

"Doesn't it make perfect sense? We plan your life, notarize whatever documents you need to make your life-changing plans, and then throw you a party to celebrate. Drug-Free and Divine."

Beth hadn't planned on laughing but once she started, it was hard to stop. "Unplanned Pregnancy? No problem. Pregnant and Poor. Let's celebrate!"

"Got it," Keith said, putting the cards in his pocket.

"As if I had a clue about how to plan someone's life. Who would hire me?"

"What's so funny?" Jennifer said, appearing at the bottom of the stairs, dressed in jeans and a thick sweater, her wet hair combed over her shoulders.

"There's my big first grader," Keith said.

Beth felt herself wince at the mention of first grade. Why couldn't she tell him? "Oh, honey, are you hiding hives again?"

"No," Jennifer said. "I want dad to take me skating. See, I even found my gloves from last year." She pulled out one purple glove from each of her back pockets. "I'm all set."

"I guess you are," he said.

"They were under all my socks."

"Very clever hiding place," Keith said.

"It opens at eleven for free skate."

"Very clever girl," he said. He walked over and lifted her up, breathed in her wet hair. "Who could say no to someone who's so smart and smells so sweet? You don't want to come with us, do you?"

Keith said, turning to Beth.

"Please, Mom," Jennifer said.

Beth didn't know what was happening, but she felt dizzy, her equilibrium suddenly off-kilter. Was there some new set of rules she was unaware of? Were they now pretending to be a family again? Keith hadn't filed divorce papers yet. There was nothing to move on from yet. "No, you two have fun. I've got too much to do around here today."

"Suit yourself," Keith said. "It'll just have to be the ice princess and the prince, then." He twirled Jennifer around and carried her to the door. "I'll bring her back before she turns into a pumpkin."

Beth shut the door behind them and waved from the window. She felt suddenly silly, as if she were saying goodbye to out-of-town company headed on a long drive back home instead of her own husband and daughter. Once again, she'd managed not to tell Keith that she'd been homeschooling Jennifer. And once again, he'd managed to stop by without giving her any child-support money. She stopped waving and shut the blinds.

The truth was that despite how much Winter had planned for her to do for the rest of the day, Beth didn't want any part of it. After Keith and Jennifer drove off and she finally walked away from the living room window, the weight of this fact hit her.

Each of Jennifer's absences created its own set of impossible expectations. How much could she accomplish in the next six hours if she actually tried? Staying at home meant work that felt optional no matter how she squinted at it. There was only Winter, no real boss checking in with her periodically, no co-workers clicking away at their keyboards in the next cubicle or punching numbers into their phones, and, most important, there was no actual paycheck to look forward to twice a month. She should have asked Keith about money instead of worrying so much about telling him about homeschooling. Now she was stuck with Winter's ideas.

Today she had a list of tasks Winter had written out for her. She'd stuck it under a pile of magazines and pulled it out now to look at it. Winter had listed each item for her, as if she were a child, with big blue letters, One, Two, Three, Four.

She was supposed to research setting up a website and getting a listing in the next Yellow Pages. This was ONE! Then, she was supposed to HEAD OUT! (TWO!) and leave small stacks of their cards in gyms, at the organic bakery, at some kind of self-service legal office on Bellflower, and at the DMV. And she was to post it on those community bulletin boards at health-food stores and every coffeehouse in Long Beach that had one. THREE! She was supposed to network online, GET THE BUZZ OUT! Winter wrote.

Beth felt like the child for whom the list might have been written, not like someone who had a marketing degree and several years working in promotions. She didn't want to do any of these things on the list. *Because I didn't feel like it,* she imagined telling Winter, even though, when the moment came, she knew she'd make up much more elaborate excuses. Maybe she'd even cite her marketing degree, explain how, for a new business to succeed, the founders needed seed money and the ability to handle monetary losses for at least the first year.

In the kitchen Beth opened up the bottle of wine she'd stuck back in the refrigerator. She drank half a glass, just enough to help her work up the nerve to call Patterson. As his cell phone rang, she imagined her number or maybe even her name displayed on his screen. She felt stupid and exposed. What if he was with a client or if he was home and Winter picked up?

"I need your help," she said when he picked up.

"What's wrong?"

"Something's broken."

This was what they did. Each time, one of them pretended they needed something, and then it was just an accident that they fell into each other. Even when they'd gone to the beach together one unseasonably warm February afternoon, they went because there was something about the ocean that Patterson said he needed to show her. They'd ended up face-to-face floating together on his surfboard behind the waves, even though he'd turned his back when she stepped into the wetsuit he bought for her as if she were stepping out of her bathing suit instead of pulling on a thick layer of neoprene.

"The garbage disposal," she said now. It had been months, maybe even years, since the thing had worked. The garbage can under the sink was filled with broccoli trimming, orange peels, rotted tofu. It all stunk. Every day it stunk, an unintended compost heap in the kitchen. "I don't know how much longer we can get by without it."

"Give me an hour," he said. "I'll have a look at it. Can you wait an hour?"

"I can try." She hung up and looked back into the refrigerator for something, anything. What was that joke that Darla had told her about married women getting fat because they looked in their bed and, disgusted, went to the refrigerator, while single women looked in the refrigerator and, disgusted, went to bed? Which one was she now anyway?

Beth balled up Winter's to-do list and stuck it down deep into the garbage can, hidden under all that rotted food, and then she washed her hands and lathered up her forearms with dish soap. *You are not the boss of me*, she thought. Very mature. Could she get any worse?

She went upstairs. The blankets were pulled back, the sheets creased. She crawled back into bed. Apparently she could get worse. She opened a *Homeschooler Today* and tried flipping through it the way Winter flipped through magazines, dismissing each page she deemed unimportant.

But how did Winter know if something mattered or not? Was teaching your child how to dye her own wool more or less important than returning your suburban backyard to the water-saving sustainable coastal desert it once was?

Soon Patterson would be here. Tomorrow Winter would find out she hadn't tackled her list at all. She closed the magazine and shut her eyes, sleepy with guilt.

Maybe this was how her lying friends felt in high school when their mothers chewed them out after finding overdue library books scattered under their beds or even a pack of cigarettes buried deep in their pajama drawers. In much deeper trouble, they were relieved to be discovered for their least important offense.

CONFIGURATIONS

The waves had turned bad. The normally reliable bend of the ocean in San Clemente was choppy and sporadic one morning, flat and baylike the next. Sheathed in early morning fog, Patterson floated around on his belly with the other surfers at what felt increasingly like a failed cocktail party, the alcohol gone too early and only those with nowhere else to go still lingering around the last few stale chips. One by one, each surfer paddled to shore and went on his way, while Patterson lingered to think.

It turned out it was not God who had been missing from his life. It was Beth. Each weekday morning, he left his sleeping house an hour before he had to, his board strapped to the roof of his car, hoping he was wrong and trying to re-create the connection to God and the ocean that he'd once felt.

Disoriented by his failed early morning attempt at surfing, Patterson could no longer be reassured by the predictability of his office life. Rumors had begun to circulate that the insurance agency he worked for was giving up on California and relocating somewhere in Texas. And he couldn't blame them. While he underwrote individual life insurance policies, his company had bigger issues to consider. Droughts, mud slides, earthquakes, and wildfires didn't make it easy to be profitable issuing home insurance policies. The way Patterson saw it, the entire state of California was never really any better off than a cancer patient in remission.

And now, on top of this, he was being blackmailed by a Mr. Mom of a man. Blackmail was what it amounted to, even if neither one of them called it that. Patterson had reread the email TODAY! so many times, he had it memorized.

Thought I spotted you at the beach today, but I didn't want to bother you out there on your board. Looked like you two were having too much fun.

Jesus. The man didn't look like he had it in him to be a blackmailer.

But what besides being blackmailed could compel Patterson to promise to stop by another man's house on the way home tonight and look at the mess he'd made of things when his wife had plenty she needed him to do, when his boys would be clamoring for him to take them out to toss a football?

He finally gave up on the ocean and showered off on the beach before changing into work clothes in the public bathroom, a routine that felt somehow seedy when he hadn't caught any actual waves.

At work, he got online and opened up what he assumed was a work-related email from an office mate entitled COUNT ME IN. But instead of reading a response to the carefully crafted memo he'd sent out the day before about escalating lung-related health risks for retired longshoremen exposed to coal dust, he stared at a photograph of a huge stone mansion somewhere in Texas that was listed for not much more than the price of the SUV that Winter had been after him to buy.

Real estate porn was all any of it amounted to, and Patterson deleted it as quickly as he would have a picture of a naked teenage girl. But just like porn, the image lingered. Texas. You could buy a house like that in Texas. He had seniority and would be included in any move. All he had to do was relocate with his company.

The only thing more looming than Texas was Beth, even if, instead of growing larger each time he saw her, she shrank in size. *There's going to be nothing left of you for me to grab onto*, he told her the last time they found themselves locked together. He'd gone over to fix her garbage disposal but couldn't. The motor was dead. Still, he told her, he could save her money by replacing the thing himself.

Don't call a plumber, he whispered to her in the kitchen, her underpants on the floor by her feet.

I wouldn't even know who to call, she said.

She never knew who to call. Unlike Winter, there was nothing capable about Beth. Every day she needed rescuing. It seemed impossible that her husband could have left her. Stranded her, was the way he thought about it.

And here he was, thinking about Beth again instead of working, the way her underpants, so loose at the hips now, always wound up at her feet when they were alone together. She could ruin his life if he let her. Several times a week he spent dangerous time he didn't have speeding down the freeway, driving to her house and back on his lunch hour. Despite the fact that no one knew better than he did that each time you got in your car, each time you got on the freeway, your risk of death or dismemberment or disability increased exponentially.

He tried to imagine Winter wandering through their new Texas mansion's empty rooms with her magazines and their decorating tips, taping up her paint swatches and wallpaper samples. He saw his boys wearing cowboy hats and running wild in their big flat sunny Texas backyard with maybe a horse or two off in the distance, grazing. All of it would have appealed to him only months ago, but now he couldn't stop imagining what he would be leaving behind.

Maybe it was time to think about leaving. Two years ago his parents sold their Temecula home and moved to the outskirts of Houston. Surely they'd be happy to have their grandchildren closer in their retirement years.

Patterson roamed through the trash bin of his email, looking for the Texas McMansion he now regretted deleting so quickly. He pulled up the picture of the slick new house. *Thirty-eight hundred square feet*, he read. He could stick two of their current house inside of it. The house was surrounded by tiny new trees and sod so green he wondered if it was that new fake turf he'd considered rolling out in Beth's backyard if the dog business had lasted, the kind a dog could safely urinate on without leaving a burn spot, the kind you could hose off like it was plastic sheeting at the end of each day.

He imagined the digital appliances in the house mystifying Beth, the maintenance requirements for new wood floors setting her back days. He could buy it for Winter—or a house like it—and move his family before he ran their current life into the ground completely.

Do you have a realtor already? he typed back to his co-worker, a man who chatted away about his stock-buying strategies for seven hours straight when Patterson had made the mistake of carpooling with him to a conference in Palo Alto.

He could have just walked down the hallway to ask, but he wanted a more succinct answer. *Is this move really a go?*

Hell, yes, baby, he read.

At 6:30 p.m., Patterson stood in what was once the dining room of his blackmailer's house and turned away from the designs spread out on the table. He'd called Winter on the way home to tell her why he'd be late and could barely hear her with his boys shouting at each other in the background.

"I swear they filled the Sprite machine at the movie with Mountain Dew today," she said, her voice calm as always. "Boys. Quiet down now. I'm talking to your father."

"I'll probably be about an hour late," he said. "I'm helping that David guy, Mr. Mom Homeschool. Seems he got in over his head with some home repairs."

He could hear Winter draw in a breath, but she wasn't the kind of wife who would say "no" and tell him to come home on time. "That's nice of you," she said. Once again, he tried to be grateful for her.

From the outside, David's house looked normal enough, and for a minute, he'd almost looked forward to the break that entering this house would give him before going home to his wired-up boys. No matter how much he missed them, he felt assaulted by Aiden and Nolan every time he walked through the front door.

But with the holes knocked through walls and construction debris in piles, the inside looked more suited for squatters or crackheads than a family. David's three girls sat in the living room on the couch watching cartoons as if nothing was out of the ordinary.

"We're thinking about Design #2, minus the added-on sunroom," David said, pointing to one of the childlike drawings spread out on the dining room table. "We can let go of that."

Patterson looked at David. Was he kidding? A laugh track roared out from the living room.

"I've had to lighten up a little on the TV policy," he added, "just during the renovations."

"You've made a real mess of this place, buddy," Patterson said, looking around. "It'll take some doing to put things back together again."

"I know," he said. "Can you help?"

"The first thing you have to do," Patterson said, "is forget these." He folded up the drawings and handed them to David. He'd spent his summers in high school and college getting paid under the table for doing grunt work for a contractor in Anaheim. He could show David how to hammer a few nails, but that was it. "Let your little girls color the designs in if they want, set their Barbie furniture on top of the rooms."

"We don't play with Barbie in this house," David said.

Patterson looked at the three girls. He remembered their surprising quick turns on the ice at the Lakewood Ice Palace, their wasteful full plates from Hometown Buffet. The two older ones were wearing overalls. He could see the filthy bottoms of their bare feet resting on the coffee table in front of them. The little one sat with knees pulled up to her chest, a big shirt pulled down over her legs. She scratched her head aggressively. Beth's girl, Jennifer, looked nothing like these girls. She might as well have been a different species.

"My point is," said Patterson, "I'm not an architect or a contractor. If you shell out a few bucks for supplies and a licensed plumber, maybe an electrician, we can work on smoothing down the edges of your new open floor plan. Let's put it that way."

"I was thinking about bartering for the plumber," David said. "But I wasn't sure what to offer. Maybe some organic-gardening advice. The girls and I have some lettuce coming in right now if the snails don't get it all, that is. We haven't had much success with our wire blockades. Now we're trying some nonalcoholic beer to keep the snails away."

"Is that right?" Patterson said. He could use a beer himself, a real one, but so far David hadn't offered him anything. Clearly, manners weren't high on his homeschool priority list.

"Follow me," David said. "I'll show you."

He followed David out through the back door. Surrounding the raised bed of lettuce were plastic soda bottles with little flaps cut out of the sides. The bottles were filled with what looked to be an inch of urine.

"It may not look particularly appetizing to us," David said, "but the snails love the stuff. At least they're supposed to love it. Not that we actually nabbed any snails yet. Here, take some home." He broke off several long, unruly leaves of lettuce. "Even your boys might eat salad if they knew it grew in an actual organic garden."

Patterson doubted it, but he held onto the leaves, not knowing where to put them. They felt mossy, more like rabbits' ears than lettuce.

"I just finished reading a fascinating article about an entire homeschool network outside of Portland that operates its own barter system. I was thinking about setting one of those up right here in Long Beach," David said. "What do you think?"

"Is that a fact?" he said, annoyed and half listening. David rambled on the way Winter did when she got excited about a vaguely formed idea. "As long as we're both clear on what you're offering me."

"Offering you?" David said. "Man, I'm not sure what I have to offer. Did you ever just get in over your head and not know how to get out of it?"

"As long as we're clear," Patterson said.

"I mean, I used to have my own money, my own life. Now, look at me."

Patterson looked at David with his scruffy beard and pouchy belly. His despair felt contagious. "Look. I can come by on Saturday mornings and help you. Do we have a deal then?" He thought about putting out his hand to shake on it, but his right hand was still holding tight to the lettuce leaves.

"You should know we're moving to Texas," Patterson added, not sure whether or not he was lying. "Probably in the next few months, so my time is limited."

"Texas," David said. "That'll be a change."

"Anyone with half a brain leaves Southern California when the opportunity presents itself," he said, a near-verbatim quote from his co-worker's last email. "Take the money and run and all that."

"You know, I always thought I'd wind up in the Northwest or maybe the Bay Area," David said. "I never thought I'd live here again. I'm trying to embrace it now, though, have a new attitude about So Cal. A place is at least partly what you make it, right?"

David sounded as if he might want to have a long, heartfelt conversation or perhaps cry right there, and suddenly the idea of his boys leaping on him and dragging him out to the yard to see the latest casualties in the cemetery they'd constructed out of toothpicks for all their tiny dead toy soldiers seemed far more appealing than it had fifteen minutes before.

"I'll see you Saturday morning," Patterson said.

At home, Winter brought him a cold bottle of beer while the boys watched him count their latest casualties.

"It's nice of you to help that poor man get started," Winter said.

"You should see how he's wrecked the place." He took a sip and swallowed quickly, trying not to think about the layer of warm piss beer the snails were supposed to drink.

He stared at the hunk of yard in front of him, a sun-baked mud cemetery, while Aiden and Nolan argued over which tiny graves each of them had dug. It seemed like the soldiers' cemetery had grown exponentially over the past weeks.

"Maybe you should plant a garden or something," he said to Winter. "Grow some vegetables." He had opened the window on the way home from David's and dropped the lettuce into the street, and now he wondered if he should have brought it home, how it might have tasted on top of a hamburger.

"Right. In all my free time," she said.

Right, he thought, *exactly*, but he didn't say it. In truth, besides starting up small businesses that quickly fizzled, he had no real idea what his wife did most of the day. But he knew better than to comment on it. It was his idea to homeschool, and, while Winter hadn't held it against him yet, he was careful not to push things.

"How do you feel about Texas?" he asked as the boys ran off to their room to find more army men to bury.

"Isn't that the state where women are always going nuts and killing their children?"

"It's the state where my parents live."

"And?"

Patterson looked at his wife. Her skin was tight and lips perfectly outlined in pink. She was wearing a black sports bra under her pink tank top, tight exercise pants that stopped right above her knee.

He tried to appreciate the sheer wonder, the flat-out luck of his life. "I just thought we should visit them soon. It's been nearly a year. They miss the kids."

"Why not?" Winter said. "We can make it educational, maybe show the boys some real cowboy history and a working farm or two."

"Exactly what I was thinking," although he hadn't thought of any of those things. All he'd been thinking about was the skill it would take to keep his job, work on another man's house, and sneak over to see Beth as often as possible.

The boys would soon come running back out, their hands full of tiny green plastic army men. Patterson finished his beer, and while his wife went inside to get hamburgers going for dinner, he knelt down on the packed dirt and tidied up the uneven rows of toothpick crosses on the boys' graveyard. As soon as he finished, the boys reappeared and got busy lining up more army men to shoot. Patterson picked up a football and tossed it toward his sons. "Go long!" he said. "Who's got this one?"

ORGANICS

While Keith had had moments in the past seven months when he'd felt homeless, the truth was he only understood how close he was to the actual prospect when a janitor found him sleeping on the couch in his office, a microwave plugged in by the window and an open suitcase, which he'd come to think of as a drawer in the way someone driving cross-country might think of their car as home, on the floor.

"You can't sleep here," the janitor said, turning on the overhead light, a heavy set of what Keith would have sworn in his half-sleep were jagged-edge jailer's keys jangling on a chain in the man's hand. "No one's allowed to live here. It's against the rules."

Keith bolted up from the couch and then sat back down, sleep quickly shaken off the way beer buzzes had been back in high school when someone's parents came home unexpectedly. He was thirsty and had to pee, but he didn't get up. He kicked a stray black sock under the pilly couch the previous tenant had left behind and smiled in a way he hoped seemed nonchalant.

The janitor stared down at what felt to Keith like the side of his head. He wasn't the regular janitor, the stoned aging hippie with a ponytail. The regular janitor never got to his office until at least 9 a.m. After working late one night, when Keith had once opened the door still in his pajamas, the janitor had flashed his usual halfhearted peace-sign greeting and then emptied Keith's trash can into the large bag that hung from his cart without comment.

This janitor was a middle-aged man with a square head and a buzz cut, and Keith took a chance. "Just had a little fight with the wife. You know how it is."

"It's not legal," the janitor said, still not looking right at him.

"It's the middle of the night, isn't it?" Keith asked. He picked up his watch from the floor and checked it, raising his eyebrows in what he hoped looked like surprise. "Seven already? How'd that happen? I guess seven qualifies for morning." He forced a tight little laugh that came out sounding like *hey hey*.

"I'm usually on floors two, three, and four, but Jimmy was sick so I'm here on five, six, and seven, too. Double-time but no overtime."

Keith laughed without planning to this time, but instead of smiling, the man just looked at the side of his head and frowned. He saw his mistake. The man was plodding and slow-witted. "I'm sorry," he said. "I know I shouldn't have slept here. I promise to follow the rules from now on."

"I have to report you," the man said, walking away now. "I'm supposed to. No smoking. No cooking. No staying overnight in the offices."

Keith got up quickly and followed him out the door, but the janitor was already wheeling his cart down the hall. "Wait!" he shouted, but the man had turned the corner.

He spent the next night at Eleanor's. He fell asleep quickly after dinner while they watched a documentary on the birds of Central America, so he was able to avoid asking her if he could stay over, lately a more and more humbling request. But the next night when he called her, she claimed to be busy with a new Arabic cooking intensive, and he didn't see her at all.

After considering the cost of a hotel room and nearly falling asleep in the laundromat watching his clothes dry, he put a chair up against his office door after locking it and slept on his couch again. He didn't really think the chair would keep anyone out, but he hoped the sound of it tumbling over might wake him before the janitor did, and he could pretend to be hard at work in his darkroom. Still, he was on edge and slept in short, fitful blocks of time.

On the third day, when he'd nearly convinced himself that he'd over-reacted and the janitor was too slow-minded even to remember him, he opened an official-looking envelope from building management slipped under his door and read that this was his FIRST AND FINAL WARNING. He could keep his office as long as he never slept in it overnight again. BUILDING ZONED FOR BUSINESS USE ONLY.

He'd chosen the office because it was cheap. There was nothing official about the building—no doorman, no automatic door into the lobby, only one dark elevator—and now he was staring at this official-looking notice. A few times, he'd seen women he was nearly certain were prostitutes wobbling around the lobby in tight skirts and high heels in the middle of the day. Did they get warnings, too, or did their work qualify as business?

On his way to pick up his daughter, he drove past several blocks of apartment buildings, some with FOR RENT signs out front. He stopped and took a few flyers from a box in front of a duplex that needed to be painted. The flyer was full of everything the apartment didn't include or allow—No Pets, No Washer/Dryer, No Short-term Leases. Overpriced and depressing. He folded the flyer in half and stuck it under the seat of his car.

He knew he should be making up flyers of his own to advertise his photography. His business was going through one of its dormant periods. It wasn't unusual not to have every weekend filled in the spring, but his summer calendar worried him. He should have been double-booked months ago, but he still had a free Saturday in July and two in August. He knew eventually the novelty of sticking with film and shooting only in black and white would wear off, and he suspected this was happening now. He'd have to invest in new equipment and go digital and work with color if he intended to keep up.

Keith was relieved to find Jennifer waiting on the front stoop when he drove up. He could avoid going in and facing Beth for now. He'd contacted a lawyer about divorce, but the retainer was out of reach. So far, he'd managed to keep up with the mortgage and the bills, but he hadn't given Beth any money for several weeks now, and, after a brief period of what almost seemed like friendship, he'd begun to keep his distance from her again, waiting in the car for Jennifer whenever he wasn't forced to get out and knock on the door. This was, he suspected, how he looked to Eleanor lately: furtive and broke.

You're the one who left, Beth wrote to him in an email. *Did you think this would be easy?*

Of course not, he wrote back, but he hadn't given nearly enough thought to the level of difficulty. When he did now, he envisioned the way ski slopes were labeled: novice, intermediate, expert. He'd taken photos of a bride and groom at Snow Summit once, a January wedding. They'd rented out the lodge for the ceremony but wanted to be photographed on the slopes. They rode up on chairlifts, the bride and groom, both snowboarders, in front of him, holding hands, the seat next to Keith filled with his equipment.

The couple wore ski jackets, his black, hers white, and they posed by a sign at the top of a mild slope that read "Novice." The sun reflected off the snow at odd angles, eliminating half the shots the couple wanted, but he'd managed to take enough that they liked. They bought the negatives and used one in their thank-you notes.

It was a corny premise, but now it seemed ingenuous, too. Marriage should be off-limits to novices. Certainly, leaving your family and starting over was an Experts Only slope. Not only was moving out expensive, but his daughter seemed to miss him less and less each time he saw her, and, now that the initial rush had ended, it was nerve-racking to be dating again.

The past several times he'd spent the night, Eleanor had pushed him out of bed in the morning with her small, buffed feet, shooing him out the door so she could get ready for a pilates or yoga class. He wondered if she'd shooed away her three husbands, and her grown son in Seattle, this same way.

"I'm ready to go skating," Jennifer said, sliding into the back seat of the car and placing a large bag Keith recognized as one of Beth's old purses on her lap.

"What, no hello, no kiss?"

She leaned over the seat and kissed the air by his cheek. "Now can we go skating?" she asked. "See, I remembered to wear my knee socks and everything." She leaned back and stuck a socked foot up on the back of the seat next to him. "I've got my mittens, too. See?" He heard the purse snap open, and she held up her covered hands.

"No skating today, honey. I thought we could do something else." He drove away from the house, heading out slowly in no particular direction, an all too usual feeling lately. He hadn't figured out what the "something else" was yet, but he hoped it would come to him.

The morning was overcast, thick with a marine layer, as good a morning as any to be indoors, but he was tired of watching Jennifer's tedious progress as a skater. They'd gone several weeks in a row, but she still clung tightly to his sleeve, letting go for a second or two at a time and grabbing onto the wall for support when he did a lap or two by himself. The rink was cold, noisy, and shining white, and he had no interest in going back there today despite the marine layer. What Jennifer really needed, he suspected, was lessons, and he couldn't afford to pay for those right now.

Besides, taking Jennifer to the rink used to mean the possibility of running into Eleanor, but her skating class was over and she'd moved on to new things, Arabic cooking in the evenings and birding during the day, heading off with her binoculars into the local woods with the new group she'd joined.

"How about a nature hike instead?" Keith asked. "That sounds like fun, doesn't it?"

"No."

"Oh, come on. It does, too."

"Whatever," she said, but her voice was quieter now, and he could tell she'd go along with the plan.

"Maybe you'll like it and surprise yourself. Remember how you used to love the woods?"

"No," she said, her voice a whisper.

Keith didn't remember either. But he did remember that they used to like to try new things together, and now they didn't. Or maybe he only remembered that she used to like him and now she didn't. The rare times he'd taken her out alone when he was still with Beth, he felt as if he'd broken her out of some kind of child prison.

Keith passed the turnoff for the multiplex and thought briefly about going there instead, sitting in a cool, dark theater with his daughter, drinking sodas and eating popcorn and not having to try to make conversation for two whole hours. But he kept driving.

He didn't see Eleanor's little car in the parking lot, but he did see two official-looking green vans parked next to each other, and he thought maybe her birding group had met somewhere else and drove together in the vans to save the five-dollar parking fee.

As they walked over the bridge toward the nature center, they stopped to look at the turtles sunning themselves on platforms in the murky water. Beth's old purse hanging over Jennifer's shoulder made her look smaller than she was and prematurely old, like someone's grandmother.

Keith was relieved to remember that Beth and he had taken Jennifer here years ago, that he hadn't been lying about the woods. She'd been quick and unpredictable, not much older than a toddler. The nature center had been nothing but a study in worry for Beth. First, there was the possibility of Jennifer falling through the gaps between the fence rails over the bridge. Now these gaps were covered over with wire mesh. Maybe she'd been right. A child had fallen in, or, more likely, a more vocal parent than Beth had threatened a lawsuit.

After they made it over the bridge, Beth had fretted about Jennifer toddling away from them after a squirrel or rabbit and falling, or getting scratched by the berry bushes she kept reaching out to touch, or being covered in poison oak.

"I remember about the turtles now," Jennifer said.

He took a chance and reached for his daughter's hand as she peered down through the safety wire. She was still wearing her skating mittens even though the marine layer was gone and it was warm enough that other children were dressed in shorts and flip-flops. She didn't squeeze his hand but she didn't let go either. A small victory. He held tight to her hand as they walked toward the building that housed exhibits.

"Welcome to Organic Foods Day," a woman said as they walked inside. She handed them a flyer, which he crammed deep into his pocket. Being accosted by organic food people didn't feel much different to him than being handed religious flyers. Food was loaded with enough issues and problems when he was with Jennifer. He didn't need to consider new ones.

"Gluten-free bread sample?" a bearded man asked as Keith trailed behind Jennifer, who'd headed quickly to the touch tables against the wall.

"No thanks. She's got a lot of food allergies."

"This is the perfect bread for allergy-ridden kids."

Keith stopped and took a piece of gluten-free bread. He hadn't eaten breakfast yet and didn't realize how hungry he was until he swallowed. Although the bread tasted disarmingly gummy, he grabbed another sample and stuffed it in his mouth when the man turned to look at someone else walking past. Why hadn't he taken Jennifer to IHOP on their way here?

"Jenny?" the man said. "What a surprise."

Keith followed the gluten-free bread man's gaze down to a spot next to him. His daughter was standing there now, back from the touch table, a fox pelt draped around her shoulders, the fox's face pointed up in the direction of her chin.

"You know my daughter?"

"He's David," Jennifer said.

"You're looking very glamorous today, Jenny," he said.

She centered the fox pelt around her shoulders and blushed a little.

"I know Beth," David said. "Her mother."

"Right," Keith said. Maybe he'd been wrong about his wife and Winter after all. "She's quite popular, Beth. I'm Jennifer's dad, Keith. Her father."

A speaker of some kind that was attached to David's belt loop sounded, and he took it off and talked into it. A walkie-talkie. Keith hadn't seen one of those since he was a kid, was surprised that in a world full of smartphones, they even still existed. "I read you," David said. "Come check in with Poppa, Mad girl."

"My girls," he said to Keith. "They wanted to do the mile loop instead of standing around with their old man."

"Go figure," Keith said.

"They're not used to the weekend crowds. They know the trails, but I have to keep track of them with all the schoolers around."

Before Keith could ask him what he meant by *schoolers*, the door opened and three children pounded in, wearing hiking boots and yellow hard hats. They walked in a row, short to tall. They carried sticks and wore T-shirts and baggy jeans. Walkie-talkie antennae stuck out of their front pockets.

"What's she doing here?" the littlest one asked, taking off her hard hat and scratching her scalp.

Keith put his arm around his daughter and pulled her in close, feeling as if he needed to protect her from what felt like a primal force of some kind—a sudden gale-force wind or an impending tsunami.

"You want to try one out, Jenny? Nothing more fun," David said. "Come on, girls. Someone lend Jenny one of your radios."

The middle girl handed Jenny hers. "You have to take off your mitten," she said. "Don't switch channels. We're all on three."

The oldest girl was cramming down the bread samples now. *Mine,* Keith thought. *My bread.*

"I'm going to try it. Okay, Dad?" Jennifer said, sliding off a mitten and putting it into her big purse.

"Don't go too far," he said, although he wanted to take the walkie-talkie and hand it right back to the girl. They hadn't even gone on their nature walk yet. He was starving. He looked around the room. There were three more food booths to try. "I'll wait in here for you."

"I'll take that," the littlest girl said, stopping to scratch her head long enough to pull the fox pelt off Jennifer's shoulders and lay it over her own.

"The pelts and skeletons can't leave the building," David said.

While Jenny practiced talking back and forth with David, Keith checked out the booths. One gave out tiny cups of thick, foggy juice that he rejected on principle. The girls were behind David's sample table with him now. They all wore animal pelts, their tangled hair draped over the fur. Their hard hats gleamed in bright plastic contrast.

"Are you sad? You can have your fox back now," the smallest girl said to Jennifer, who'd paced back to their booth with the walkie-talkie. "I like the raccoon better." She tried to hand Jennifer the fox skin, specked with pieces of nut from the trail mix.

"No thanks," she said. David stared down at its little pointed sinister-looking mouth as the girl draped the pelt back around her own shoulders.

"They're all hides from animals found dead near the trails," David said, as if answering Keith's question.

"Too bad the kids didn't get to hunt them down. On Survival of the Fittest Day."

David looked at him.

"That was a joke," Keith said. "I was kidding."

"Tell your mom that as soon as Patterson's done helping me get the house back together, we're going to have a party," David said into the walkie-talkie. "A housewarming. Tell her to expect an invitation. You've got it, Jen. You're free to leave the building."

Keith thought about saying one of a number of things. *Who are you to tell my daughter she's free to go anywhere?* Or, *How do you know my wife?* Or, *Who the hell is Patterson?* Or, *What about* my *invitation?* But instead he watched as Jennifer headed outside with the walkie-talkie tight in her one unmittened hand.

At a booth near David's, Keith managed to grab a bowl of some kind of nutty salad without making eye contact with the volunteer. Initially, the salad tasted okay, but it had a lingering acidic aftertaste, and he longed for something nonorganic to wash it down with.

At the last booth, a woman handed him a flyer with his baggie of trail mix. "You can make it yourself," she said. "The list of ingredients is right on the flyer. Be sure to use carob chips, not chocolate, unless you want to be hyped up when the hike's over."

She said this last line in an automatic kind of way that let him know she'd said it many times already that morning and would say it many times again. He thought about challenging her. *Would a few pieces of chocolate really "hype up" a grown man? Where's the proof?* But instead he stuffed a second bag of the trail mix into his pocket for Jennifer. While she couldn't have the nuts, she could at least safely pick out the carob chips.

"You haven't seen a group of bird-watchers come through this morning, have you?" Keith asked, chewing an unsalted almond.

"I couldn't say," she said. "We're not supposed to ask people why they came to the nature center. We just give out samples."

"But you would have noticed a group of adults with binoculars, though, right?"

"Lots of people have binoculars." She turned away, handing flyers and bags of trail mix to David's three girls. The middle one made her flyer into an airplane and whisked it across the room, where it came close to clipping the ear of a mother bending down to tie her son's shoe. The older girl knocked on her sister's hard hat. "Watch out, idiot."

It struck Keith that their walkie-talkies were alarmingly silent.

"Where's Jennifer?" he asked the oldest.

She looked at him blankly.

"Jenny. Where's my daughter?"

The littlest one was still wearing what he couldn't help thinking of as Jenny's fox pelt. She dropped pieces of her trail mix on it as she chewed. He watched as a carob chip lodged itself into the fox's open mouth.

"We turned ours off," the middle girl said.

"Because we're inside now," the oldest one said loudly and clearly, as if he might be as thick-witted as the janitor who reported him for living in his office.

The smallest girl took off her hard hat and scratched deeply at a section of her scalp and stared intently at a spot below Keith's nose. "You've almost got a mustache," she said. "My dad's got a beard."

"Where is she? Where would she go?" Keith said to the oldest, but she was already turning away. The two other girls followed her to the next booth, where they all downed several tiny cups each of free juice as if they were drinking shots. Why did no one in this place seem to know anything? Why hadn't he told Jennifer to stay close? It was the aquarium all over again—the spongy odor of organic samples might as well have been the stench of dead mackerel.

"Where's my daughter?" he asked David. "Call her now. Call her on that thing."

"Relax," David said. "I'm sure she's just taking in her surroundings." He took the walkie-talkie out of his pocket and lifted it to his face. "Come in, Jenny. Can you read me?"

Keith waited, but no one answered. "She doesn't know what that means, 'read me.' Just ask her to pick up and answer."

"Jenny, pick up if you can hear me, honey."

Honey. Who was this man to his daughter? Keith felt a piece of raw cashew wedged in his throat and thought he might puke the way he had in the aquarium months before.

He grabbed the walkie-talkie from David and spoke in a voice he barely recognized as his own. "This is your father telling you to answer me right now, Jennifer."

Keith looked around the room in case she was lurking somewhere close by, but all he saw were strangers. Lines had formed for the food booths. He walked out to the back porch, the way Jennifer had left. He squinted into the sun toward the hiking trails, not sure which direction he should take.

"I lost it," Jennifer said, next to him now. "I put it down because it was hard to hold, with my purse."

"Where were you?"

"Over there," she said, pointing to the spot where the trail started in the woods.

"Without the walkie-talkie? By yourself?"

She nodded.

"Christ," he said. "You have to stop doing this to me."

"Shh," Keith said when Jennifer started to cry silently. "I didn't mean to get mad. I was just worried."

"Can we go home now?" she asked, wiping her face dry with the side of her mittened hand. "I want to go home."

"Roger, Jen girl," Keith said, but without a walkie-talkie the words felt flat. "Over and out." Keith looked at his daughter, hoping for a smile he didn't get.

"I wanted to go skating," she said as they walked back to their car, her big purse tucked under her arm.

"We did this instead," he said, scanning the lot for Eleanor's tiny car. Maybe she and the other bird people went to Bolsa Chica or Huntington Gardens or wherever people with time on their hands went to look for birds. Or maybe they were still out there in the woods. He knew he should be happy to have his daughter back and safe, that he should take her skating now because that's what she'd wanted to do. But all he wanted to do was drop her at home and go find Eleanor.

"I got you some trail mix," he said when they got in the car, pulling the bag out of his pocket. "You can eat the chocolate chips. They're actually carob."

"I hate carob," she said, handing the bag back to him over the seat.

"Your loss." He started up the car and drove away, not slowing down when he saw in his rearview mirror gluten-free man running out toward the car, shouting *Hey!* and waving him back.

"He wants his walkie-talkie," Jennifer said.

"Well, it looks like he's not getting it."

"Aren't you going to tell him I lost it?"

"Nah," he said. "Let's be outlaws and just keep driving."

"Cool," Jennifer said from the back seat.

Keith realized he had hit a new low in parenting, but at least he hadn't lost his daughter or poisoned her with food she was allergic to. He poured the trail mix directly into his wide open mouth, pieces hitting the back of his throat like sleet.

PEDICULUS HUMANUS CAPITIS

At first, he had attributed his littlest duckling's scalp itching to a nervous habit. Katie was his rule-follower. David worried the scratching was a coping mechanism she'd developed to get through the chaos of construction. But when Emily and Madeline began to claw at their scalps, too, he'd finally taken out a flashlight and peered deep into their hair shafts. Hidden close to their scalps were hundreds of sticky white eggs. He'd initially misdiagnosed the eggs as dandruff until a magnifying glass illuminated live, crawling bugs.

The irony wasn't lost on David that his homeschooled daughters all had developed head lice, a plague that regularly swept through entire elementary schools. At least his daughters would be spared the humiliation of lining up in front of the nurse's office and being sent home in the middle of the day.

He'd looked backward at their blurred days until he became convinced that they'd first come into contact with the lice at the Santa Ana Children's Museum during Half-Price Homeschool Wednesday several weeks before, when Katie had tried on every hat in the dress-up box. Possibly they'd spread the bugs at the nature center when they tried on the animal pelts. He'd call both those places later in the week, after they'd cleared the worst of it, offer a semi-anonymous tip.

Opened up by construction, the house had become as infected as the girls' hair. Not by lice, but by cockroaches, black ants, and mealmoths. The kitchen was particularly verdant. The moths, though light as ash, had the capacity to chew straight through plastic and somehow survive even the sealed cool of the refrigerator. Reaching into a bag to grab a handful of granola had become such a hazardous task that even his brave Emily had begun to trust only food taken directly out of the freezer, crunching down on frozen fruit leather when she wanted a snack.

He knew the bugs were a reminder of the role of nature in their lives and their place in it. But it was one thing to confront bugs in the garden, where, despite their best organic attempts at dissuasion, worms bore their way through tomatoes, and snails drilled into lettuce leaves, and another thing entirely to confront an overfed cockroach scurrying across the kitchen floor. It made no sense, but he couldn't help but think of the cockroaches as giving birth to the tiny lice crawling around the girls' scalps. The combined infestation of his tomatoes, his house, and his daughter's scalps filled David with a vital sense of outrage.

When it looked as if the construction wouldn't be finished anytime soon—even with Patterson coming by most weekends to work alongside him—he decided to confront the insect problem while the house was still opened up. Deborah was spending more and more time at work and had threatened to move into a hotel if she saw another cockroach in the kitchen when she came in to get her morning coffee.

"Alone?" David had asked, imagining the relief he'd feel if she stopped coming home after work for what increasingly felt like little more than nightly progress inspections.

"With my girls," she said.

He couldn't even begin to imagine being in the house without the girls. "Your girls?"

"Well, who had them?" she said. "It's an expression. Sometimes you act like you gave birth to them yourself."

The girls were still sleeping in their room, but David glanced over into the living room just in case one of them had padded in and was nestled on the couch. He didn't believe in having this kind of discussion in front of them. Neither did Deborah, but lately she'd been less than tactful. He imagined her leaving for work with the residue of a fight lingering over both of them and decided to take the high road and let it go.

"Does your head itch?" he asked, dropping the word "too" from his question at the last minute. Deborah hadn't seemed to notice the infestation, and pointing it out to her felt like a mistake.

"Don't be silly," she said. "Was I scratching?"

"No. Just wondering. You know, there's some dust from the construction."

Deborah rolled her eyes. "Of course I know. Who wouldn't notice it?" She took a final sip of coffee and left the cup on the table for him to clean up. When had she stopped bringing her own cup to the sink?

When the girls woke up, he'd already begun researching holistic methods to rid a house of insects. "We have a new project," he said as he carefully poured their cereal, checking for moths before adding the soy milk. "The whale tracking will have to wait just a little bit longer."

David found an outlet that hadn't been disconnected in the living room and blasted his favorite Irish folk music for inspiration. After their initial complaints, there was something almost festive about the way the girls joined in to help.

Emily filled pieces of cheesecloth with cedar chips that Madeline sewed shut, and little Katie crawled up on counter tops and stuffed the homemade sachets into the far reaches of their food cabinets. Just in case the cedar chips didn't do it, the girls cut strands of kite string and hung open pieces of spearmint gum from shelves. "That should take care of the moths," David said with a confidence that was only partly faked.

To scare away the cockroaches, they cut mint from their overgrown, neglected vegetable garden and shoved sprigs near wall openings and under the sink, along with cloves. They left eucalyptus oil, crushed garlic, sliced lemon, and cucumber peels along the paths on the kitchen counters where the ants last marched, and they taped mint tea bags to the floor by the back door. Then the girls settled down on the couch to watch an episode of *SpongeBob*.

After all their efforts, David thought the kitchen smelled exotic. He felt both nauseated and hungry. He craved Middle Eastern food, humus, tabbouleh, baba ganoush, and even lamb, something he hadn't eaten in over fifteen years, when he'd seen a film that highlighted the particular cruelties of the ways lambs were raised and slaughtered. He longed to tell the girls *good work* and *let's go celebrate*, but the April afternoon was so bright that he worried the sun would highlight for complete strangers in the Mediterranean Café the lice roaming around in his daughters' hair.

The remote had disappeared months before, but he still looked for it reflexively on the table before walking over to shut the TV off. "Back to the kitchen, ducklings. We have to take care of one more problem," he said, "before we leave this house again." He couldn't bring himself to say the word *lice* in connection to his daughters. He knew it was silly to feel stigmatized by the infestation. Lice didn't know anything about social status, and, in fact, he'd come across some evidence that the bugs actually preferred clean hair to unwashed hair. Still, it felt like the childhood equivalent of herpes, stigmatizing no matter how you rationalized it.

After researching several organic parenting blogs, he drove to Albertson's for supplies and came back and soaked his daughters' hair in olive oil, wrapped plastic wrap around it, and tied the wrap down tight with bandanas. Then, armed with a metal nit comb, he unleashed their oil-soaked hair and had one daughter hold a magnifying glass and the other shine a flashlight. "Did you know that lice have been recovered from prehistoric mummies?" he said.

"What's a mummy?" Katie asked.

"It's a very old dead person, stupid," Emily said.

"You're the stupid head," Madeline said. "A mummy doesn't have to be old. It's just the way some people are wrapped up in bandages after they die, right Dad?"

"None of you girls are stupid," he said. "Since when do we use that kind of language in this house? Why don't you go look up your own answer while the olive oil soaks in some more. How about trying our reference books first this time. Let's not forget about the primacy of books."

"Computers are way faster, Dad," Emily said.

"It's true. Books are too slow," Madeline said.

"I'm scared of mummies," Katie said. "I don't want to look."

"Then you stay here with me and I'll work on your hair some more," he said. "I'll give you the super-duper special youngest-duckling treatment while your sisters do their part to allow books to fall into total decline."

He patted the seat in front of him and Katie sat back down. The lice chair. That's how he thought of it now.

Katie had shown the first signs of having lice, and her case seemed tougher than either Emily's or Madeline's. The sticky white eggs slid easily off their oiled hair, and David had extracted only three or four live bugs from each of them. But poor little Katie was a lice sponge. He wished that lice could fly or leap, that he could hook up a fan and blow them away from his baby's hair, where the eggs had burrowed in thick and deep.

"Did you know a female louse can deposit eggs at a rate of about six per night. Up to one hundred eggs total per female," he said as he worked on his daughter, squishing live lice between his fingers.

"What's a louse?"

Katie's question sounded like a setup for a raunchy joke, or maybe it was just that David was in desperate need of a shot of adult humor. With his email homeschool inquiries to answer and the possibility of meeting up with other adults at various homeschool activities nearly any day of the week, he had rarely missed adult company. But the rigors of the construction project had isolated them, and working alongside Patterson on Saturdays hadn't exactly been a boon in the conversation department. Patterson worked in a brooding silence that David supposed was macho or at least manly. It reminded him of why he generally preferred the company of women.

"A louse is singular. One bug," David explained. "The plural, lots of bugs, are lice. So that means if I find one bug, I found a. . . ?"

"Louse!" Katie shouted.

"And if I find more than one, I found lots of. . . ?"

"Lice!"

David did a final run-through of his daughter's hair with the nit comb. The smell of olive oil mixed with the garlic and lemon created a claustrophobic hunger. He shouted to Madeline and Emily. "Go wash out the olive oil, girls. Let's get out of here."

The drive down the coast to track whales didn't have to take them through Belmont Shore. But David had seen an ad in the paper that morning for a rare weekday-afternoon open house right smack in the neighborhood where he had imagined they might be living by now. Knowing that it was impossible to sell their house in its current deconstructed state even if they had the money to move, he imagined simply leaving it, the way people sometimes gave up on repairs and abandoned a car on the side of the road. Lately the word *foreclosure* had rattled around in his head with the word *lice*. Ugly, going-downhill-fast words, taking up the space where he used to plan educational activities to fill his girls' days.

While he packed the sandwiches for a picnic in La Jolla, the girls ran water and fought loudly in the bathroom about whose turn it was at the sink. David assumed they'd rinsed most of the olive oil out of their hair before they left, but their hair seemed wetter than it normally did after they'd showered, and it hung in thick, oily looking clumps. They looked slightly wild, feral, nothing like the JC Penney catalog models Deborah had surprised him with before he began the remodel.

The smell of their hair made him hungry for something more substantial than the peanut butter and jelly sandwiches he'd packed for the afternoon. *Italian*, he thought, *not Middle Eastern*. He thought briefly about making a U-turn at the light and heading north to Lakewood instead of south toward the beach. In the glove compartment, he had a cache of restaurant coupons, and he was pretty sure he had one for the Olive Garden that hadn't expired yet.

But he kept driving. He'd sunk all of his own money into his charities, and he was completely reliant on Deborah, who had been tracking their spending lately. She claimed to be working on a new budget, and David was supposed to use his ATM card, not cash, when eating out. The plan felt more punitive than practical to David with *the man* tracking their days, and he rarely took the girls out to lunch since the plan had been implemented. He suspected that this may have been the point. He took a sandwich from the bag in the seat next to him and took a bite.

"How come we're going this way?" Madeline asked.

"I just have a quick stop to see someone."

"I don't want to stop!" Katie said, scratching at her head. "I want to see a whale."

"How come you're eating already?" Emily said. "I thought we were going to have a picnic."

"Sorry," he said, putting the sandwich back in the bag. "I just took a bite." Sometimes it felt like they were all watching him, his three girls and, from a throne on high, De-BOR-ah.

"I don't want to stop anywhere," Emily said. "Why can't it just be us today?"

"It's always just us," David said.

"There's their house, Dad," Madeline said, leaning forward in her seat and tapping him on his shoulder. "You almost drove right past it."

David pulled up to the curb in front of Beth's house, a place he had not intended to stop at. In truth, he'd planned to drag his girls into the open house he'd seen in the paper, but now as he looked at his daughters with their hair hanging in thick clumps, olive oil staining their T-shirts, all of them still clawing at their scalps, he realized this would be an exercise in humiliation as they were rushed through and back out. Leave it to Madeline to remember the house they had gone to once months ago for the kitchen-supply party. Only eight, she already had a mature grip on her surroundings.

Dragging the girls into an open house to look at a place they had no intention of buying suddenly felt ridiculous no matter how they'd be treated. An exercise not just in humiliation but in pure capitalistic capitulation. One of his girls always had a way of steering him back on track when he got lost. "Let's just see how Beth and Jennifer are making out," he said. "A real quick stop, and then we'll be on our way."

Emily bolted out of the car as if she had been stashed inside of it for hours, not minutes. Although they took regular field trips that required much longer car rides than this, his middle duckling was definitely not sedentary. As a baby, Madeline had been lulled to sleep by the quiet motion of the car, and little Katie rarely complained about being cooped up on road trips. But Emily was always the first one out.

He imagined the conferences he might have been called in for by her teachers if she were in school. She would have been in first grade now, at school from nine to three, stuck at her desk most of that time. Emily was the kind of inquisitive kid teachers deplored on principle because she questioned before doing, because, to her, a desk made a much better fort to hide under than a surface to hunch over. He shuddered to think of the harm a confined classroom would have inflicted upon her.

He lifted Katie up so she could ring the doorbell. The last time they'd been here, the house was full of women and children taking advantage of the free snacks at that overpriced kitchenware party. The time before that, he'd come alone, and the doorbell had set off a cacophony of dog barking. This time the house was silent. There were two cars parked in front, so David took a chance and rang the bell himself.

When Beth finally came to the door, David worried he had awaken her. She wore a loose T-shirt and sweatpants, and a clip hung out of her hair.

"Oh, I thought you were Darla, that maybe they were back early from the rink. You never know with Jennifer. When she might have eaten the wrong thing, gotten sick."

"No, just us. We were passing through the neighborhood. Just wanted to say hello, see how everything was going. The girls wanted to say hello to Jenny."

"I was just taking a nap," Beth said. "Darla took the kids this afternoon. Lauren's only in half-day kindergarten, although sometimes I think Jennifer likes playing with Jeremy more than Lauren."

He had no idea who Darla and Lauren and Jeremy were, but Beth didn't seem to notice.

She pushed a clip back into her hair. "I'm sorry. I should invite you and the girls in."

"Don't be silly," David said. "Homeschool parents need to enjoy their kid-free time. So how's everything going?"

"Good," Beth said. "Good, good, good."

"Everything okay with Jennifer?" Slight and frail, Jennifer might have been seven, but she was smaller than four-year-old Katie. He remembered lifting her up by one arm when she fell at the skating rink, surprised at how light she was.

"Perfect," Beth said. "Everything's perfect."

How could everything be perfect? Last fall she'd been one of his triple threats: no job, no husband, brand new to homeschooling. And didn't Jennifer have a whole host of allergies? What had happened to Beth? He remembered her being a more substantial person, but the woman standing in front of him was nearly as wispy as her daughter. David wanted to come in and talk to her, make sure she wasn't sleeping her days away, too depressed to remember to eat.

If he hadn't been so distracted with the construction project, he would have done a better job of checking up on her, of keeping up with all the people who reached out to him on the internet or by phone. Some days he didn't even check his messages anymore.

Do you need help? he thought about whispering, as if someone inside were holding her hostage. The air around her smelled salty and furtive. He looked over her shoulder into her empty living room.

But she was already slowly closing the front door on him. "Thanks for checking on us," she said as it shut.

David stared at the door for a moment and turned back to his girls. "Jennifer isn't home."

"We heard," Madeline said. She scratched at her scalp, and in the gleaming sunlight, David saw a tiny louse skirt across the top of his oldest daughter's head. Emily and Katie were turning cartwheels on the browning lawn. Their hair, thick and greasy with the residue of olive oil, picked up pieces of loose grass that stuck to the tips.

"I have an idea," David said.

"What idea?" Katie said, right side up and slightly breathless.

"You'll see. Everyone back into the car."

"I thought we already had our idea. We were going to trace the whales' mutation patterns today," Emily said as he turned the key.

"We are going to trace the whales' *migration* patterns," he said, careful not to correct his daughter directly, "but first there's my other idea. A surprise."

"I thought we were having a picnic first," Madeline said. "I'm hungry."

David passed the bag of sandwiches behind him. "Dig in, girls," he said. "Car picnic."

When they'd safely left the confines of Long Beach, David slowed down. He drove through conservative, family-oriented Seal Beach. Still too close to home. He knew several Christian homeschooling families that lived here and didn't want to run into them. Sunset Beach was the nearest safe bet. The nicest houses were beachfront property too expensive for homeschool families to buy, and the run-down apartments by Pacific Coast Highway were too marginal for them to rent.

He had a place in mind and was relieved to see the business hadn't shut down or transformed itself into a frozen yogurt shop. The sign next to the tattoo parlor read HAIR CUTS $10 BUCKS/WALK-INS WELCOME. He smiled at the familiar redundancy of $10 bucks as he pulled into the parking lot.

"You're happy because we're getting tattoos?" Madeline said.

"I'm scared of tattoos," Katie said. "I don't want a tattoo!"

"I do!" Emily said. "I want a tattoo."

"Don't be silly," David said. "We're getting haircuts, not tattoos."

"But we already had haircuts," Katie said.

"With Mom," Madeline said.

"They grew out," Emily said.

David heard the car doors slam and felt his ducklings walking in line behind him.

David wanted it short.

He wanted to cut off the bangs and the bugs and the oil.

The beauty parlor was empty. They wouldn't have to wait until he lost his nerve or little Katie had time to object some more.

"The shorter the better, right girls?" he told the beautician, if that's what she was. Her thin arms were snaked with tattoos, long ropes of what looked to be black roses. David suspected she worked part-time at the tattoo parlor next door, or at least hung out there plenty.

"For summer," he said. He looked around for another beautician or even a customer, who might nod in agreement, but it was three o'clock on a Wednesday afternoon in April, and they were definitely the only ones there. "It's a surprise. For the wife." *Deb-OR-ah*, David thought. *The wife, the man.* David was about to blow a full week's allowance in one visit to the hairdresser.

"Cool," she said. "Who's my first victim?"

David looked at his girls. He hadn't raised them to be vain and silly. They knew hair was dead, and that there was always more where it came from, that it would grow back at the rate of approximately an inch and a half per month. That cutting it off should be no more meaningful or permanent than clipping their fingernails. But for a moment there was silence, and he worried that he'd misjudged, that no one would go along with his plan.

"I'm first," Emily said. She climbed up into the chair.

The beautician took the length off in a few quick scissor strokes and then asked him what came next. David wondered briefly and too late if the lice could live on her scissors, if she would pass them on to her next customer. But weren't beauticians supposed to disinfect their tools, like dentists? Wouldn't that technically be her fault, not his, if she didn't?

"You want me to use the clippers?" she said to David, catching his eye in the mirror. He saw the brief flash of a studded tongue when she spoke this time. David wondered what his life would have been like if he had married her instead of Deborah.

David prided himself in being something of a renegade, homeschooling his daughters while his wife supported the family, but what if it turned out he had done the safest, most predictable thing in the world? If, instead of Deborah, he had married the beautician with the skinny arms and tattoos, a woman who seemed to ask only the most basic of questions. Who knows where life might have taken him? *What's a louse?* he would ask her, and she'd know the raunchy joke that should follow.

The beautician turned and looked down at Emily, who was running her fingers through her new short length. "No more brushing or snarls. Just run your hand over it."

"Yes!" Emily shouted before David had even finished processing her question about the clippers.

He put his hand on his own hair as he listened to the electric shears buzz over his middle daughter's head. Clippers. That's what clippers were. He'd imagined something else when she had said the word, old-fashioned-looking wooden scissors, although he realized that made no sense. Certainly nothing so quick and electrical and irreversible as what buzzed close to his daughter's scalp now.

David had given himself haircuts for years. He let the girls be his mirrors, positioning themselves around him and pointing out spots he'd missed. They made a game of who could sweep up the most hair off the kitchen floor when he was done. They threw the hair outside in the backyard, hoping birds might line their nests with it. Once they made androgynous cut-out cardboard figures and glued his hair to paper-doll heads. He hadn't heard the sound of actual clippers since he was a child.

David was in way too deep, but he couldn't stop. His daughter was getting something that resembled the buzz cuts David's mother inflicted upon him when school got out each June. He would go next. What choice did he have?

"You're a rock star," the hairdresser said to Emily. Then skimmed a spoonful of gel over Emily's head and flicked a louse off a point of her freshly shorn hair. "They don't stand a chance anymore," she whispered loudly. "Nowhere to hide."

David turned away, pretended to be fascinated by a hummingbird that lit on an overgrown bird of paradise that grew outside the window, and oblivious to the wildlife laying eggs on their scalps.

In the end, only he and Emily ended up buzzed, their hair sticking out a stubby inch and a half over their scalps. He told the hairdresser to take off his beard, too. "Why not?" he said. "Have at the whole thing."

After staring at them both, Madeline had opted for an asymmetrical scissor cut that David thought, or hoped, made her look slightly cock-eyed or, at the right angle, Eastern European. And Katie, at four, had been the most sensible. She had insisted on no layers at all, just a straight chop below her ears.

"Will that work?" he asked. "Is it short enough?" Buzzed, he felt strangely embarrassed in front of her, this woman who knew their secret, that they had all been infested.

"Does the trick every time. It's the killer hair gel."

David cringed at the phrase. The hair stylist had slathered his girls' heads with enough killer gel to undo all of his years of natural foods, environmentally friendly soap, and organic cotton clothing. He over-tipped her, grabbed the girls, and walked out as soon as she'd finished with Katie, before she could get out the blow dryer.

Outside, he ran his hand over his clean chin and his newly shorn head. But instead of feeling clean, he felt dirty, as if he'd taken his girls to a porn film or maybe to the tattoo parlor next door.

"Mom's going to die," Emily said in the car. Her giggle sounded strange to David, slightly off-kilter like Madeline's haircut.

"Mom's going to kill YOU," Madeline said.

"She will not," Emily said, but her sentence ended up sounding like it was a question.

"If Mom kills anyone, it will be me," David said.

It was nearly rush hour now, too late to continue down the coast and get home in time for bed, let alone dinner. David turned the car in the direction of home. The girls were too distracted discussing their new haircuts to complain or even to notice that their plan to study whale migration had been postponed once again.

"Emily looks weird," Katie said. "And Dad looks bald."

"I like looking weird," Emily said.

"She doesn't look weird," David said. "I look weird. Emily looks beautiful." It was true. With her hair buzzed short, Emily looked like an entirely different child. He noticed her eyebrows for the first time, fierce, dark bridges over her eyes. She was almost beautiful and some-how more feminine. The haircut fit her personality and her face, he decided.

"I look foreign, right, Dad?" Madeline asked.

David wasn't used to any of his girls needing his approval. They had opinions of their own, all three of them, but he sensed something newly hungry in them now.

"Absolutely," he said. "Like a Romanian movie star in a black-and-white movie."

"Where's Romanian?" Katie asked.

"Rom-an-i-a," Emily said.

"I want to buy a prom dress on the computer when we get home," Katie said. "So other girls can be pretty, too."

"Not today," David said.

"Are we too poor to help other people now?" Madeline asked.

"How come you won't let us buy anyone a cow or a bicycle anymore?" Emily asked.

"Or a prom dress?" Katie added.

"Because we're poor," Madeline said. "Right, Dad? We're poor because we have to pay for the house to get fixed after we broke it."

All three girls sat quietly in the back seat of the car, waiting for his answer. He'd recently read an article about tiny houses, living smaller, making less of a carbon footprint. What had he been thinking tearing open their perfectly fine house? "Of course not," he said. "We just have to finish the house up before we go back to our other projects."

He thought briefly about stopping by Beth's again on the way home, checking in to see how Jennifer was doing. But he'd been bearded for four years, and his newly shaved face was starting to itch. He could think of little else than racing to the medicine cabinet and pulling out the huge tube of aloe vera. This new itch may have been raw and mean, but at least there were no more bugs crawling around his girls' scalps.

David glanced at them in the rearview mirror. He decided all three of the girls' new haircuts suited them. Why couldn't he surprise his wife the way she'd surprised him just months before? He was anxious to get back to the house before she came home from work. Maybe he'd hide the girls in their bedroom, have them pop out and surprise her.

Really, what had he done differently except let their ducklings decide for themselves how they wanted to look, unlike Deborah, who brought his girls home processed and homogenized, anyone's little girls in middle-class America. Maybe his wife would be pleased instead of angry. At least he could hope.

"When we get back home, we'll get out the atlas, and I'll show you where Romania is," David said, feeling more like himself again now.

"I want to look up more stuff about mummies," Emily said.

"I want to look for Romania online," Madeline said. "Reference books are way dated, Dad."

Their rhythm as a family was coming back. It was still the four of them, newly shorn, that's all, on their way to the next thing.

TRANSPORTATION

Jeremy lived directly across the street, but he should have lived with Jennifer. She wouldn't call him a baby and fill his pickup truck with Barbie shoes and plastic baby bottles the way Lauren did. If he had been born her brother, not Lauren's, Jennifer would have never locked her bedroom door to keep him out when she had a friend over. She would never need to have a friend over, because she would have had Jeremy.

Although Jennifer knew babies weren't actually delivered to houses even though people used the word *delivery* when they talked about them, she still felt an important mistake had been made when it came to Jeremy. He may have grown in Darla's belly, but he should have grown inside Jennifer's mother.

She decided she would take Jeremy when she ran away with Ursala to her grandmother's house in Pennsylvania. If Jennifer's life was bad now that her father had left them and loved Eleanor the witch instead of Jennifer and her mother, and she was stuck with the evil twins all day, Jeremy's life was deplorable. *Deplorable* was a vocabulary word from the list Winter had given her to learn in February. She hated the fake-excited way Winter gave the new words to her at the beginning of each month, hiding the list behind her back as if she had an actual present. But she liked the words themselves. Especially some of them, like *deplorable*, which fit a lot of situations, including Jeremy's. For one thing, his own sister hated him, and, for another, his mother didn't even seem to notice.

If Jeremy lived with her, his life would not have been as deplorable, but it wouldn't have been perfect. Not now that there were the evil twins and Winter and even her mother who kept getting skinnier as if she were on her way to disappearing altogether. But if she and Jeremy lived with Ursala and Jennifer's grandmother in Pennsylvania, they'd make snowmen and drink hot chocolate that didn't come from a vending machine and go to the Franklin Institute on the weekends, and none of their lives would be deplorable at all.

Besides, Jeremy liked Ursala, too. Darla took them to the rink sometimes on Wednesday afternoons after Lauren got home from kindergarten, and he actually stopped trying to skate long enough to watch Ursala practice her spins and jumps in the middle of the rink. "Show off," Lauren always said and kept right on going. But not Jeremy.

Jennifer had talked to Ursala two more times since meeting her in the bathroom at the skating rink. The first time, she'd sat down next to Jennifer to unlace her skates on the bench, and Jennifer had said *hello* so quietly that Ursala hadn't heard her.

When Ursala walked away in her woolly boots on plain ground, she looked almost like the other homeschooled teenage girls. But none of them talked to Ursala. And her tutor handed her a protein bar instead of money to buy something from the machine. Maybe, Jennifer thought, Ursala had allergies, too.

The second time she'd been close enough to Ursala to talk to her, she spoke louder. The twins were there, and she was supposed to stay with them so they could help her if she fell while Winter and her mom talked to the manager about posting flyers for their business.

But Aiden and Nolan went chasing after the three girl-boys, and Jennifer skated right to the middle of the rink without falling once. She watched Ursala practice spinning. "Doesn't that make you dizzy?" Jennifer asked when Ursala stopped.

"You have to find a point and focus," Ursala said. "Or else you're fucked."

Jennifer nodded and tried not to look surprised that Ursala said the word *fucked*. She had Ursala's barrette in her box of souvenirs at home under her bed, and she felt bad about it for a minute, but today Ursala was wearing a thick hair band, and she looked like she didn't need the barrette.

She wasn't sure if Ursala remembered her from the bathroom where she had told Jennifer she would kill her if she told anyone she smoked. But she decided she should tell her that she wouldn't in case she was worried. "I won't ever tell on you," she said.

"Tell on me?" Ursala asked.

"About smoking," Jennifer whispered.

"Fuck you," Ursala said. And then her coach was back and she skated away from Jennifer and snapped her gum while she listened to him tell her everything she was doing wrong.

The evil twins were what her mother and she both called Aiden and Nolan now behind their backs. Her mother smiled when she said it, like it was a joke, but Jennifer never did. And her mother still let them come over every morning. Jennifer had to sit with them at her own kitchen table and make lists of rhyming words on the little chalkboards Winter bought for them. She had to take field trips with the evil twins to the Santa Ana Children's Museum and the monkey zoo, and she had to take the free Saturday boat tour with them around Long Beach Harbor to see the oil islands up so close that they looked like nothing special at all anymore.

Winter always came over with the twins, but Patterson usually came over by himself. Sometimes he came to their house when only her mother was home so he could fix things. When Jennifer walked in the front door after her father dropped her back off, Patterson would just be leaving, but first he'd pace around a bit like he might decide to stay after all.

Patterson was nothing like Jennifer's father, who put his feet up on things and left Cheetos bags on the floor of his car. Patterson smelled like soap mixed with Pledge and stood straight and tall like he might salute instead of saying hello. And he paced instead of sitting.

"He's a very busy man," her mother said when she asked why he never sat down, what was wrong with him. "He's got a lot on his mind."

Jennifer had a lot on her mind, too, so she tried to be tolerant about the pacing. *Tolerant* was one of the vocabulary words Winter gave her in March. She had used it on her father. "I am *tolerant* of your messy car," she told him when he'd picked her up on a Saturday morning.

She'd missed almost the entire year of first grade, and her father hadn't noticed. She wondered if she would miss second grade, too, and if he would notice that. If she went back to school, she worried she'd have to repeat first grade, and everyone would think she was stupid. Or maybe she could start in second grade in September with all her old friends. But that might not be good either, because maybe they wouldn't remember her anymore, or she wouldn't know anything and would have to go to the special class that had three teachers but only ten kids.

She wondered if it was really legal what her mother was doing, keeping her home, and if one day the police would come and arrest them both. Sometimes, late at night when she got tired of moving her pillow around so the streetlight could make different shadow shapes on her wall, she invented stories to tell her teacher and friends about her missing year.

In one story, she was in Africa with her father taking pictures of people getting married on lions and giraffes. In another, she was so sick she almost died and had to live at the hospital. And in her favorite story, she'd spent the year training to be an ice skater and almost got to go to the Olympics with Ursala.

Jennifer kept the homeschooling secret from her father, and she kept the secret of Eleanor being her father's girlfriend from her mother. She kept the secret of Patterson coming over by himself to fix things when Winter and the evil twins weren't there from Winter.

No one told her these were secrets and to keep them, but she wasn't stupid. She knew what a secret sounded and felt like, muffled and heavy.

Like Patterson, she had a lot on her mind.

Still, she didn't feel sympathetic to him, *sympathetic* being a vocabulary word from just a week ago. "I am not *sympathetic* to Patterson's pacing around," she told her mother.

"You don't have to be sympathetic. Just be tolerant," her mother said, smiling.

Jennifer didn't smile, even though she understood they were playing a game now with vocabulary words, and she'd started it. None of their games was really a game anymore. They were all about learning something. Even checkers, it turned out, was about logic and math strategies. She'd heard Winter explaining that to her mother while the twins ganged up on her with their red men, yelling *King me!* when they jumped her.

What Jennifer wanted was to get away from Aiden and Nolan and Patterson and Winter. She even wanted to get away from her mother and father, who didn't act the way they were supposed to anymore. Her mother was supposed to worry about what she ate and where she was every minute, and her father was supposed to be fun. But her father wasn't fun anymore, and her mother sometimes slept so late that Jennifer had to make her own breakfast. And her mother didn't even look much like her mother anymore. She was almost as skinny as Winter. There was nowhere on her to cuddle up. And even though Jennifer was seven, sometimes, especially when she was sick with asthma, she still wanted to cuddle.

Winter wasn't coming over, and Jennifer and her mother were both free the morning she decided to leave for Pennsylvania. Her mother had told her the night before when she'd kissed her goodnight that they'd both have the day off. "Winter's taking the boys for their physicals. I think I'll sleep in. How about you?"

"I don't have to go?"

"Don't be silly. They have different insurance. You don't even go to the same pediatrician."

Jennifer nodded. She didn't know what insurance was, but she had learned not to ask too many questions. Ever since her mother had started to homeschool her, the answers she got to her questions were so long, she was almost always sorry she had asked. All that mattered was that she didn't have to go for a checkup with the evil twins, that her mother was sleeping in, and that she would finally have time to sneak away.

For a long time, Jennifer hadn't gotten what she wanted. She hadn't gotten a dog. She hadn't gotten a little brother. No one signed her up for ice skating lessons. And she hadn't gotten to go back to school.

While her mother slept that morning, she got dressed and pulled her first grade backpack out of the closet where it was mixed in with her old shoes. She hadn't opened it since her last day of school in October. And when she opened it now while her mother slept in, she found a bright yellow notice about Picture Day!!! and how much money to bring for it crumbled at the bottom of it. She had missed Picture Day!!! When she used to get notices, she couldn't read them, but she could read this one now, and she thought maybe she had learned something this year even though she didn't go to regular school.

Jennifer thought maybe one of the reasons her mother decided to homeschool her was because she hadn't given her the most important paper of all. Probably the **Picture Day!!!** paper wasn't an important paper, but she smoothed out the notice just in case and left it on her desk.

Jennifer stuffed her mittens in her first grade backpack with two pairs of underwear, her snow hat, and the yellow inhaler she kept on her night table. She pulled her souvenir box from under her bed and took out the walkie-talkie she'd told her dad she lost at the nature center and Ursala's small, pink barrette, which she decided she would give back to her when they got to Pennsylvania and it was too late for her to be mad about it. And she took the little turtle eraser her father bought for her at the aquarium, just in case Jeremy got bored on the long bus ride and needed something to play with. Then she slid the box back under her bed.

She thought about getting the hive medicine out of the bathroom, but the medicine cabinet squeaked when it opened, and she didn't want to wake her mother. Besides, the cap was the kind she couldn't screw open herself even if she did the trick of pushing down hard.

She opened her night table drawer and took out the two twenties her grandmother had tucked inside her last birthday cards, one twenty for each of the past two years. Every year of her life her grandmother put a twenty-dollar bill in her birthday cards. Jennifer would have had a lot more money if she had been smarter when she was younger and hadn't wasted it on toys she couldn't even remember anymore.

When she'd asked her mother how much she would have had, her mother made her count by twenty seven times. But Jennifer couldn't remember the answer anymore, and she didn't feel like counting on a day she had off.

Whenever her mother and father took her to visit her grandmother, it was Christmastime and it was cold. She didn't know how long winter lasted in Pennsylvania, but she hoped it would still be cold in April.

If they still had a TV, Jennifer could put on the Weather Channel, and if she watched long enough, someone would probably say something about Pennsylvania and she could find out. But they'd given the TV away to the Goodwill store after homeschool had started. And even if they still had one, it would be in her mother's bedroom, and if she turned it on, she'd wake her up.

She didn't know if this would be true, but she hoped when she got to her grandmother's house, she could wear her mittens outside where mittens belonged and show Jeremy what snow looked like. And they could both watch Ursala skate on a real frozen lake and take off their mittens to clap when she did spins, so she'd hear them.

"Can Jeremy come with me to Ma and Pa to get ice cream?" Jennifer asked Darla while her mother slept in.

"Ice cream at 9:30?" Darla said. "Sounds like a party to me. Where's your mom? In the car?" She looked out at the empty street.

"I thought we would walk."

"By yourselves?"

"I go there all the time by myself," Jennifer said. This was a lie, but she thought it could be true, so maybe it wasn't a complete lie. Ma and Pa was a little store only three blocks away. Even though she'd never walked there by herself before, she went with her mom when they needed something fast, like when they ran out of sugar right in the middle of making lemonade. It cost more than a regular store so they only got their emergency things there, and they usually drove because they were in a hurry. Jennifer was pretty sure, though, she knew the way if Darla asked her the route they were taking. It was on the same street as the bus stop that she always checked for whenever her dad drove her back home.

"Please, please, please, Mom," Jeremy said.

"Well," Darla said, "I just don't know."

Jennifer heard Darla's phone ring.

"Your mother really lets you walk to Ma and Pa alone?"

"Sure. All the time," Jennifer said.

"Come right back, then," Darla said. "And hold Jennifer's hand!" she shouted to Jeremy as she rushed back inside to catch the phone before it stopped ringing.

"I want ice cream for breakfast like you're having," Jeremy said. "I want my kind to be chocolate." He reached for her hand, and Jennifer walked with him in what she hoped was the direction of the Ma and Pa store.

She hadn't exactly planned on buying him ice cream before they took off on the bus to get Ursala at the skating rink and take her with them to Pennsylvania, but now she saw that Jeremy was counting on it.

"I can't eat real ice cream," she said. "I have allergies, so I get Tofutti."

"I have Tofutti, too," Jeremy said. He squeezed Jennifer's hand, and she squeezed his back. "I have allergies," he said even though this wasn't true.

"I'm going to take very good care of you. Don't worry," she said.

Jennifer found the house with the red door and black shutters that her mother always passed in the car on their emergency trips to the store, and she made the right turn to get to the Ma and Pa store. The Tofutti box in the store's freezer was empty, so she bought two chocolate fudge bars and paid with one of her twenty-dollar bills.

The man behind the counter counted out her change slowly as if he were trying to teach her something, just like her mother and Winter always were. "And that makes sixteen twenty-five. Your change, young lady," he said, laying each bill and the quarter into her palm. She pushed the folded-up money and change deep down into her pants pocket.

Outside the store was a bus stop sign, and Jennifer decided they would get on the bus there instead of the other one she had planned and tell the driver to take them to the skating rink to get Ursala.

She sat next to Jeremy at one of the picnic tables outside in the sun. To keep the sun out of their eyes, they faced the store and the bulletin board with the pictures of missing dogs and ads for things like maids.

She recognized her mother and Winter's business card pinned there. No one called them for their new job where they were supposed to make parties and plan things, but the card was still there, and she felt like Winter and Beth were watching her eat the fudge bar.

Her father thought she made the whole thing up about food allergies, and that her mother started it. That's what he told Eleanor. She heard them talking right in front of her at Eleanor's apartment when they were watching a cooking show on TV full of things Eleanor wanted to make one day that Jennifer couldn't eat.

"I like Tofutti," Jeremy said, chocolate dripping down his face.

"This is chocolate," Jennifer said. "They were out of the Tofutti."

"I like chocolate," he said, and she nodded in agreement.

"Do you like cold weather?" she asked. "Can you imagine ice skating outside?"

Jeremy shook his head *no*, and she hoped he was saying that he couldn't imagine ice skating outside, not that he didn't like cold weather.

Nothing itched yet, and she thought maybe her father was right, that she had made the whole thing up. Maybe in Pennsylvania when she lived with her grandmother and had a little brother and a big sister, nothing would ever itch and she would never get asthma.

Jennifer reached over and wiped Jeremy's chin with a napkin. "Do you like buses?" she asked.

Jeremy nodded. "I like trains," he said.

"Me, too. But there aren't any trains here." She threw their ice cream sticks away in the outside garbage can. "Let's not go home yet, okay?" she said. "Let's go on a bus instead."

Jeremy reached for her hand. His hand was sticky from where the ice cream had dripped, and it stuck to hers a little as she looked both ways and walked him across the street.

UNDERWATER PHOTOGRAPHY

Keith had never shot an underwater wedding before, but he was desperate. He hadn't worked in weeks, and he still hadn't found an apartment despite receiving a second notice from the building management, a redundant but nevertheless threatening Last and Absolutely Final Warning.

Keith had bought a security chain for his office door so a janitor wouldn't be able to surprise him again. He reasoned that, if nothing else, he could at least hear the pull on the chain and look like he was hard at work instead of fast asleep on the couch. But apparently one morning, the janitor had managed to peer in at him asleep without waking him, and he'd been reported to management once again.

When the couple emailed him, telling him they wanted something different, a wedding held underwater and shot in black and white, he'd thought about it for only an hour before typing back his answer.

To explain their very short notice—two weeks—they offered him what amounted to a romantic sob story. They'd met on a snorkeling trip in Waikiki. The groom had proposed underwater on a scuba trip to St. Croix. They wanted their wedding shot underwater, and they *loved* the timeless look of black-and-white film.

They had planned a destination wedding in the Cayman Islands in August and lined up a photographer there, but one by one, friends and relatives began backing out. People couldn't get their passports in time. Plane fares had doubled. Children were too old to travel for free and too young to be left for more than a night or two.

Finally, they decided to forgo their deposit, send out an email cancellation/invitation, and hold their underwater wedding at Diver's Cove in Laguna Beach on a regular Wednesday morning when they might at least see a sea cucumber or two and have the place to themselves. They wondered if Keith would be interested. An instructor would be there to guide him. He wouldn't need scuba certification to shoot the wedding, since they'd be so close to the surface.

Do you have any diving experience? All we need to make our day perfect is you saying "yes"! They wrote before signing both their names to the email.

Often, just the woman wrote to him, but sometimes they signed their inquiries together, the most entangled engaged couples. Keith imagined them hunkered down together over the keyboard, running each sentence by each other.

Although he had no actual diving experience, he typed the word *Yes*, answering only their second question about whether he'd do the wedding. He'd done his share of beach weddings and taken the requisite fake-candid shots of the bride and groom holding hands, walking by the ocean, stopping to kiss, but this would be his first underwater wedding.

Even though he needed this wedding, Keith remembered to make a list of his terms before pushing *send*. Short-term notice required a rate increase of fifteen percent. The couple would be responsible for the cost of renting the additional equipment he would need, including the watertight housing for his camera. And they would have to pay for the wetsuits for both his assistant and him. And since there was no way he could reload his film underwater—and he assumed one of the reasons they had chosen him was because he was a film man, a wedding artist—the number of shots taken during the actual ceremony would have to be limited to thirty-six.

Sounds perfect! They wrote back so quickly that Keith realized he'd asked for far too little. *We're so lucky we found you!*

So here he was, 10:30 on a Wednesday morning in April, still winded from climbing down a steep hill carrying his equipment, standing on the beach, shooting the bridal party and guests as quickly as he could before the overcast morning clouds blew off and the sun glared into his camera lens.

He had considered hiring a different assistant for the day since Eleanor had never caught on to swimming, but she had insisted she'd be fine.

"It'll be good for me," she'd said when he told her about the wedding, "confronting those old swimming fears."

He had wanted to tell her that whether or not it would be good for her wasn't his primary concern. *This is my job*, he thought. *Work*. But he just smiled and said, "Terrific. That's great."

He had to admit that she looked pretty cute in her wetsuit. Their nonworking relationship had slowly deteriorated on a good week into a single weekend date that may or may not come with sleepover privileges depending on Eleanor's whim. Still, after several weddings they had a certain rhythm working together.

While primarily selfish in most aspects of her life, Eleanor had a way of anticipating his needs as a photographer, passing him a roll of film just as he finished his last shot, positioning an umbrella at the right angle to block glare. "Your job is fun!" she said to him once as they left together after a wedding, amorous in the seat next to him, cuddling in beneath his shoulder. "Makes me almost wish I had had a career."

Today, though, she was clearly nervous. The ocean had never been flatter, but she didn't seem reassured by this. Even walking near the water caused her to seize up and look over her shoulder as if perhaps a tsunami were on its way.

There was only a lone surfer out there, and Keith had to keep adjusting his groups of wedding-goers so the surfer didn't ruin his background. He wished the man would just come in already, but instead all he did was paddle over to the right and then slowly float back.

"Asshole," he whispered to himself as the surfer drifted back into view. He moved the mother and father of the bride four steps to the right. He took the mother's glass from her hand with its lipstick imprint on the rim. He was so distracted that he almost left it in the picture. The angle of the sun wasn't as good now, but he snapped several shots anyway while he had the chance.

"Maybe he's enjoying this," the bride said, turning and waving at the man now.

"He's probably one of those people who figures out a way to get into the background of everyone's vacation snapshots," the groom said, laughing.

The mother looked soused and maybe a bit mean, but this couple who had lost their deposit on a wedding in the Cayman Islands were so genuinely happy and good-natured that Keith felt like peeling off the wetsuit they bought him and walking away from the whole thing. Usually, he could see the seams in a relationship, the places that would divide the couple later. And he hated to admit it, but he took a certain satisfaction in privately predicting the timeline of each marriage's eventual demise.

He wondered if he had somehow been able to photograph his own wedding, would he have seen the way his marriage would dissolve? But he'd been as stupid as any groom, standing with Beth under a flower trellis outside the reception hall. They had just bought their house, and they decided to have a small wedding in California, where they'd met in college. Only their immediate families had flown out. The friends and relatives who didn't make it sent them presents that they'd opened a few a day for weeks. Wrapping paper and gift boxes got mixed up with takeout cartons and moving boxes.

They'd laughed and given up trying to keep things sorted, finally sending generic thank-you-for-the-gift notes. Keith set up a tripod, and Beth and he agreed that the thank-you notes were made personal when they included in each a black-and-white photograph of the two of them smiling in front of the mess.

Unaccompanied by anxiety, Beth's disorganization had seemed free-spirited back then, even sexy. He remembered them eating dinners with fondue forks when she accidentally returned the silverware they'd been given instead of the second set of baking dishes. He remembered her underwear strewn around the bedroom. But maybe her worries about her inadequacies had been there all along, even before Jennifer was born. If Keith had shot the wedding himself, maybe he would have seen them and the way they would slowly drive him away.

"Are we ready to go under?" the groom asked, and Keith waited for an answer until he realized the groom was asking him.

"I think I got everyone," he said. "Let's do it."

She wore a wetsuit and would have all the same equipment, but Eleanor wasn't planning to stay under with him. As his assistant, she would be on standby, ready to walk out and get his backup second camera in a watertight housing if he wasn't able to capture the event with the first thirty-six pictures. Although Keith had no experience at all with scuba diving, he had slightly more with underwater photography. He'd taken a class once years ago through the community college that had culminated with the group putting on snorkeling gear and shooting photos of rubber fish in the college's pool.

Now an instructor of some kind was hooking scuba gear onto them both and explaining how to breathe. He remembered the woman giving lessons at the health club where he met Eleanor. He looked at Eleanor, hoping she might be giving him a conspiratorial glance, but she was looking past him at the ocean, focused and squinty and scared, as if she were trying unsuccessfully to stare it down.

"You remember how this all goes, right, dude?" the man said. "Just relax and let the equipment do the work for you. The mistake people make is they fight it, or they get afraid when they hear the sound of their own breathing. But that's all it is. Just the sound of your own breathing."

"Okay," Keith said. "Sounds good."

"You, too, Miss. Just breathe naturally," he said to Eleanor.

"You guys will barely be in over your head," the instructor continued as he adjusted their straps. "Remember, you can always stand up, float up a few feet, and get your bearings if you need to."

"Your phone's ringing again," Eleanor said, turning to him now.

"Should I get it?"

Keith shook his head. It was probably just Beth again. He'd return the call when the job was finished. Lately, she'd been calling him almost daily, often with a small piece of information about Jennifer. She'd tell him how well Jennifer had begun to read or how she'd made her own electrical circuit out of leftover telephone wire. He knew he should be interested, but it all felt insubstantial. He ended up putting the phone down each time feeling like he had missed something or that there was something more important that she had left unsaid.

Maybe the vague nature of their separation was part of the problem for both of them. Keith knew he needed to file divorce papers, make the separation legal, and as soon as he found an apartment and got set up in a way that felt more official, he would begin the process.

But now the bride and groom and a man they had introduced as Minister Bob, all in wetsuits with compressed air tanks, were walking out wearing swim fins. They looked as alien as astronauts. Maybe that's what was next for him, space marriage. Anything to keep a paycheck coming in.

The instructor finished hooking on their compressed air tanks, pulled up their hoods, and helped them adjust the masks around their faces. "Open wide," he said to Eleanor, and Keith watched him stick a mouthpiece between her lips. She handed Keith his camera, sealed in its waterproof housing. He wondered how he'd ever shoot a photo as weighted down as he was, but the instructor was hooking something called a weight belt around him now, telling him that without it, he'd be nearly weightless underwater.

Keith put in his mouthpiece and looked out at the drifting surfboarder through the sheen of his diving mask. Although he'd never been much interested in surfing himself even back in college, when half his friends wouldn't enroll in morning classes because they didn't want to miss the best swells, he found himself envying the surfer's streamlined equipment now. Just a wetsuit and a board. The man glared back at him, and he considered giving him the finger.

Keith felt a hand press on his back—either friendly encouragement or a push, depending on how he chose to interpret it. He decided he might as well try to join in the aggressively good-natured spirit of day and consider it a pat on the back. He turned to Eleanor, who stood shivering in her wetsuit even though the sun was out in full force now. He decided it would take work and time, but he would get her back. When this wedding was over, maybe they'd get a hotel room on beach, a place with a hot tub. Forget about renting an apartment. Just one more month. He gave Eleanor a thumbs-up and together they began their slow walk under.

TEACHER SUPPLIES

When Beth woke up at 10:30, she thought at first she was in huge trouble. On an ordinary weekday morning, Winter and the evil twins would have been here for nearly two hours already. The kitchen table would have been turned into a study table. And Beth would be serving as Winter's assistant teacher, getting out the colored chalk or water-based paints, depending on the lesson plan for that morning. Or, at the very least, she'd be making healthy snacks for break time.

Sometimes Winter sent her out on errands. Beth had to pick up powdered laundry detergent so the kids could make a snow collage, or a bag of raisins from Ralphs to be used as both a reward and as manipulatives for addition and subtraction problems.

Winter had lots of ideas.

Beth had no idea which of her ideas were sound and which were foolish. She spent long hours late at night reading articles about homeschooling and ways of teaching—or not teaching. The more she read, the more she felt confused about the possibilities and contradictions.

She considered talking to Winter about buying a curriculum, maybe one with a money-back guarantee, but she didn't know how to bring it up without insulting her. Besides, she wasn't sure which one to suggest. She suspected she was much more drawn to holistic approaches than Winter was. She leaned toward the curricula that talked about the whole child, even though she worried whether they actually covered enough material. Although she wasn't sure what material they should cover.

When Beth came across an article touting the benefits of combining music and learning, she was stunned that she hadn't even considered this idea before. While she read, the fist that had lodged itself in her throat months ago swelled up. They had no piano in their living room for kids to pound out notes as they learned to read music while they learned to read words, no half-sized violins scattered throughout the house. She'd never even bought Jennifer a simple wooden recorder.

"Education is to light a fire, not to fill a bucket," she read.

It was easier to buy fabric paste to glue buttons onto sock puppets and bags of plastic-coated paper clips from Staples so the kids could build their own human genome chains than to argue that most of the activities Winter came up with seemed either too juvenile or too advanced. Instead of facing how far she was from knowing anything about the right way to homeschool her own daughter, or even whether or not she was doing the right thing at all by trying to homeschool, Beth thought about Patterson while she shopped, wondered what repair emergency might bring him over most quickly after Winter left late in the morning to take the twins home for lunch.

If she was uncertain, Winter made up for this with unbounded confidence in everything she tried. Her word lists, her Styrofoam planetary systems, her field trips to the electric and gas companies. And Beth was relieved to shut up and go buy the raisins.

This morning there would be no running out for materials or hovering behind Winter, waiting to be put to good use. They had the morning off, and Beth felt the way she did as a child when she'd forgotten it was President's Day. A weekday holiday was better than an unexpected snow day. There was no need even to listen to the radio to hear if her school was closing or not.

Beth grew up in Pennsylvania, with seasons, and while she remembered most acutely the claustrophobia of summer and winter, trapped inside by extremes of temperature, she sometimes wondered if she had denied something important to Jennifer. "Let the world be your child's teacher," was a sentence that rang in her head this morning, next to, "Light a fire." But could the world be your teacher when you lived in only a small, sheltered part of it?

Beth sank back into her pillow, imagining Jennifer sinking deeply back into her own pillow in her bedroom down the hall. Before she went to sleep the night before, she'd finished reading the last essay in a collection written by "the true experts" (as the blurb on the back of the book read), homeschooling parents themselves. Now she wasn't sure if this sentence—"Let the world be your child's teacher"—stayed with her because it made good, clear sense or because it had the same cheery rhythm as a familiar military recruitment advertisement.

Maybe she and Jennifer both needed a break from thinking about anything. They could do something really different today, something with no educational value at all. She imagined taking Jennifer to the toy store at the mall, the one that always had the big discount signs, letting her pick out whatever cheap plastic toy she wanted and then buying her french fries and soda for lunch.

"Jennifer," Beth shouted from her bed. "Honey, are you awake yet?"

When she didn't answer, Beth walked down the hall to her room and then down the stairs to look for her. Beth knew she overreacted. Jennifer was always fine in the end. Even when she had to go to the hospital during a particularly bad asthma attack, she was herself again by the time they left. And now Beth promised herself she wouldn't begin to panic until she checked the backyard.

"Jennifer!" she shouted after she found the backyard empty and silent in the hollow midweek way that she experienced only when Jennifer used to be in public school. Still, she wasn't truly panicking yet, and she felt oddly proud of herself. She was doing the right thing, yelling. Anyone would be worried by now. Her daughter might be nearby and not know Beth was even looking for her.

She remembered how Jennifer had loved to hide when she was a toddler, so she stopped yelling and did a methodical walk through the house, opening up each closet and checking under long coats and piles of sweaters that had found their way to the floor. "Ollie, ollie oxen free!" she called.

Beth walked out the front door and peered down the block, where Jennifer often played hopscotch or handball or hide-and-seek with Darla's children, all of them trained to be careful to watch for the occasional car on the street, which suddenly felt too quiet. "Jennifer!"

Maybe, she thought, she'd screwed up and Keith had gotten her. But that didn't make any sense. As far as he knew, Jennifer was in school today. She called his cell phone anyway. Listened to it ring. It was a Wednesday, midweek, no holiday, no reason to be home.

It made more sense that Jennifer was still asleep, that this was one of those awful dreams about losing her, the kind of dream Beth was so afraid of having that she'd stayed awake for hours each night when Jennifer was little. But in those dreams, a fault had split the earth open right under their house and sucked in an asthmatic Jennifer, and there was nothing she could do. Now Jennifer was missing, but the house was whole, and it was Beth who felt her lungs seize up.

"Aren't they back yet?" Darla said, outside now and running down her front steps. "I thought they'd be back by now, too. Shoot. I knew I should have told them not to linger."

"Back?"

"From Ma and Pa," Darla said. "It must have been over a half hour already."

"Ma and Pa?" Beth said. "What are you talking about?"

"My God," Darla said. "You have no idea, do you?"

Beth felt Darla look her over. She stared down at her bare feet and legs. She was wearing only a nightshirt. Her toenails looked yellowed in the sunlight. She should polish them, she thought. When had she last polished them?

"Jennifer said she had your permission," Darla said. "She said she'd walked there by herself lots of times. She just wanted to take Jeremy for ice cream."

"Ice cream?" Beth said. Jennifer couldn't eat ice cream. And she couldn't go to Ma and Pa by herself. What was Darla thinking? What was wrong with her?

"I'll get them," Beth said. "I'm sorry. I had no idea. It's all my fault. Everything." She could see now what the problem was. All of Keith's telling her not to worry so much was backward advice. All wrong. The problem was she hadn't worried nearly enough, and she hadn't worried about enough things.

Beth took off running. She felt her feet pound into the sidewalk. It would have been faster, she realized too late, to get her keys, get in her car. But she was halfway there. She had an image of herself, a crazy lady running in her nightshirt down the block.

She turned at the intersection, hoping Jennifer remembered the right spot, where to turn. Before all the cars came whipping by. My God. All the cars.

They'll be sitting right there in front of the store at a picnic bench, she willed herself to think, as she ran the last block. *Later, after I calm down so I'm not yelling at her, Jennifer and I will have a long mother-daughter talk about this.*

But the picnic tables were empty, and Beth ran by them into the store. "Did you see two children?" she asked. "Were two children here by themselves?"

"A little while ago," the man behind the counter said, "some kids came in for ice cream. I thought I recognized the girl. She's yours, right?"

Beth held onto the counter. She'd seen movies where people were told to sit down before bad news was delivered, and now she understood. "They were here?" she said. "Now they're gone?"

"Do you want me to call someone?" he asked. "I'm sure they're on their way home."

"Do you really think so?" she said. But she knew it wasn't true. Jennifer knew only one route. They always went the same way. She reached for her pants pocket. But she'd left the house wearing only a nightshirt. She didn't have a pocket or a cell phone or shoes or her daughter. "Help me," she said.

"Use my phone," someone said behind her. She didn't know anyone was there, but a cell phone was in her hand now, and she was pushing buttons, and Keith's phone was ringing and then his voice mail picked up.

"She's missing," Beth said. She wanted to yell, but her voice was quiet. Words were barely coming out. "Jennifer," she said and hung up.

Darla was there now, and Beth and Darla were being rushed into the back seat of a car, and people were calling the police, and Beth heard sirens, and she made herself focus. Darla was crying, and people were asking them questions. About time, about what the Missing Children were wearing. Beth knew she needed to help Darla, but she couldn't talk and she didn't know any of the answers anyway. "I was asleep," she finally said. "I was sleeping in today. We were taking the day off."

"From what?" Darla was yelling. "Taking the day off from what! What do you do all day anyway now? I should never have shut your stupid dog-sitting business down. All day long those damn dogs barking and barking. But at least Jennifer wanted to stay home for once."

Beth felt as if she were falling back to sleep again right here in the back seat of someone's car with Darla sitting next to her screaming. She would talk to her daughter about scaring everyone. Keith would, too. She'd have to tell him about the homeschooling part first. It would be a relief, finally telling him. And then they would sit down at the table in the backyard. And, after everyone was safe and everything was back to normal, they would talk to Jennifer together.

But Darla was screaming at her now about dogs and barking and the children missing and how all of it, all of it, was Beth's fault. And Beth couldn't speak because maybe she was awake and maybe she wasn't. She opened her mouth but nothing came out.

Where did Jennifer take Jeremy? Would Jennifer get in a stranger's car? Would she? Would she? She should have been at school! None of this would ever have happened. You're crazy. Those goddamned dogs. I should have known. Look what you did. Look at you.

RELIGIOUS STUDIES

Patterson thought if he could just find his way back to surfing, if God would plant his hand firmly on his shoulder one more time as he rode a wave into shore, the sun rising in the distance and the fog lifting to reveal the full mystery of the world around him, he might find his way back to Winter.

Not that she'd actually noticed he'd left her.

But really, why should she? He hadn't left physically. He still shared a bed with his wife, made love to her when she sidled up against him under the covers, kissed her goodbye each morning, and left his coffee cup in the kitchen sink when he went to work.

It was during the day that he took most of his risks. He made excuses to leave, many of them involving Winter or the twins, and then got on the freeway and drove to Beth's house for what he knew was a bogus emergency of one kind or another. The rest of the time, it was only his thoughts that were elsewhere.

And even if Winter never noticed, he wondered if his infidelity was about to be pointed out to her. His homeschooler blackmailer had let him go, fired him from his job of rebuilding his house after only four Saturdays. David had done it cheerfully enough, over the phone, telling him he'd broken down and hired an entire crew of workers. But

Patterson was waiting for the catch. Had he really been freed up?

Winter was after him to decide about Texas, now that it was official. She had adjusted quickly to the idea of a big new house, had already started calling the twins her cowboys. He couldn't imagine leaving Beth, even though he knew he should take the offer, that it made mature, good sense to take his family while he still had one, and leave with the company he worked for while he still had a job.

Again last night, after she put the kids to bed, Winter asked him what he planned to do.

"You know my vote," she said, staring at him hard across their living room.

"What about our lives here?"

"We'll take our lives with us. What couldn't we take that really mattered?"

"What about your homeschool group?" he asked.

"What group? You mean Beth. I do all the lesson plans. I map out the field trips. Every single home-business idea is mine. Beth's got to learn what to do without me one day anyway."

Patterson felt his shoulders tighten at the mention of Beth's name, but, as usual, Winter seemed oblivious. He thought about bringing up her latest home business, a venture that, in truth, he could barely remember, and how difficult it might be to move it to Texas. But he knew this was a sore spot. Before they'd decided to homeschool, she'd been dead set on going back to work, and he didn't want the conversation to get sidetracked into a lament about the real job she might have had by now.

"What about my surfing?" he said, feeling foolish even as the sentence left his mouth.

"By all means," she said, opening up a magazine and ending the conversation. "Absolutely. Let's base our decision around that."

As if to prove a point, now here he was, sitting on a surfboard in his wetsuit, late for work, God's hand nowhere near his shoulder and no good waves in sight. He'd decided to try a new beach this morning, to head farther south to Laguna to a spot his old instructor had taken them to once for a field trip.

But the water was flat here, too. And he wasn't completely sure he'd even come to the right beach. He couldn't remember the exact place. Somewhere off Cliff Drive in Laguna. That's all he remembered for certain.

Earlier that morning, he'd slowed down as he passed Shaw Cove with its familiar-looking, understated residential entrance, a small sign with various warnings. Worried about getting a ticket for some kind of parking infraction he wasn't aware of, he kept driving and parked at a little stand of meters. He was closer to the entrance of Diver's Cove now, another understated sign. He carried his board over and then peered off to his right, at Fisherman's Cove. He couldn't remember where they'd surfed, having followed his instructor with the thirteen-year-old boys in his class. Patterson studied the sign by Diver's Cove, with its warnings about scuba divers and surfers avoiding each other. SCUBA DIVE AND SURF WITH A BUDDY he read. OBSERVE WATER ETIQUETTE.

The cove was bordered by rocks he didn't remember. But he'd already parked his car and filled the meter, so he kept walking down the paved path of the cliff anyway, his surfboard tight under his arm, hoping he might stumble across a decent surf break.

Without a watch, it was hard to know the exact time, but he knew he'd been floating on his board too long. He should have at least called in to work by now, made up some story about a kid's earache or a car problem or at least miserable traffic. But all he had with him was his car key, sealed tight in an internal pocket built into his wetsuit. His cell phone was in his car with his briefcase and work clothes, and the effort to hike back up the steep hill and get it felt overwhelming.

He was alone in the ocean, apparently the only surfer foolish enough to even look for a wave, but a small group was gathering on the shore as the morning fog lifted. A woman wore a white wetsuit that emphasized her hips and breasts. She carried a bouquet of flowers, and the sound of her laughter moved across the water and reached him.

Several other people—all men, and one small woman or maybe an older child—were wearing wetsuits. But the rest of the group was dressed for a fancy, daytime event. A woman was in a white suit. Men were in Hawaiian shirts and blazers. A small child, about the size of Jennifer, wore a pale pink dress.

A beach wedding.

A photographer in a wetsuit was setting up equipment, and the child-woman in a wetsuit handed him a tripod. The photographer arranged people in various groups, the wetsuited bride and groom, who looked like slick, upright seals, at the center of each photo.

How could people make such a farce out of marriage? He knew he wasn't in any position to judge, but he disliked this wedding on principle. His own wedding had been traditional, serious business, the way weddings should be.

Still, where had he ended up? Late for work, sitting on a surfboard at a waveless diving beach, hoping a woman who wasn't his wife would call him after lunch with a fake emergency so he could risk his job and his family once again by going to her.

So he could cheat on his wife with a woman he hoped would call him to fix a toaster when he was in bed with his own wife? So he could work four consecutive Saturday mornings remodeling another man's house and get outed anyway?

Patterson wanted to come in now. The beach wedding had ruined his mood entirely. The morning was shot, and he was late for work. The last thing he wanted was to end up in the background of these photos, so he paddled as far as he could to the right, away from the group.

He knew what he had to do, God's hand on his shoulder or not. His cell phone was locked in his car, and he had to get back to it quickly before he changed his mind. Patterson sat on his board and looked over his shoulder in vain for a wave that might take him in to shore.

TRANSFER CLASSES

Two teenage boys without helmets skateboarded up and down in front of the bus stop where Jennifer and Jeremy waited. Jennifer wanted to say something to Jeremy about how he should always wear his helmet, but she didn't want to be rude and say it in front of the teenage boys, so she saved it for later.

When the bus pulled up to the curb, the boys flipped their skateboards up under their arms, and Jennifer took Jeremy's hand and walked with him up the steps behind the boys. Jeremy was three and good at steps now, but he still had to pay attention on them, so she held onto his hand tight in case he slipped.

"You want to hold my board for me, little brother?" one of the boys said to Jeremy as he dug in his pocket for money for the bus driver. The other boys laughed, and Jennifer hoped Jeremy didn't think they were laughing at him, even though maybe they were.

"Ninety cents for you, Missy," the bus driver said. "The little guy is still free."

She pulled all the change up out of her pocket, careful not to take the dollars out, too. She couldn't remember how much change the man at the store said he gave her, and it would take too long to count it now, so she handed all the quarters and nickels to the driver, and he shooed her on. The bus wasn't crowded, but there were other people in some seats, so she chose two empty seats next to each other in the back.

"You can have the window," she told Jeremy. She looked around for a seat belt to latch over him, but there weren't any. She remembered now from a field trip in kindergarten to a farm that there weren't any seat belts on that bus either.

On that trip, the children were supposed to sit up straight just as if they had seat belts, and they had to be quiet, too, so they didn't distract the bus driver. Jennifer decided that this bus driver looked like a very careful, slow driver, so she let Jeremy sit on his knees so he could see out the window better.

Jennifer had seen a movie once where the bus driver announced things, like the names of stops, but this one just opened the door to let people on and off without saying anything. She hoped she'd see the ice rink and know when to get off, but nothing looked familiar and she wasn't sure.

A man in the seat across the aisle was reading a thick book and underlining in the same kind of yellow highlighter pen that Winter used to mark vocabulary words in their sentences. He looked to Jennifer like an important person who might know things, so she decided to ask him where to get off for the skating rink.

"What's the skating rink's name?" he asked.

Jennifer couldn't remember the name. "It's near the Walmart," she said. "Next to the bowling alley."

"You have to transfer buses," the man said. "At Ximeno."

She wanted to ask more questions, but she didn't know which ones to ask. She didn't know what he meant at all. She thought maybe she'd start to cry if she tried to talk, so she turned around and looked straight at the seat in front of her.

"I live kind of out that way," the man said. "I'll show you when we get off. Just follow me."

Jennifer remembered about not talking to strangers unless it was very important, but this was important. Someone had written something on the back of the seat in front of her with a black marker. The writing looked like a picture and a word put together, and she couldn't understand what it said.

"I like the bus," Jeremy said. "I like when the doors open."

Jennifer felt her stomach getting hot and itchy, and she wished she'd brought the hive syrup even though she couldn't open the bottle herself. Maybe it would be okay to ask a stranger to open it for her. She tried not to scratch and to concentrate on taking good care of Jeremy instead.

"Look at the trees," she said. "Those are palm trees and that's a lemon tree." Jennifer leaned over next to him and pointed out the window. "Where my grandmom lives, the trees are different. Sometimes there's ice on her trees and the ice makes the branches look like they're made out of glass."

"Oh," Jeremy said.

Now she felt the top of her legs getting hot, too, and she knew they were getting ready to itch. She wished they hadn't been out of Tofutti. Jeremy didn't have any allergies except maybe one to cats. His mother didn't know yet for sure.

"This is the Ximeno transfer stop," the man across the aisle from them said. He was sliding his big book into a backpack and hoisting the thing on.

Jennifer took Jeremy's hand and followed the man to the doors closest to them and down the steps.

"We can wait right there," the man said. He pointed to a bench and Jennifer put Jeremy on the side of her away from the man, and the three of them sat down.

"It shouldn't be long," the man said, but even so he got out his book and started reading again. "Big test tomorrow," he said, although she hadn't asked him anything. "Grad school is a bitch. Don't let anyone tell you otherwise."

She followed close behind the man onto the bus when it came because, even though he used bad language, she could tell he knew a lot about buses and where they went and the way things were supposed to work.

This time she handed the bus driver a dollar bill because her change was all gone, and he handed her back one dime. Her mother said today was a day off, but there was a math takeaway problem in her head as she walked with Jeremy down the bus aisle.

The seat across from the man was taken, so they sat behind him. She looked at the back of his neck. He had a small tattoo of some kind of bird, a bat maybe. She wanted to touch it to see if that part of his skin felt different, but she put her hands in her lap and kept them to herself. She wondered if everyone in grad school had tattoos on the back of their necks and what exactly grad school was and if she would ever go there or if her mother would homeschool her for that, too.

"You like my tat?" he said, turning around. "It's cool. I can feel when people are looking it. It's kind of a sixth sense I have."

"Is it a bat?" Jennifer said.

"You got it," he said. "My girlfriend did it. She's a tattoo artist. Down in Sunset Beach. Cuts hair, too. Gave herself a tat on her thigh of a lioness. Mouth open."

"Did it hurt?" Jennifer said. "The bat?"

"Shit, yeah," the man said, turning back around in his seat.

Jennifer thought she might get a tattoo of an ice skater on the back of her neck one day, even though it would hurt. And she'd wear her hair in a high ponytail so anyone sitting behind her on a bus would see it.

"I have to go potty," Jeremy said.

"I am sympathetic," she said, one of Winter's big vocabulary words coming out of her mouth now. "But you have to wait. Can you be a big boy and wait, Jeremy?"

"I don't have diapers," he said.

"You're three," she said. "You're a big boy. Aren't you?"

Jeremy did something with his head that might have been a *yes* or might have been a *no*, but she decided not to ask him which it was and just hoped very hard it was a *yes*.

This bus was louder than the first one and bumpier, and she told Jeremy to sit up straight and not to sit on his knees this time to look out the window.

The man with the tattoo on the back of his neck stood up with his backpack to get off the bus, and Jennifer said, "Wait."

"This isn't you yet," he said. "Stay on until the end, the last stop. Don't worry. It's all good."

The man with the tattoo on the back of his neck got off the bus, and Jennifer watched him walk away down the street. Her legs were itching hard, all the way down to her feet, and she felt like crying now that he was gone, even though she didn't know him very well at all.

A fire truck and an ambulance sped by the bus, and Jeremy got excited and pressed his face to the window. He forgot to sit up straight and still, and Jennifer decided not to remind him. Instead she looked out the window, too. She didn't know this part of town or if they were in the same town or a different one now. When she concentrated on the buildings she didn't recognize, she didn't think as much about how hot and itchy she was.

When the bus driver yelled, "End of the line!" she remembered about getting off at the last stop. "Time to get off," she said to Jeremy.

He stood up and walked behind her down the steps in the back of the bus behind the rest of the people who got off there.

"Do you still have to go potty?" she asked, looking around for the ice rink. She remembered that upstairs at the rink the boy's bathroom was right across from the girl's. There was the picture of the boy skater wearing the scarf on the door instead of the word *Boys*. But maybe she'd just take him in with her to the girl's room. Probably he wouldn't care since he was only three. And then she could help him and make sure he remembered to wash his hands with warm water and soap.

"No," he said.

Jennifer looked at him and saw that the front of his shorts was all wet. Lauren called him a baby when he wet his pants. She was a mean sister and didn't deserve him the way Jennifer did. "It's okay," Jennifer said. "It was an accident."

Jeremy smiled and took her hand. "You got bumps on your hands," he said.

The hives had moved all around, the way they did when she tried to hide them for too long. She took off her backpack, unzipped it, got out her mittens and put them on. "There," she said. "All better now."

Jennifer breathed in and out hard, listening for a crackle, but she didn't hear one, so she kept her inhaler in her backpack and zipped it back up.

She wished the man with the tattoo who knew so much was there so she could ask him where the ice rink was, which direction to walk.

Some new people were waiting for a bus across the street now, so she waited for the light and walked Jeremy over to them.

"Excuse me," she said to a lady who sat with her pocketbook in her lap and her hands over it. Jennifer remembered that the man knew the Walmart and thought maybe other grown-ups did, too. "Where's Walmart?"

"Where's your mama?" the lady asked, looking up at Jennifer suspiciously. "She working? You supposed to meet her for lunch or something?"

Jennifer nodded, which wasn't the same thing as telling a complete lie, and the lady pointed down the street. "See it?" the lady said. "You be careful now, crossing the street, you two."

They walked past a McDonalds and Jeremy said, "Please, Jennifer, please!"

Jennifer took him in and ordered french fries and water. "Soda is very bad for you," she told him. "It's all sugar and chemicals."

"Check you out," said the girl who took their order.

Jennifer didn't know if she was supposed to say something back or not, so she took her mitten off for a minute so she could reach in her pocket for money. She gave the girl a five-dollar bill, stuffed the change back and put her mitten back on to hide the bumps. She could see for herself now how you could spend a lot of money without even thinking about it. That's what her mother always said whenever they went anywhere.

It was airconditioned inside, and she tried to eat a french fry with her mittens on, but the fuzz came off the mittens onto the french fry. She took her mittens off and put her hands in her lap quickly after she ate so Jeremy wouldn't be scared of her bumps.

"Next we go to your grandmom's house," he said. "Where all the ice trees are."

Jennifer nodded. He remembered everything. If Jeremy were home-schooled, he was so smart he'd probably be doing kindergarten work by now. She put her mitten back on and let Jeremy finish up the french fries by himself because he looked very hungry. "That's right," she said, "but first we have to get Ursala."

"Right," he said. "First Ursala."

ABNORMAL PSYCHOLOGY

David decided Deborah was still capable of taking him by surprise. When he chopped off his daughters' hair, he thought she'd be furious. He didn't know she'd be sad. And he certainly hadn't expected her to cry. He hadn't seen her cry in years, but there she was, standing in their bug-infested, ripped-open kitchen, still in her business suit, her briefcase in her hand, thick, silent tears running down her face.

"My God," she'd said. "Look at you, at all of you."

The girls stood close to David. Even little Katie didn't go running to her weeping mother.

"I look Eastern European," Madeline said.

"My God," Deborah said. "What have I done?"

"We did it," Emily said. "You didn't do anything."

"We like us," Katie said. "Don't you like us?"

"My God," Deborah said, and she dropped her briefcase on the kitchen floor and walked away, back toward the master bedroom.

David told the girls not to worry. He set them up on the couch, found a cartoon on television, and told them he'd be back soon.

Deborah was under the covers shivering, fully dressed still in her suit. She'd come home and cried like this after she'd taken the bar, certain that she'd failed. Then, he'd crawled in bed with her and comforted her by smoothing her hair away from her face. He'd kissed her, his hand moving down her back and into the space where her jeans pulled away from her waist. Back then, he knew how to comfort her. Now he only seemed to know how to cause her pain.

"It's my fault," he said, standing by the bed. "Don't punish the girls."

She sat up in bed, pulled a pillow up over her chest. Her face was mottled, but she'd stopped crying. Her eyes moved over the split-open ceiling, the hole in the wall where David had intended to expand the closet. "We need help, don't we?"

David nodded. He thought about mentioning a marriage counselor he'd met at a recent homeschool get-together, a beach clean-up morning. He'd liked the woman instinctively, with her loose, peasant-style shirt, floppy sun hat, and slightly husky voice, and he thought Deborah would like her, too.

His wife looked sexy, crying in their bed, her suit jacket still on. He wanted to touch her, unbutton her shirt, reach his hand inside, but it had been too long since he'd done this. They touched at night, when the house was dark, the girls asleep. And they hadn't touched at all since he'd smashed in the ceiling over their bed weeks before.

His wife was already on the phone, making a call.

He didn't know what kind of help line she could possibly be calling. He was always on the other side of these phone calls. Now, here he was, the cause of the problem, shaved raw, his house split open, his daughters huddled in front of the television alone in the living room. "Yes. Tell me about your lines of credit," she said. "What can you tell me about your loan products?"

A week later, a crew of El Salvadoran construction workers were hard at work putting their house back together, an exterminator scheduled for the following week, when the holes in the walls would be patched up. And David and the girls were on their way to the Wednesday-afternoon Homeschool Ice Skating Day. At first, he felt that he should work with the men, but his Spanish was only good enough to allow him to ask questions, not understand the answers. And he wasn't sure what their hearty laughs were about when he shrugged and walked away. So instead he'd taken to supplying them with the occasional pizza, periodically complimenting them on what he hoped was good work.

It was certainly better work than he was capable of doing. He knew that much. And it was a relief not to have Patterson, with his slamming hammer and macho silence, around on Saturday mornings anymore.

He'd even relented on the exterminator after the cockroaches began to feast on the lemon and cucumber peels the girls and he left out to ward off the ants. And at least one mouse had showed up to eat the mint leaves left out to discourage the cockroaches.

With the problems of the house taken largely out of his hands and the money supply loosened up, he'd begun taking the girls out for lunch again. The four of them once even surprised Deborah at her office in Cerritos and drove her to the Towne Center for an Indian buffet. She'd smiled while they ate vegetable curry and discussed what they'd learned about India and its reluctance to abandon its caste system. David had the sense that they had entered a new phase as a family, one that felt oddly like dating, with all five of them on their best behavior.

All the girls but little Katie had permanently abandoned their construction hats after Deborah and he had hired an actual construction crew. And now, on the way to the Ice Palace, only Katie wore hers. Madeline was bare headed, her off-kilter Eastern European hairdo sprayed on one side with temporary orange hair dye.

He was glad Emily had chosen to wear her stocking cap to the rink. Although he still thought she was striking with her crew cut—and even Deborah had taken to it, stroking first David's head and then Emily's for luck before she left for work each morning—he wasn't in the mood for the stares and questions the haircut provoked in people. *No, she didn't donate her hair so some poor child might finally have a wig.* Worse were the stares, the questions that hardly anyone dared to ask. *No, she didn't have cancer. No, she hadn't had surgery for a brain tumor.*

"I'm hungry," Madeline said as they drove past McDonalds.

"You're always hungry," Emily said. "I want to skate. We only have two hours of free skate left, right, Dad?"

David nodded. "Let's compromise. Hungry ducklings can hit the machines as hard as they want at the rink today. All limits off. All healthy eating rules suspended."

"Yeah!" Katie said. "I want Sweet Tarts! I want Sour Skittles!"

David pulled into the parking lot, past the McDonalds and Walmart. The whole suburban landscape was what he was up against. Lately, despite his many political objections, he'd been tempted to stop at Walmart and finally check it out. Other homeschoolers bragged routinely about the deals they got on laundry detergent, apple juice, and even kids' bicycles, apparently oblivious to the greedy corporate culture they where perpetuating.

David had always tried to shop locally, but he wondered if anyone in Southern California even noticed the difference. His house was full of construction workers, most probably illegal immigrants who were being paid less than minimum wage under the table by their contractor, a man who, after their initial two-hour meeting, showed up once a day to point out to the workers their mistakes and then drive off in his gleaming white truck.

In college, David had skipped classes to protest the working conditions of Mexican migrant grape pickers, and now this, in his own house. Life suddenly seemed full of compromises he'd never considered making before. Next week, their house would be blasted with toxic pesticides. Letting his daughters fill up on junk food from vending machines seemed almost reasonable.

He parked the car and emptied the change out of his pockets, handing it all to Katie. "You divide it up, honey. Give your sisters the same amount you get."

"She's so slow!" Emily said.

"Give her a chance. She's not slow. She's younger than you."

"One quarter for you," Katie said, handing one to Madeline. "One quarter for you," she said, handing one to Emily.

Her counting and sorting did feel slow, but he smiled at Katie in a way he hoped was encouraging. He felt the afternoon sun gleaming down on his stubbly head. Later, he'd have a sunburn. He should have worn a baseball cap.

Inside the rink, the girls ran ahead to get their snacks and rental skates while David paid their admission. He saw Beth's daughter walking up the stairs to the bathroom holding a little boy's hand and what looked like a walkie-talkie in her other hand. For a minute, he wondered if she had stolen the one he'd lent her that day at the nature center but quickly dismissed the thought. He wanted to call up the stairs after her, but he had the distinct feeling he'd frighten her if he did. She might not even recognize him if she turned around.

He walked over to the rink and stared out at the ice. He climbed up the bleachers and settled himself into a middle bench seat. His girls were already out there, Emily's stocking hat flying out behind her, Katie and Madeline trailing just behind in her wake.

He hadn't spotted Beth yet, but he was glad to know she was here somewhere. Although he'd seen her just over a week ago when he'd stopped at her house on the way to getting the girls' haircuts, the visit had been unsatisfying and furtive. He planned to really talk to them both at the rink today, find out what was happening in their lives. Maybe he could help.

"Dad!" Emily yelled. "What's wrong? Come skate with us."

He decided he would just sit up in the bleachers for once. He shook his head. "You girls have fun," he said. "I want to watch you today." He was in the market for a new perspective, and he figured he might as well start now.

ROLE MODELING

"This is kind of like her office," Jennifer said, walking with Jeremy up the stairs in the skating rink. "When Ursala's not skating, this is where you can find her."

Jennifer felt the catch in her throat. She pushed her words out in quick bursts between the catches. She didn't want to scare Jeremy, but she was beginning to feel breathless and dizzy, the way she always did when her asthma first started up.

They'd walked in without paying after waiting for the ticket seller to notice them. But the woman never even looked down. She just took money from the next people in line instead. Jennifer wanted to set a good example and didn't want Jeremy to think that sneaking into places was okay. But she was happy to hold onto some more of her money. She didn't know how much bus tickets to Pennsylvania were going to cost. And it seemed fair that they didn't pay since they weren't even going to skate.

The hives on her arms had gone down, but her belly still felt hot and itchy. She pulled her shirt down low and held tight to Jeremy so he wouldn't get lost. She'd taken the walkie-talkie out of her backpack and held tight to it, too. If she got sicker, she'd press the button the way David had shown her and someone would come rescue Jeremy.

"It's the girl's room, but it's okay if you come in with me," Jennifer said. She breathed in fast and hard to get enough air for the rest of the sentence. "Because you're still young enough, even though you're a boy."

Jeremy nodded and held tight to her.

The bathroom smelled smoky when they pulled the door open, and Jennifer tried not to breathe too much so she wouldn't get sicker. "Ursala's here, I think," she whispered to Jeremy. "She smokes even though smoking is bad and she shouldn't."

"I have to pee," he said, and Jennifer took him into a stall and helped him with his shorts. Jennifer saw that they had almost dried in the front where he'd wet them a little while ago. She was happy because only a very bad babysitter would have let him walk around in wet shorts. But Jennifer didn't have any shorts to change him into. She wished she'd thought to bring clothes for Jeremy, too. She'd have to get her grandmom in Philadelphia to buy him some when they got there. Maybe even before they went skating.

Jennifer flushed the toilet for Jeremy and opened the stall door. Ursala was there now, leaning over the sink, looking in the mirror and pushing at a spot on her forehead.

"Fucking zit," Ursala said. She looked at Jennifer in the mirror and then turned around and looked at her head-on. "Take a picture," she said. "It lasts longer."

"Ursala," Jennifer said. "Jeremy and I both think you're the best skater ever."

"Whatever," Ursala said. "Skating's boring. I'm into hip-hop now, or I would be if anyone would let me."

Jennifer nodded. "Me, too," she said even though she wasn't sure what hip-hop was. She hoped Ursala didn't totally hate skating and would still want to skate on an actual outdoor frozen pond.

"You're all sunburned and messed-up looking," Ursala said.

Jennifer put her hand on her cheek. Her mitten smelled like french fries. She could feel her cheek's heat through it. She was glad Ursala was blocking the mirror because she didn't want to look at how ugly her allergies had made her.

"I want to go now," Jeremy said. "I want my mommy."

Jennifer looked at him. He was about to cry, she could see. She should have been paying more attention. Her vocabulary word, *sympathetic*, was still in her head. As soon as she told Ursala about her plan, she'd focus on Jeremy again. "We're going to Philadelphia to my grandmom's, and we're going to skate on a real frozen lake, and we want you to come," Jennifer said all at once before her breath ran out.

"Sounds like a party," Ursala said. She sprayed peppermint breath mist into her mouth and walked toward the ladies' room door.

Jennifer grabbed Jeremy's hand and followed her, but instead of walking toward the exit after she came down the stairs, Ursala sat down on a bench and put her skates back on.

"You have to come to Pennsylvania, too," she said.

"That's sweet but truly fucked up," Ursala said. "I don't even know you."

"It's part of our plan," Jennifer said. One of the boy-girls sat down on the bench and began tightening a skate. Jennifer could hear her breath, fast and hard from skating. The sound covered up her wheezing. She wore a long stocking cap with a pom-pom hanging off the end. The girl finished with her skate and pulled her hat off by the pom-pom and stuffed it in her jacket pocket. "It's crazy hot out there," she said, "once you get moving."

Jennifer saw that the boy-girl was almost bald, that the places on her head that used to have hair were now all prickly looking, like her father's chin and cheeks when he didn't shave in the morning. Even though her hair was missing, the boy-girl didn't seem to mind. She still had her same face, and Jennifer remembered she was the middle one, Emily, who knew everything about bugs.

"I know you," Emily said. "You're the one with the mom."

Jennifer nodded even though she wasn't sure exactly what Emily meant about being the one with the mom. "You have the dad," she said.

"He's just watching today," Emily said. "Up there." She pointed at the bleachers. "Where's your skates? Only an hour left." She pushed herself up off the bench. "I didn't know you had a brother."

Jennifer wanted to say something back about how she didn't really have a brother but she wished she did. She wanted to tell her she was taking Jeremy and Ursala if she decided to come with them to see real ice and real snow and skate on a real pond. She looked over at the spot where Ursala had been, but she was gone now, already walking toward the rink, her trainer there next to her, the two of them laughing together like they were friends and maybe Ursala didn't really hate skating completely.

Something was happening inside Jennifer's throat now, and she couldn't find the place where it made a catch to talk around it. She wanted to yell at Ursala to come back, not to forget about the real ice and the real snow. She wanted to tell her that she had her barrette in her backpack and she'd give it to her once they got to Pennsylvania. But no matter how hard she tried, she couldn't talk at all, even all at once. She pushed the button on the walkie-talkie and tried to shout into it. *Help me*, she thought, but no words came out of her mouth.

"What's her problem?" someone said, and Jennifer couldn't feel Jeremy's hand anymore when she tried to squeeze it, and she couldn't tell if her eyes were open because she couldn't see anymore either.

She thought Jeremy's name as loud as she could. Maybe he'd hear that, and he'd stop crying. She could still hear, and he was loud now, crying for her, and she hoped he wasn't wetting his pants again. She wanted him to stop being afraid because she was there to take care of him. She heard the walkie-talkie hit the ground and felt herself falling down backward off the bench, like she was falling through the air from so high she might as well have been flying. And it hardly hurt at all when her head hit the floor.

REFLEXOLOGY

When a wave finally materialized that was big enough to carry him to shore, Patterson didn't even try to stand up. Too many days of a flat ocean had screwed up his reflexes, and the muscles in his arms felt flabby with lack of use. He rode in on his belly like a little kid, not even bothering to steer himself away from the small wedding party.

Half of the wedding-goers had waded into the water, women holding their dresses up high in one hand as they splashed out a few feet from shore, men with their pants legs rolled up. With the ceremony itself happening underwater, the group in the water laughed and squinted down. But this was Southern California, not Fiji, and Patterson doubted they could see much through the murk of the Pacific Ocean.

If he'd been invited to this wedding, Patterson would have stayed with the group on the sand, drinking his own tall glass of whatever it was they were consuming.

"Hey, come join us for a drink," a woman shouted as he carried his board under his arm out of the ocean.

"The creature from the black lagoon himself," she said, handing him just the kind of tall, wet glass he had in mind. "You know, you nearly ruined all our shots by floating around out there."

Patterson took a large sip of orange juice spiked with something. And then another sip. He looked up to thank the woman, maybe join in her spirit and make a little joke about the drink taking the edge off an otherwise ruined, crappy morning, but she'd already moved back to the party. Not knowing what to do with his empty glass, he set it on the sand.

When he stood up, his head buzzed from alcohol, not an entirely wholesome feeling at what couldn't have been much later than 10 a.m.

"Hey, let me borrow that, man!" someone said, grabbing Patterson's surfboard from under his arm.

"Wait," he said, but the man had already taken off toward the water in his slacks and Hawaiian shirt, paddling out over a set of small, choppy waves. "What the hell."

"I heard she can't swim." It was the same woman who had handed him the drink, someone's mother, he guessed, a well-preserved, sunburned sixtysomething in a white suit with matching white lines etched around her eyes and mouth.

"Then why get married underwater?" Patterson asked.

"The photographer's assistant," she said, "not my daughter."

"Oh," Patterson said. "I'm sorry."

"Please," she said. "What are you apologizing about? At least you didn't ruin the wedding by all this drowning nonsense, did you? All you did was float around out there. Now everyone's punching 911 on their cell phones. No one's even touching the appetizers. You know, they were supposed to get married in Fiji. I always imagined my daughter getting married somewhere indoors. I suppose they're going to want to have underwater births, too."

Patterson stared at the woman, trying to figure out how much she'd had to drink, if she was joking, and if he owed her a laugh because she'd given him a free drink. But the woman turned away from him and stared out at the ocean. The bride and groom were surfacing now, pulling off their goggles and spitting out water.

"Someone help!" the bride screamed, a piece of thick seaweed wrapped in her long hair. "Is anyone a lifeguard, a doctor, a medic?"

Patterson was none of these things. He was an insurance salesman who was so sure God was talking to him the first time he caught a wave and took it all the way to shore without the guidance of an instructor that he pulled his children out of school. Now, he wasn't sure of anything. He was a man who cheated on his wife every chance he got even after he'd been caught and blackmailed for it and maybe now was about to be turned in. He was a man who had no idea how to save a drowning woman.

Apparently the only kind of emergencies Patterson could handle were the domestic ones Beth invented for him, and even then he couldn't always be counted on to eliminate completely the squeak of a closet door or the faulty connection that caused a ceiling fan to switch itself on and off.

The man who had commandeered his surfboard was holding onto it with one arm now, looking under the water with the groom's goggles.

"He can keep the surfboard," Patterson told the bride's mother. "Tell him not to worry about it."

"That's very kind of you," she said.

"Not at all," he said, "I'm done with it anyway. I'm moving to the center of Texas. No surfing there." He walked away toward the steps up the hill. His car was parked up there. It was easier to get his key out of its sealed inner pocket without juggling his surfboard, easier to climb back up without carrying the board. He could see his car as he turned the corner, halfway there now. The small row of metered spots was full of cars that weren't there when he'd parked, and his appeared to be smack in the middle of them all, as if he were an actual invited guest.

The sun was out in full force now. He hadn't looked at a clock yet. It might have been eleven, even noon. It was too late to go to work and, on a normal day, too early to drive over to Beth's house. But his wife and boys were at the doctors' office this morning, and maybe Beth had sent Jennifer across the street to play and was home alone. Maybe she'd left him a message on his cell phone with an imagined emergency or was home waiting for him to figure out the score and show up and surprise her.

Patterson heard an ambulance siren begin in the distance and come closer. A helicopter was circling above now, too. Soon, real men, men who knew what to do and how to do it, would land on the beach in their helicopter, run down the cement slope with oxygen tanks and stretchers and whisk away the drowning photographer's assistant who didn't know how to swim. Patterson pushed his remote key and watched his headlights blink back at him.

ANAPHYLACTIC

They took Beth home and a policewoman sat with her in her living room by the phone, a second kitchen headset next to it now. Her cell phone was on the coffee table, too, all three phones not ringing. Darla was at her own house, across the street, and Beth listened for her phone, too. Sometimes she could hear it with the windows open and the houses quiet. But the house wasn't quiet when the policewoman assigned to her talked on her walkie-talkie.

Jennifer's EpiPen was on the coffee table between the phones. Beth sat on her hands and rocked and stared at the EpiPen as if it might be the thing that rang first. She wanted to open its plastic case and stab the needle into the policewoman, who acted like a bored houseguest. When she wasn't talking into her walkie-talkie, she was tying knots into a loop of string that Beth had left out for Jennifer to play with. Wendy, she said her name was. *Call me Wendy.*

When she was able to talk again, Beth told the police that when Jennifer was younger, she used to hide. And they tore the house apart looking for her in the back of closets, under beds. Someone even crawled through the dirt under the house.

But they only looked really worried after Beth told them about Jennifer's allergies. Before that, they were joking. She heard them talking as she sat in the car outside the store. Did this happen before or after they searched the house? They were sure no one had taken them. *Kids who run away are not kidnapped,* someone said. Someone—that person or someone else, Beth didn't remember—had laughed about the backpack probably being full of doll clothes. Or had Beth imagined this? Was joking possible?

"No sign yet," Wendy said, clicking off her walkie-talkie. "I'm sure it's just a matter of time. Let's go over it again. What houses might they have gone to? No cousins or grandmother? No school friends? Are you sure I have them all?"

"That's it," Beth said. How could this have happened? Only two possible houses for her daughter to run to? "I already told you. Darla's and mine and Winter's maybe, but I don't think so."

Winter was at home with the boys waiting by her phone, too, but Beth knew Jennifer would never go there or call her. The evil twins. What was she thinking, spending every day with a woman she disliked and making her daughter spend every day with her annoying children?

"And the father's domicile after your separation. Let's go over that again."

"I told you. Keith stays at his office. And it's too far. They'd never be able to walk there. You have all that."

"So you're saying you separated eight months ago, and he still doesn't live anywhere else?"

"He's looking," she said, feeling defensive, although she often asked him the same question herself. "It isn't easy to find something affordable." She repeated what Keith told her.

"He doesn't answer his cell phone," Wendy said. "Are you sure he had no reason to take Jennifer? No arguing recently over child support, visitation, custody?"

"No. He can see her whenever he wants. He wouldn't kidnap her. I don't think so." She hated the way the woman made her wonder about Keith. Was he tired of scraping up the money to give her every month? Could he have taken Jennifer and disappeared?

Wendy was on her walkie-talkie again, and then over-and-out, she'd hung up. "No one's at his office. Our guys just checked it out. The janitor said he's caught him sleeping there. There was a blanket and a pillow on the couch."

"I told you he slept there. That's his do-mi-ci-le." Beth stretched out the ridiculously inflated word, the kind of word Winter might have put on one of Jennifer's vocabulary lists.

"And the girlfriend? Still don't remember anything else about her?"

"I don't know where she lives," Beth said. "In an apartment somewhere. Jennifer said it was on the top floor. They took an elevator, parked on the street." *It looks like a witch's house*, she thought about adding, but stopped herself. Why would she let her daughter go somewhere that looked like a witch's house? Why didn't she know where her daughter went? What was wrong with her?

"I just thought you might have remembered something else," Wendy said.

"It looks like a witch's house," Beth said quickly before she could stop herself. "That's what Jennifer said. I'm sorry," she added, chastened now and ashamed. "That's all I know." Obviously, she didn't know nearly enough about her daughter's life.

When her phone rang, Wendy pointed the antenna of her walkie-talkie at it, and Beth picked it up. They didn't expect a kidnapper, but just in case, Wendy picked up the other headset at the same time, the way they had planned.

"What's the emergency this time?" Patterson said, "because I can't wait to see you."

"No," Beth said. "This is different."

"Honey," he said. "Tell me."

"Jennifer's missing," Beth said. She started to cry.

Over an hour had passed since Jennifer and Jeremy had disappeared from the Ma and Pa Store. The police had said they'd have them back in an hour. They were out there in their uniforms, driving slowly and walking up and down the streets of the neighborhood, but the kids were still missing.

"I'm coming over," he said, and the three of them hung up.

"You didn't tell me about the boyfriend," Wendy said.

"He's not a boyfriend," Beth said.

Wendy took out her pad of paper. "What is he then?" she asked.

"He's a friend. Winter's husband. He just cares about us, that's all."

"Does Winter know how much he cares about you?"

Beth shrugged. "Look, Winter is my homeschool partner. We all spend a lot of time together. Our families."

"Right, the homeschool thing," Wendy said, the word *homeschool* sounding foul tasting coming out of her mouth. She wrote something on her pad of paper. "Has Patterson ever been alone with your daughter?" Wendy asked. "Does he like little girls in particular in any way?"

"My God," Beth said. "What are you asking?"

Everything rang at once before Wendy could answer. The cell phone, the home phone, Wendy's walkie-talkie.

"Your daughter," a man said when they picked up the home phone. "My Emily found her at the rink. She's on the way to the hospital."

"Ma'am," a woman said when Beth answered her cell phone. "Your daughter is on the way to Memorial."

Beth rode in the front of Wendy's car to the hospital, siren blaring. She held the EpiPen tight in one hand, her cell phone in the other. It was too late, but she brought the EpiPen anyway. Maybe she'd never let go of it. She'd buy a chain and punch a hole in the plastic EpiPen holder and wear it around her neck. She'd stick it deep into her own thigh and leave it there, ready to pull out and save her daughter's life the way she should have done.

"Just take a deep breath," Wendy said as she drove. "Your daughter needs you to be calm."

"Fuck you," Beth said, breathing hard. She never talked this way. Even in labor, she hadn't cursed at Keith. But now she wanted to yell at Wendy the way she'd read about other laboring women yelling at their husbands when they reminded them about their Lamaze breathing instead of getting the anesthesiologist to hurry the fuck up and start an epidural.

In the waiting room, Darla, who had somehow gotten there first, was holding Jeremy, rocking him back and forth. "He's fine," she said to Beth. "They just checked him out to be sure. But he's fine."

The fact that Jeremy was fine, and Darla didn't seem to hate her anymore, should have been a relief, but Beth couldn't bear to look at Jeremy in his mother's arms.

Fine. Jeremy was fine. Wendy was leading Beth past Darla and Jeremy, holding onto the top of her arm as if she were a criminal, escorting her back to her daughter. They passed a bald man who looked familiar somehow, three children with butchered haircuts sitting on the floor by his feet playing poker. The man smiled at her in a way that might have been a hello. They looked ragged but fine, all four of them.

Jennifer was not fine. She was down a long hallway in a room that was really just a curtain drawn around her bed. She was covered in a plastic tent, breathing into a smoky tube. An IV was dripping into her arm. She was asleep or half asleep. She didn't even blink when Beth leaned over her as close as the clear plastic would allow. A nurse was adjusting things, liquid that dripped into her daughter's vein, a blood-pressure cuff on her arm. Jennifer was way too small for all of this, for this bed. She had never been the right size here. Always, it was as if she were playing hospital.

They'd been to Memorial before many times. They'd sat in the emergency room and waited their turn, sometimes for hours. They'd been surrounded by victims of superficial knife wounds; cramping pregnant women who may or may not have been miscarrying; children with throats so sore and swollen that their mothers wrapped their necks in warm towels while they waited.

On those visits, Jennifer had been wheezy and coughing and full of hives, but they'd never been rushed into the emergency room. They'd sat with everyone else and waited, watching the true emergencies—the gunshot wounds, the drowned children, the car crash victims—being whisked passed them on stretchers, grateful, at least, that Jennifer wasn't as bad off as they were.

Jennifer hadn't been the emergency in the emergency room since she'd been an infant and came close to choking on her own breath, her allergies still undiagnosed. This was the beginning of the list of off-limit foods. They said Jennifer was sick from drinking Beth's breast milk.

Beth had made her daughter sick from the absolute start, from the first day she was born. Probably before. It made sense that she wanted to run away. "I'm sorry," Beth said to Jennifer.

The nurse shook her head. "Shh," she said. "You're her mother, but there's nothing you can do, nothing to apologize for."

"I'll find you in a bit," Wendy said. "So we can clean up the details, close the case so we can file our report."

Wendy disappeared, but when Beth finally looked away from Jennifer, Winter was in her place, her head poking in the door, her shiny fingernails waving a little. Her other hand was over her mouth holding a word, something, back in.

"I brought the EpiPen," Beth said to the nurse or Winter or Jennifer, she didn't know who.

The nurse wrote something on her chart. "We don't need that right now. They gave her epinephrine already. In the ambulance. She's on albuterol, too, and the saline drip, and the docs are going to start her on prednisone soon, I think."

Beth nodded, comforted momentarily by the familiar, reassuring words. Albuteral, saline, prednisone. Jennifer had had this course of treatment in the past when she'd had severe attacks. Everything except the epinephrine, but she'd always been awake in the past, too, holding tight to Beth's hand and staring right at her instead of looking at the nurses or medications.

The nurse left the room, and the twins were standing in the doorway next to Winter now. They stared at Jennifer's bed, with its side rails and oxygen tent.

"Cool. I want a bed like that," one of them said.

The other dropped a tiny crazy ball that bounced up to the ceiling. He ran in to find it.

"Cut it out, boys," Winter said. "Remember your manners. Aiden and Nolan made Jennifer a collage picture while we were waiting to hear. While we were waiting for our good news. Didn't you, boys?"

Winter unhooked the clasp on her purse and pulled out a folded piece of paper and handed it to Beth "See," she said, pointing. "The boys are playing with Jennifer in the picture. She's all better. She's been like a sister to them, you know."

"We used spaghetti to make her hair," one of the boys said. "Broken up," the other said.

"Uncooked."

"Glued on."

"She has a sink in here and everything." The boys ran over and one turned on the water.

"Turn that off, or you're both going into time-out," Winter said.

"I still can't tell them apart," Beth said, "no matter what you say about Aiden having the longer chin."

"What are you saying?" Winter said.

"It's true. They look exactly the same to me."

"You're not yourself," Winter said. "I'm not going to take this personally."

"No children. Only immediate family in here," the nurse said, back again now and shooing the boys and Winter back to the doorway.

"Oh," Winter said. "Come on, boys. Aiden. Nolan." Winter said each of their names slowly as she touched the top of their heads, as if pointing them out to Beth. "We'll wait in the other room."

"They'll probably be moving her up to the ICU when a bed opens," the nurse told Beth. "They can keep a better eye on her up there."

Beth nodded. She wanted to ask what was wrong with her daughter. Why she wouldn't open her eyes. But she couldn't. "We need help," she said instead.

"It's okay, honey. A doctor will find you in the waiting room and talk to you soon," the nurse said. "Catch you up to speed."

"File his report," Beth said.

"Excuse me?" the nurse said.

"Never mind." It all blurred. Their voices. What they wanted from her. All Beth wanted to do was wake her daughter up and take her home.

"Why don't you wait out there with your friend," the nurse said. "We need to change the IV, and moms usually don't want to watch this."

"She's not really my friend." Beth held tight to a rail on her daughter's bed. "I don't even like her."

"Then maybe you should call someone else to wait with you," the nurse said, busying herself now by scrubbing her hands in the sink, pulling on a pair of latex gloves. "Someone you do like."

"I'll be just outside," Beth said.

"Don't worry," the nurse said. "She's in the right place now."

In the waiting room, Beth sat down near the television, so she could pretend to be watching it, so everyone would leave her alone, but the man with the shaved head came over.

"It's amazing they got all the way to the rink by themselves," he said. "You've got to give her credit for resourcefulness. Yourself, too, for instilling that confidence in her. That's something they definitely don't teach in school."

"David," Beth said. It all made sense now. "I didn't recognize you. Or the girls."

"We had a little image change," he said. "Some anti-makeovers, I guess."

Beth nodded. "You're the one who found her? At the rink?"

"Emily did," he said. "No one told you what happened?"

"I don't think so," Beth said.

"She passed out, and Emily got me, and we called the ambulance. I found your number after they paged you and no one could find you at the rink. We didn't have a clue about any of it. So there you have it."

"There you have it," Beth said.

"We'll just wait over there for a while," David said. "Make sure everything's okay before we leave."

Darla and Jeremy were gone, but Winter was back with the boys, who were eating little cups of ice cream with white plastic spoons. "That cafeteria is outrageously overpriced," Winter said. "It's like an airport in here."

"It's nothing like an airport," Beth said, wishing she and Jenny were waiting for a plane somewhere, the buzz of travelers all around them. "It's not a thing like an airport."

"Aiden," Winter said, putting her hand on his head, "Nolan," she said, putting her hand on the other boy's head, "why don't you boys go sit down over there so Miss Beth and I can talk privately."

"I don't want to talk privately," Beth said. "I just want to sit right here by myself and wait for the doctor to give me his report, to come out here and tell me what's going on with Jennifer and when I can take her home."

"Well, we're right here if you need us," Winter said. "I phoned Patterson, and he's on the way, too. I'm going to take the boys down to the children's ward so they can play in the waiting room over there for a bit, get some of the old energy out, but we won't be far."

Go far, Beth thought. *Go very far.* But she shut up. Awful things were coming out of her mouth, and it was better not to talk. She'd managed to get dressed at some point this morning, but she couldn't remember what she was wearing. She looked down and was relieved to see she had on a big sweatshirt and jeans. She drew her knees up to her chest under the sweatshirt, hugged herself tight and put her head down.

When Jennifer did this, she called it her turtle house. Turtle, tortoise. Just a few days ago, Jennifer had told her a joke that relied on word play, rhyming "tortoise" and "porpoise." *What's a tortoise called when it swims in the ocean with a sea mammal? A tortoise with a porpoise.*

A helicopter circled overhead, loud enough to hear through the layers of hospital floors. The emergency room was full of noisy commotion, but Beth kept her head down, her eyes closed. The worst possible thing had already happened. There was no point in looking for relief in someone else's tragedy.

SALINE

Keith rode on the helicopter even though he wasn't the husband. He climbed on after they carried Eleanor up on the stretcher, and later the paramedics called Eleanor *your wife*. He knew he wasn't supposed to be there, that he was barely even a boyfriend anymore. But there he was, the helicopter noise so much louder than his own breathing underwater had been. Not that Eleanor seemed to notice.

She had panicked, everyone figured. Why else would she rip out her mouthpiece and drop it, breathe in salt water instead of compressed air? The water had been just a foot over her head, but her weight belt had held her down in place. Keith should have noticed, but he'd been too busy shooting and trying to get comfortable with the whole situation, the sound of his breath amplified, his thick mask, the waterproof casing on the camera, which made the camera feel like it belonged to someone else. Like he was borrowing his own camera.

The bride finally pointed and did her best to shout underwater. *What?* Keith had mouthed back to her. *What?* Something was all wrong. Finally, he'd looked behind him and saw Eleanor, her eyes pleading, and her arms flapping up and down at her sides but her body not moving anywhere.

She grabbed at them as they tried to help, the bride and groom, the underwater minister, Keith. And then she stopped grabbing and flapping and her eyes stopped pleading. At first, they couldn't figure out what was holding her down, a rope tangled by her foot, maybe? And then, after they figured it out, they had to work to get the weight belt released.

My God, it was like drowning in the bathtub, someone said as they finally got her belt off and lifted her onto the surfboard. *My God, my God, my God.*

"She never learned how to swim!" Keith shouted over the noise of the helicopter.

"She doesn't look good," a paramedic told him. "How long was your wife under?"

Everyone was confused. The paramedics thought Keith and Eleanor were the ones getting married. "On your wedding day, man," someone on the helicopter said. "Don't worry, man. We're airlifting your wife to the best trauma care in the area."

Nothing looked good, none of her vitals, but Eleanor was still breathing a little when they landed on the pad outside the hospital, when they ran inside with Eleanor on a stretcher. She was still in her wetsuit, the top ripped open where they tried to shock her heart into waking up again. She smelled like salt and blood. The whole helicopter, animal, mineral, machine.

Keith ran with them through the emergency waiting room, his wetsuit almost dry now. Still barefoot, he felt fast and slick and foolish, a grown man dressed in a superhero costume. As if he had forgotten his special space boots.

"Wait!" someone said. It struck Keith as odd and not odd to hear that word shouted in the waiting room. But they were already through it, passing back into the real rooms with their curtains and doctors pushing him out of the way and telling him to wait outside, they'll come get him with news. Again, that word. *Wait.*

Keith paced in the waiting—wait—room, watching his feet, his sandy hairy toes. He thought about his equipment that he'd left there on the beach. Where? He didn't know. He hoped someone had put it somewhere safe for him. He hoped the tide wasn't coming in over it now.

While he paced, he thought about the money he wasn't going to make on this wedding, and how he should probably give back the deposit. None of these thoughts were the right ones to have, and he knew it, but he couldn't help it. All he'd thought about was Eleanor up until this moment, and now he couldn't stop thinking about his money, his cameras, how he'd never get enough money together for an apartment now. How he was going to blow it all on an expensive hotel room anyway. He sat down in a plastic chair, put his head in his hands, stared down at the floor.

"Keith," a woman said, whispering next to him. He was afraid to look up. He felt like he'd vomit, like his stomach was the one full of ocean. The woman kept talking anyway. She didn't seem to mind. "You made it. Good. She needs you. She might not say it, but she really does. She's not herself. She's just not."

Keith finally looked at the woman with her small gold hoop earrings and pulled-back hair, her matching turquoise sweatpants and jacket. "I know you," he said.

"Winter," she said. "Beth's friend. We came as soon as we heard."

"Really?" Keith said. "How did you hear?"

"The police called me directly," she said. "I was one of the first people they called. I mean, they called you first, of course, but you didn't answer your cell."

"My cell?" Keith had left that on the beach, too. His cell phone, his wallet, everything in his camera bag when he waded out into the ocean. "You know Eleanor?"

"What are we talking about here?" she said. "Who's Eleanor?"

He sat up straight and shook his head to shake water from his ears, clear his thoughts, his hearing maybe. He looked around the waiting room. Two familiar-looking identical twin boys crouched on the floor on opposite sides of the room, pretending to shoot each other with plastic spoons. A shirtless teenage boy in oversize gang-style jeans stretched out across four chairs, an ice bag on his forehead. A vaguely familiar-looking buzzed-cut man and three children in odd mismatched clothes, one wearing a long stocking cap—boys? girls? Keith couldn't be sure—sat on the floor playing some kind of elaborate card game. A young woman sat with her hand on her lower belly, tears running down her cheeks.

And then Keith finally saw her. Beth. Her head was down the way his had been, but he recognized the slope of her shoulders, her sneakers, the same ones she wore when he'd left so many months ago. "What's going on here?" he asked.

"You don't know?" Winter said, not whispering anymore. "You're kidding, right. You don't know about Jennifer?"

"Keith?" Beth said, looking up now. "They found you. Good."

"Found me? What are you talking about?"

"About Jennifer running away and eating lord knows what and making herself so sick she's here. That's what she's talking about," Winter said. "Now do you believe she has allergies? Now will you finally respect her off-limit foods?"

"I'm sorry," Beth said. "We were supposed to be sleeping in, and she went across the street and got Jeremy and they just left."

"Why were you sleeping in on a Wednesday? Didn't she have to be at school?"

"We were taking the morning off," Winter said. "The boys had a doctor's appointment. A checkup."

"We have to talk," Beth said. "There's some things I haven't told you. Yet. I mean I planned to and everything."

"What the hell?" Keith said. "What is this, Beth?" He was shouting at her across the room now, and the man sitting on the floor playing cards with the children was up now and walking over toward him.

"Calm down, buddy," he said. "These are stressful times. We all need to keep our heads, for Jennifer's sake."

Keith remembered now, the guy from the nature center with the bread samples and the walkie-talkies. But he had a beard then, longer hair. "Are you in on this?" Keith said. "Are you in on this, too?"

"No one's in on anything," he said. "We all just care about Jennifer and want the best for her."

"I want to see her," Keith said. "I want to see my daughter." He was walking back into the rooms with the curtains, and the receptionists were busy checking in new emergencies and no one stopped him. Keith looked in the curtains until he found her, his daughter with an IV in her arm and a tube in her mouth. But when he looked through the clear plastic cover, he saw that her eyes were wide open. Jennifer looked back at him, smiled a little with the tube in her mouth still. "I'm here," he said.

"You must be the father," a nurse said. "She's doing much better, our little Jenny. She had us all a little scared for a few minutes there."

"I'm right outside," Keith said. "With Beth. With your mother. We're both here now, honey."

Winter was talking now to a tall man in a wetsuit, arguing with him in loud whispers in a corner of the waiting room. Keith heard the man say, *See how much they need us,* and Winter say the words, *Texas* and *getting yourself fired first.*

"You were the surfer," Keith said. "At the wedding. Thanks for leaving the board. I mean it. They brought her in on it."

"Patterson," he said, extending a hand.

"Keith."

"Right," Patterson said. "I get it now."

Two women were sitting with Beth, one in a police uniform, the other in what Keith suddenly thought of as civilian clothes, black pants and a blouse. She called Keith over. "We just need to review a few things with you, too," she said. "The father."

"Review?" he said.

"It's pretty standard in these kind of case," the policewoman said. "Are you a surfer?"

Keith shook his head, and then he remembered about his wetsuit. "Scuba," he said.

"We just have to make sure the child is going back to a safe place," the civilian woman said. "That this kind of thing isn't going to happen again."

Keith saw the picture she wore around her neck. The words SOCIAL WORKER under it.

"Your wife says that you're separated and Jennifer lives with her," the social worker continued. "Is that correct?"

"Yes," he said.

"And you're looking for an apartment?"

"Right."

"And has this happened before while she was in your wife's care? Jennifer disappearing this way?"

"Never," he said, thinking about the times she disappeared in his care, at the aquarium, the nature center. He thought about pointing out that he was the irresponsible one, but decided it was better not to mention it. "Beth is a very good mother," he said. "Jennifer's everything to her."

"We'll be following up, of course," the woman said, standing up now. "We'll be visiting the home. Homeschooling is perfectly legal in California, but we'll have to see that everything's in order. All the paperwork. The home environment. What's happening there."

"Of course," Beth said, staring hard at Keith. He knew what that look meant. *Don't talk. Don't say anything now. Wait.*

Keith nodded.

"What the hell, Beth?" he said when they had signed all the reports and the women were finally done with them.

"I've been meaning to tell you," Beth said. "I was just looking for the right time. It's not like you were exactly present at her school, what with your new scuba diving hobby. You might have noticed by now."

"It's not a hobby. I was on a job," Keith said. "An underwater wedding, and Eleanor, my assistant, was air-vaced here, nearly drowned."

"I'm sorry. I didn't know."

"It looks like Jennifer's out of the woods," a doctor said to Keith and Beth. "We'll move her up to ICU, keep her the rest of the day just to be sure."

"Come on, boys," Winter said. "Aiden. Nolan. We're leaving now. Let's give Miss Beth and Mr. Keith some space."

David's girls stood up as if Winter had called them, too.

"Hey, there, man," David said to Patterson. "It's all under control now. Thanks for the help."

Patterson looked at Beth and then back at David. "What are you saying?"

"The construction crew, they're working out great."

"Excellent," Patterson said. "I'm glad to hear it. So that's it?"

"Yep," David said. "But I appreciate the help."

"We're hungry, Dad," the girl in the stocking cap said.

"They've been very patient," David said. "I like the way you girls waited."

"Just let me know if you need anything," Patterson said to Beth. "If there's anything at all I can do."

His wife had too many new friends for Keith to keep track of. All he had was Eleanor, and now this.

"Come on, Patterson. Leave her alone now," Winter said. "Will you just leave her alone." And then they were gone, all of them.

No doctor or nurse had come out and told him anything about Eleanor yet, and Keith didn't ask. He'd told a nurse about the son in Seattle and someone had found his number and called him. In a minute, Keith would ask about Eleanor, but for now, he decided to sit tight with Beth and savor this one piece of news, this singular piece of good luck.

NAP TIME

Jennifer was supposed to rest, but she didn't feel like resting. She had been resting ever since she got home from the hospital three days ago. Her bedroom was full of flowers, and her grandmother in Pennsylvania had sent her a bear holding the kind of small shiny balloons that took a long time for the air to leave. GET WELL, a balloon read. I MISS YOU! Jennifer read on another one.

Ursala had come by with one of her tutors to bring her a present in person. It was a card with an ice skater on the cover, and when you opened the card it played Christmas music. Inside the card, Ursala had crossed out HAPPY HOLIDAYS and written in bright pink, GET BETTER QUICK! Jennifer was surprised by the bright pink and the exclamation point. She thought Ursala looked like the kind of person who would write in black and use a period at the end of the sentence. Jennifer's father said you never really knew the people you thought you knew, and she thought maybe that was true.

Jennifer had been asleep when Ursala had come by to deliver her card, and she didn't get to see her. Now, she tried to stay awake while she was resting just in case there was anything else going on that she might not want to miss.

Yesterday afternoon was Eleanor's funeral. Jennifer's father had spent the morning playing Clue with her in the living room dressed in his funeral suit. When he got up to leave, she thought about saying something to him like *good luck* but that sounded wrong, so she just hugged him goodbye instead. Tonight he was bringing Eleanor's grown son, Donald, from Seattle over with him to dinner.

Jennifer didn't miss Eleanor, but she felt bad that she thought Eleanor was a mean witch who had poisoned her, so she planned to be especially nice to the grown son. She helped her mother set the glass table on the patio so they could eat together out there, the four of them, Jennifer included. But if she wasn't careful and got too excited and jumped around, her parents would take her back up to her room so she could rest some more instead.

Her father and Eleanor's grown son came right on time at 6 p.m., and Jennifer's mother told them to take a seat outside.

"I'm thinking about staying in town for a while," Donald said, "to clean up some things, and Keith here was talking to me about maybe assisting him for a wedding he has coming up, so maybe I'll stay for that. Also, there's the cat. I finally coaxed her out from under the bed."

Jennifer's mother nodded and passed the grown son the Eggplant Parmesan Surprise. The surprise part was that it was made with tofu instead of parmesan cheese, but Jennifer didn't tell Donald that, because a lot of people were unhappy with tofu as a surprise. She recognized him from a picture in Eleanor's apartment, but in the picture Donald was thinner and had more hair.

"It's just me in Seattle, really," Donald said. "Not too much going on. I planned to visit her this summer, my mother."

"Do you like Southern California, Donald?" Jennifer's mother asked. "It must be very different from Seattle."

"Yes," he said, which either meant he liked Southern California, or it was different from Seattle. Jennifer wasn't sure which.

"Next week we're having a going-away party for the evil twins," Jennifer said. "The boy-girls are coming. Everyone. They're moving to Texas where they can have more room to roam."

"Room to roam, huh?" Donald laughed, but her mother didn't.

"That's what Winter said, 'room to roam,'" Jennifer said.

"And who are the boy-girls and Winter and the evil twins

exactly?" Donald asked.

Jennifer looked at her mother and father. The two of them had had long talks over the past few days while Eleanor had been dead and Jennifer had been resting in her room. She heard them downstairs in the living room, sometimes their voices getting loud, sometimes one of them crying or laughing.

It could have been Jennifer, she heard her mother say once while she was crying. And that's when Jennifer knew that Eleanor had traded with her for being dead. Which was something a nice witch could do maybe.

Her parents had sat by the side of her bed, the three of them like a family again. Her father wasn't coming home to live with them, they told her. They hadn't decided about whether or not she'd go back to school yet, about what was the best thing. But they promised to do better, both of them.

"They're all just friends," Jennifer said. "Do you like turtles or tortoises better?"

"I don't know," Donald said. "I'll have to think on that one."

"The boy-girls have a tortoise they keep in the bathtub," she said. "Without water."

"Well, that's something, isn't it," Donald said.

It was almost summer, and it was still light out now after dinner. Jennifer could hear Jeremy and Lauren playing hopscotch outside in the street. She wasn't allowed to go over to their house by herself anymore. Darla said *Hi, Sweetie* to Jennifer when her mother walked her over. But Darla didn't say hi to her mother, and her mother never came inside Darla's house anymore. Her mother had to walk her everywhere now, even across the street, even right down the hallway to the bathroom.

"I'm getting a fish for my room because no one's allergic to fish," Jennifer said.

"Excellent choice," Donald said.

And then they all focused on their plates, the four of them chewing slowly and taking serious, careful bites.

ACKNOWLEDGMENTS

I am grateful for the walks and conversations with Teddi Chichester, Ginger Mazzapica, Marcie Moody, Kim Savage, Barbara Swain, Jan Kraft, and Anne Poppaw, and for the technical and creative advice of David Hernandez. I am equally grateful for the long phone calls with Sarah Michaelson and Gina Caruso, and for all of my other friends who keep me afloat and grounded, the best kind of paradox. You know who you are.

I want to thank my mother, writer Joyce Greenberg Lott, for raising me in a house full of books, and the rest of my family, all readers and creative thinkers—my father, Morton Greenberg; my sister, Elizabeth Greenberg; and my brother, Lawrence Greenberg. I also want to thank my own children, Joel, Claire, and Noah, for taking me places I would have never ventured to on my own and for being patient with my writing schedule.

I am indebted to my agent, Mark Falkin, who believed in *Lesson Plans* from the start, and the amazing people at Prospect Park Books: Colleen Dunn Bates, Patty O'Sullivan, and Jennifer Bastien, all joys to work with throughout this process. I am grateful for your experience, thoughtful guidance, and vision.

In addition, I want to thank the continually supportive English Department faculty at CSULB, as well as the College of Liberal Arts and the university for the release time that allowed me to write.

Finally, this book would never have found its way into print without the support of my friend and colleague Lisa Glatt and my husband, Michael Smith. There's no way I can ever thank either one of you enough for your encouragement and reading of endless revisions. But here's a try.

BOOK CLUB QUESTIONS

1. At the beginning of the novel, David suggests that "one day humans would look back at schools the way society now looked at foot binding or public stoning." Do you think his reasoning has merit?

2. Why do you think Patterson's newfound hobby leads him to consider homeschooling? Is his religious conversion temporary?

3. The book has a few different narrators. Does that enhance the story or become distracting? Which perspective do you relate to most?

4. Does the novel take a stance on homeschooling?

5. Is Keith a terrible father, the most realistic parent in the book, or both?

6. Examine the relationship between Patterson and Beth. What appeals to Patterson about Beth that's missing in his own relationship?

7. How does David's house-construction project reflect what's happening in his life?

8. What do you make of Deborah and David taking turns at giving "the ducklings" haircuts?

9. Jennifer interprets what happens to Eleanor at the end of the novel as a trade for her own fate. Do you agree?

10. Were you satisfied with the book's ending? What do you think the future holds for each family?

ABOUT THE AUTHOR

Suzanne Greenberg is a professor of English and creative writing at California State University Long Beach. Her fiction, poetry, and essays have appeared in the *Mississippi Review*, *West Branch*, the *Washington Post Magazine*, and other publications. Her collection of short stories, *Speed-Walk and Other Stories*, won the 2003 Drue Heinz Literature Prize. She is the co-author of *Everyday Creative Writing: Panning for Gold in the Kitchen Sink* and co-author of the children's novels *Abigail Iris: The One and Only* and *Abigail Iris: The Pet Project*. *Lesson Plans* is her first novel for adults.

Greenberg received her BA from Hampshire College and her MFA from the University of Maryland. A New Jersey native, she lives in Long Beach, California, with her family.

Learn more at www.suzannegreenberg.com.